Also by Frank Cottrell Boyce

Millions

Cosmic

Praise for *Framed*

'The funniest novel I have read this year' *Observer*

'The time will come when Frank Cottrell Boyce's children's titles have passed into the canon of the classics . . . *Framed* [is] a book of wonderful originality and readability . . . It's funny. It's heart-warming . . . a delight' Philip Ardagh, *Guardian*

'A wonderful, wonderful book. I absolutely loved it' Geraldine McCaughrean

'Utterly brilliant, Cowabunga!' Danny Wallace

'Every page is funny . . . fantastic' *Heat* magazine

'A cunningly constructed comic tour de force' *Books for Keeps*

'Heart-warming, life-affirming . . . it's all that and more' *Daily Telegraph*

Frank Cottrell Boyce's books are enjoyed by different generations of readers around the world. His debut novel, *Millions*, published in twenty-seven languages, won the prestigious Carnegie Medal and was shortlisted for the Guardian Children's Fiction Award and the Blue Peter Book Award. *Framed*, his second novel, was shortlisted for the Carnegie Medal, the Blue Peter Book Award and the Whitbread Award.

Also a successsful screenwriter, Frank's credits include *24 Hour Party People*, *Hilary and Jackie*, *Welcome to Sarajevo* and *Millions*, the movie, directed by Danny Boyle. Frank is a father of seven and lives with his family in Liverpool.

FRANK COTTRELL BOYCE

Framed

MACMILLAN

First published 2005 by Macmillan Children's Books

This edition published 2012 by Macmillan Children's Books
a division of Macmillan Publishers Limited
20 New Wharf Road, London N1 9RR
Basingstoke and Oxford
Associated companies throughout the world
www.panmacmillan.com

ISBN 978-0-230-76956-4

1 3 5 7 9 8 6 4 2

A CIP catalogue record for this book is available from
the British Library.

Typeset by Intype Libra Ltd
Printed and bound in the UK by CPI Group (UK) Ltd, Croydon, CR0 4YY

To Denny,
my favourite work of art

You've probably never heard of Vincenzo Perugia. But we know all about him. He was a famous art thief and we used to be in the same line of work. My sister Minnie even had a picture of him on her bedroom wall. She reckons that when Vincenzo stole the *Mona Lisa* from the Louvre museum in Paris on 21 August 1911, that was the most immensely perfect crime ever. The *Mona Lisa* was the world's most famous painting, but Vincenzo did such a neat job no one even noticed it was missing for two days. Then they did notice, and everything went mental. Everyone went to the Louvre to look at the empty space where the painting had been. They queued up to look at an empty space! Even Vincenzo Perugia queued up. And when they got to the front of the queue, they all looked at that empty space and thought about what used to be there. I can understand that. Sometimes something vanishes, and afterwards you can't stop looking at the place where it used to be.

And all this time Vincenzo had it in his little room – the *Mona Lisa* was in a trunk next to the bed.

Sometimes he took the painting out and played it funny songs on his mandolin. He didn't try to sell it. He didn't steal any other paintings. He didn't want to be famous or rich. He just wanted the *Mona Lisa*. And that's where he went right. That's why it was the perfect crime. Because he didn't want anything else.

And that's probably where *we* went wrong. We wanted something.

SNOWDONIA OASIS AUTO MARVEL, MANOD

11 February

Cars today:
BLUE FORD FIESTA — Ms Stannard (Twix)
SCANIA 118 LOW LOADER — Wrexham
Recovery

Weather — rain

Note: OIL IS DIFFERENT FROM ANTIFREEZE

My dad, right — ask anyone this, they'll all say the same — my dad can fix anything. Toyota. Hyundai. Ford. Even Nice Tom's mam's diddy Daihatsu Copen (top speed 106 mph), which is about the size of a marshmallow so you need tweezers to fix it.

And it's not just cars.

Like the time when we were at Prestatyn and Minnie wanted a swim but I wouldn't get in the water because it was too cold. She kept saying, 'Come in. It's fine once you're in.' And I kept saying, 'No.'

Dad got up, went to the caravan and came back with a kettle of boiling water. He poured the water in the sea and said, 'Dylan, come and test it. Tell me if it's all right or does it need a bit more?'

I said, 'No, that's fine now, thanks, Da.'

'Sure now?'

'Sure now.'

'Not too hot then?'

'No, just right.'

'Give me a shout. If it gets cold again, I can always boil up some more.'

Then Minnie splashed me and I splashed her and we stayed in the water till the sun went down.

He fixed the sea for us. Now that is a thing to be admired.

My big sister, Marie, never came in the water even after Dad fixed it. She said, 'Have you any idea what sea water can do to your hair?' And later on when we were playing Monopoly in the caravan, she said, 'Did you really think that one kettle of water could warm up the entire Irish Sea?'

I said, 'Not the whole sea, obviously. Just the bit we were swimming in.'

'Yeah, like that would really work,' said Minnie. 'Let me explain the physics . . .'

'Minnie,' said Mam, 'Euston Road. Three houses. Two hundred and seventy pounds, please.' Typical of Mam, by the way, cleverly changing the subject like that.

Obviously I know now that the kettle didn't warm up the sea, but that's not the point. I got into the water, that's the point. Dad looked at that situation and he thought, I can't do anything about the physics, but I can do something about Dylan. So he did.

*

He's keen for us all to learn how to fix things too. That's how I came to be helping him with the oil change on Ms Stannard's blue Fiesta (top speed 110 mph). I don't know how I came to make the mix-up about the oil.

Dad said it would probably be best if I didn't go near the workshop again. Or near a car again, really. He was quite calm about it. He said it was the kind of thing that could happen to anyone. Anyone who didn't know the difference between motor oil and antifreeze, that is.

After that, Mam said I could take over the petrol log. That's the massive red book next to the till where we write down all the petrol sales so we can track supply and demand. The book is red, with gold patterns on the front. It looks like a Bible. Mam got it in a car-boot sale (Car Boot Crazy at the Dynamo Blaenau Football Club ground) for fifty pence. It's got over a thousand pages. We only use about a page a week, so it should last us twenty years. Bargain!

No disrespect to Mam, obviously, but she was probably too busy with the new baby to make the most of that job. She just wrote stuff like, '10.20 a.m. – four gallons unleaded'. Whereas I put down all the detail – the make, the year, name of the driver, anything. I'd stay on the forecourt from home time till teatime. Sometimes Nice Tom would come and sit with me, and if he said something like, 'Mr Morgan's offside back tyre is baldy,' I'd put that down too. When Dad saw it, he said, 'Dylan, you have made a fifty-pence petrol log into a database. That is something to be admired.'

A database is very useful. For instance, when Dad read, 'Mr Morgan: offside back tyre baldy,' he sourced a new tyre and offered it to Mr Morgan. So a job that would have gone to Acres of Tyres in Harlech came to us instead. It saved Mr Morgan time and it made us money. That's market research, and I did it. 'And that,' says Dad, 'is how the Hughes family operates. Everyone has his job to do and everyone does it well. The Hughes family is an unbeatable team. We are the Brazil of Snowdonia.'

And the team sheet is: Dad – Captain; Mam – Team Manager, and Acquisitions (at car-boot sales); Me – Market Research; Marie – she's very pretty so I suppose you'd say Presentation; and Minnie, well, general Brains really. Oh, and the baby. His name is Max and he doesn't do much at the moment, but in seven years' time he will be able to play football.

Because I put so much detail in the petrol log, I only have to look at it now and I can remember anything about that day. For instance, in this entry for 11 February, I remember Ms Stannard buying that Twix, because she's my teacher and I thought, Oooh, Ms

Stannard eats Twix. And I remember that the blue Fiesta is hers because it's the car that the mix-up happened to. And the Scania 118 low loader is this immense eight-wheel truck with the beaver tailgate, lifting tackle and an intercooler engine. It came to take Ms Stannard's car away.

Like I said, Dad can fix nearly anything.

Ms Stannard's Fiesta is the exception that proves the rule.

15 February

Cars today:
BLUE BARRACUDA MOUNTAIN BIKE — man in
a balaclava (parked by the Alta Gaz)
GREEN DAIHATSU COPEN — Mrs Egerton
(parked right up against the car vac, didn't
buy petrol — tiny 659cc engine, not a big
drinker)

Weather — raining

Note: BALACLAVAS ENCOURAGE CRIME

This one is the petrol log for the day of the robbery.
The robbery was the first time any of us had seen a
criminal in action up close. So it was probably a major
influence on our later work.

A man came into the garage with a balaclava over
his face and a big sledgehammer and shouted at Dad
to empty the till. Dad knew who it was right away – it
was Daft Tom. He knew because Tom's mam had
knitted me a very similar balaclava for my birthday.
Also Tom had customized the eyeholes himself, and
the wool was starting to unravel around the nasal
area so you could nearly recognize him. Anyway, Dad
pretended to empty the safe. 'It's a time lock, see,' he
said, 'so it'll take a couple of minutes. You stay calm
and help yourself to whatever you like from the sweet
rack.'

'Just move it, Mr Hughes.' That was another bit of a clue, the robber calling Dad 'Mr Hughes'.

The final clue, by the way, was the big blue mountain bike, which was the only big blue mountain bike in town and which everyone remembers Daft Tom winning in the Christmas Lights raffle.

He was also wearing a Ninja Turtles cycling helmet, and everyone knows that Daft Tom is obsessed with the Turtles, which is unusual in a grown man. Daft Tom got into the Turtles when they first came out, same as everyone else. But when everyone else grew out of them, he carried on liking them. He was always buying Turtles T-shirts, videos, collectors' cards, the original Turtle Lair, with extra sewage piping, Ninja Choppin' Pogo 'Copters, Sewer Sledges, Shell Subs (with Torpedos) . . . He had a boxed set of super-poseable models of Donatello, Raphael, Leonardo and Michelangelo, with sixty-seven points of articulation each, and even a full-size strap-on Turtle shell.

Anyway, back to the robbery. Obviously we haven't actually got a safe. When Dad said he was opening the safe, he was actually texting Daft Tom's mam, and she came round in her little Copen. Daft Tom didn't hear or see the car pull up because the engine is so small you can only hear it if you're a bat or a shrew or something. So when she walked in, he nearly choked from shock. And when she walloped him across the back of his legs with her unnecessary Krooklock, well, he shouted, 'What the Shell!' (another giveaway) and then, well, he just keeled over really.

Daft Tom's mam wanted to report him to the police, but Dad was dead against it. 'The town of Manod,' he said, 'has the lowest crime rate in the United Kingdom. We're not going to spoil that for one mistake.'

And he offered Tom a job.

'You come and work in the garage for a few weeks and we'll say no more about it. I can't pay you, mind.'

Tom's mother was upset. She said, 'We have no way of knowing what our deeds will lead to. Look at me: I was just trying to keep my son's ears warm, like a good mother, and where did that lead? If I had not knitted him a balaclava, he might never have been seduced into criminality.'

The good thing about Daft Tom was that he could work the photocopier, which no one else could because when Mam bought it (Snowdonia Mountain Rescue Charity Shop, £20), it didn't have a manual. Daft Tom crouched in front of it and kept pressing buttons until he had it all worked out. By the end of the week, the Snowdonia Oasis Auto Marvel had become the Snowdonia Oasis Auto Marvel and Copier Centre. And Daft Tom had become Nice Tom (except to his mam).

So there's another thing that Dad fixed – he fixed Daft Tom. That was the end of his Life of Crime.

Which is funny when you think about it. Because it was probably the start of ours.

12 March

Cars today:
ROVER 3500 V8 — the Misses Sellwood

Weather — rain

Note: MANOD WEDNESDAYS

It's true that we do have quiet days at the Snowdonia
Oasis. There are three reasons for this:

Reason 1: No one knows where Manod is. There's so
much to see and do in Manod, it should have a massive sign like the ones for London or Blackpool. Sadly
there's no sign at all, not even on the A496 – close to
which the town is conveniently situated. There used
to be a sign, on the grass verge, just after the sign for
Diggermania (that's a theme park in Harlech where
you ride around on diggers), but an egg van backed
into it and knocked it over and no one's ever fixed it.
The council says a new sign is 'not a funding priority'.
Dad gets cross about this about once a week. He says
that the lack of a sign robs him of potential passing
trade.

Reason 2: To be honest, though, we wouldn't get passing trade because you can't pass our garage. The
Blaenau Road (the B5565) ends just behind the car

vac. The Snowdonia Oasis Auto Marvel is literally the end of the road. Unless you open the gate and then there's the mountain road. But that's not really a road, just a track they used to use to bring down the slate from the quarry at the top. The gate is there to stop Mr Morgan's sheep wandering down off the mountain and on to the High Street. It's part of my job to keep the gate shut or, if it is left open, chase the sheep back. If the sheep don't want to be chased I open a packet of Quavers. Sheep will follow you anywhere if you're carrying an open packet of Quavers. Try it. Mr Morgan is a customer, so sheep-chasing is customer relations.

Reason 3: The Misses Sellwood. The Misses Sellwood live on a farm halfway up Manod Mountain. Miss Elsa can drive but she can't see. Miss Edna can see but she can't drive. So what they do is, every Wednesday Miss Elsa drives and Miss Edna steers. It's not so risky on the mountain road because no one lives up there apart from them and Mr Morgan's sheep. But when they hit the High Street, they are a Menace to Society.

Some car names are annoyingly random. The Fiat Cappuccino for instance is not really a cup of coffee. The Beetle is not an insect and the Rover's not a dog. But the Rover 3500 V8 really does have a great big V8 engine, the kind they use in small aeroplanes. You could really hurt someone with it. So everyone in Manod stays off the road on Wednesdays until the Sellwoods have been and gone. They have to come through the garage to get into town to get their shopping and to have their hair turned this random shade of blue in Curl Up N Dye, the hairdresser's on Manod Road. The Sellwoods have got a great big bunch of plastic daffodils Blu Tacked to the top of their dashboard. They put them there one St David's Day and never took them down. They're getting a bit dusty now.

Because they only drive about four miles a week, they stop for actual petrol only about once a year. But as soon as they appear on the forecourt, Mam rings Mrs Porty to let everyone know that they're on their way down. On good Wednesdays they come down early and everyone can get back to normal. On bad Wednesdays they come down late, which means no one comes into the garage all day.

But even on a bad Wednesday, there's always plenty to talk about. For instance, ever since the robbery, Minnie was immensely fascinated by Tom's Life of Crime. She was always saying stuff like, 'When did you first decide on a Life of Crime?'

'Well, I didn't really decide. I didn't want to be a criminal. I wanted a career in catering, but the only catering job in Manod is the one at Mr Chipz, and for some reason they gave that to this red-headed girl who probably doesn't even like chips, or why is she so thin?'

So Tom wasn't really a criminal. He was just frustrated.

'I see,' said Minnie. 'And what attracted you to robbing garages? Why not banks, say? Or jewellers?'

'Well, you'd need a getaway car for something like that, see, and I've only got the bike.'

'You know where you went wrong?'

'I went wrong,' said Tom, 'when I tried to do a robbery. It was a wrong idea. I should never have even had that idea.'

'You didn't think it through,' said Minnie. 'For instance, that bike – everyone knows that's your bike. Everyone knows that's your balaclava. Everyone knows you. Next time you do a robbery, do it in Blaenau or Harlech. Somewhere no one will recognize you.'

'There isn't going to be a next time because I'm now totally reformed, thanks to your dad. I'm completely happy here.'

'If you'd thought it through you might have got away with it.'

'I don't want to get away with it. I don't want to do a robbery. I told you. I'm happy.'

'Come on, everyone has a dream.'

A faraway look came into Tom's eyes. 'You know I've got these super-articulated models of the Turtles?

Well, apparently they made one of Splinter too. Only you never see them in the shops. They're only available as a Japanese import.'

'Maybe you could steal one of them,' said Minnie.

'No, thank you,' said Tom. 'I might look on eBay.'

'Your trouble,' said Minnie, 'is that you give up too easily.'

29 March

Cars today:
RED FORD KA — Ms Stannard (stopped
for petrol, a Twix and firelighters)
VAUXHALL ASTRA ESTATE 1.9 CDTi —
Mr Davis (just reversing)
BLUE LEXUS — Mr Choi (stopped for petrol)
WHITE MONTEGO — Mr Evans (noisy gearbox
and squeaky windscreen wiper)
RED TOYOTA PRIUS T4 AUTOMATIC —
Dr Ramanan and family — (fill up, oil check,
air check, brake fluid and party pack of Hula
Hoops)
GREEN DAIHATSU COPEN — Mrs Egerton

Weather — wet

Note: NO BALL GAMES

This one's an easy one to remember. Ms Stannard
came round to show us the new Ka (top speed 108
mph) that she got from the insurance people and I
became the very last boy in Manod town.

I remember Dr Ramanan coming in for that big
pack of Hula Hoops because that was the last time I
saw Mohan. Mohan was the only other boy in our
school, and on 29 March he moved out.

When I first started at Manod Elementary there
were ten other boys — just enough for a game of

five-a-side, with one man on the bench. Unfortunately, five of them were the Ellis brothers, so when Mr Ellis went off to London to work on the New Thames Barrier, that was half the boys in the school gone and no more five-a-side, just three-a-side. It was OK if you had rush goalies. Then Terry Tailor's mam went off to learn to be a teacher, and Terry went with her. Then Wayne and Lewis Martin moved to Manchester because their new dad was in computers. He bought them a season ticket for City, and we were down to just kicking the ball around. Then Mr Ellis told Paddy Parry's dad that he could get him work on the New Barrier too, so off went Paddy, leaving me and Mohan with nothing to play except penalties.

The New Barrier, by the way, is this big floating wall thing that's supposed to stop London flooding again. They started to build it when the Old Barrier broke that time. Amazing that a place the size of London has to ask a little place like Manod for help to build its barriers. But that's how good Manod is, I suppose.

When he came in to pay, Dr Ramanan said to Mam, 'I won't say goodbye, Mrs Hughes, because I'll still be your doctor. We hope to see you very often.' Which is not really what you want your doctor to say.

'It's a shame,' said Dad.

'I'm sad to leave the people, but really there's nothing here for us now.'

Nothing here? There's everything here!

There's an off-licence (open from 6.30 p.m.), a Spar (only one unaccompanied child allowed in at any one time), unisex hairdressing at Curl Up N Dye, Mr Elsie's chemist's shop, and Mr Davis's butcher's shop, which has 'Always meat to please you; always pleased to meet you' written over the door. This isn't strictly true, as he's never pleased to meet you. When you go in, he says, 'Well?' You tell him what you want. He weighs it out and then he just points to the price on the till. Oh, and there's a shop called Save-A-Packet ('where *you* save money because we don't have packets'). They have these big bins full of dry goods and you scoop out as much washing powder, or corn-flakes, or whatever, as you like and then you pay at the till. We never go in there because Mam likes to know what she's buying, and of course the stuff in the bar-rels has no brand name. Or ingredients. Or sell-by date.

The best shop is the Mountain Rescue Charity Shop. They sell all kinds of things there. For instance, I got a skateboard there once for £3.50. When Jade Porty saw it, she said it used to be hers but she'd given it away 'to the poor children. And now you've got it. So you must be poor'. Which is a bit mad, because the shop isn't for poor children. It's for lost and injured mountaineers. I love looking in the window, because it's different every time. Sometimes a thing – say, a hat

19

– will be in the window, and the next day it's gone. And you can wonder about who bought it and then you'll see it somewhere in Manod – for instance, on Mr Morgan's head.

And there's Waterloo Park. That's a fantastic park that used to have a boating lake, a water feature and an indoor pavilion in case it rains. The pavilion was like a wooden house that had two ping-pong tables in it and, of course, a snooker table. Manod used to be globally famous for snooker tables. The quarry at the top of Manod Mountain used to produce the smoothest slate in Wales. It's closed now, but when it was open all the best snooker tables in the world were made of Manod slate. Minnie says there's one in Buckingham Palace and one in the Crucible in Sheffield. And there is one in the pavilion in Waterloo Park. It's still there, but you can't see it because the pavilion is padlocked and the windows are boarded up. The lake and the pavilion were closed a few years back because of all these problems with insurance. But it's still a great park. For instance, round the lake there's a great big wooden fence with a mural on it showing Scenes from the Life of Elvis Presley. That was Mr Davis's idea. He actually saw Elvis once, in Harlech Home and Bargain, when everyone else thought he was dead.

When they quarried the slate, they more or less hollowed out the mountain. They threw the bits they couldn't use all over the top of the mountain. All the other mountains around here have grass on the top. Ours is covered in broken slate. Basically they turned the mountain inside out. I mean, how many towns have got an inside-out mountain at the end of the High Street?

Slate is legend, by the way, and not just for snooker tables. You can make roofing tiles, doorsteps, fireplaces, floor tiles. Anything. In Manod, we've got slate roofs, slate doorsteps, slate window sills. There's even a slate pillar box and, by our school gates (slate), a statue of a man made of slate. And a slate bus shelter with a sign on the gable that says 'No Ball Games'. And when you go indoors, slate tiles on the kitchen floor. And a slate clock, we've got. You can write on slate too. They used to use it for blackboards in school. On the slate bus shelter, someone has written, 'GET ME OUT OF HERE!!!' in great big letters. They're only joking, of course. That's the thing about Manod people. They've got a sense of humour. As Dad says, 'They have to, or they wouldn't stay here.'

The whole of Manod – from the pub at the bottom to our garage at the top – is one colour. Slate colour. Grey, in fact. As Dad says, 'It's not the most interesting colour in the world, but it does go with the clouds.'

The only thing in Manod that's not grey – apart from the Elvis mural – is the cars. Dr Ramanan's car, for instance, was that deep red you only get on a Toyota. It looked like a big lady's fingernail.

As he started up the engine, Dad said to him, 'Manod has the lowest crime rate in Britain, Doc. You can't sniff at that.'

Dr Ramanan said, 'It also has the highest rainfall, of course. And perhaps the two are related.'

And then they went. I saw Mohan looking out of the heated rear window and I gave him a wave and thought, 'There goes my last chance of a game of footy.'

It's not that Mohan was much good. He had a left foot you could open tins with but it was a bit random, which meant that you spent most of the afternoon climbing over the wall to get the ball back and not developing your skills at all. But it was better than nothing, which is what I have now.

When the Ramanans' Toyota pulled off the fore-court, I remember thinking that the steering looked a bit mushy. I said to Dad, 'The steering looks a bit mushy.'

'I'm sure they know how to sort out steering in Blaenau.'

And as the Toyota drove away, he just kept staring at the number plate. I do that sometimes – see how far away something goes before you can't see it properly. I said to him, 'Fancy a game of penalties after tea?'

'No thank you,' he said, and went off into the

workshop and shut the door behind him, even though there was no car in there for him to work on.

Tom's mam came to collect him in her little Copen. Tom wanted to say goodnight to Dad, but Minnie told him not to bother as he was in a bad mood.

'Why's that then?' said Tom.

Minnie said, 'You know you're not supposed to count your chickens before they've hatched? Well, imagine if you waited till they hatched, and then you fed the chicks and made sure they had water and antifreeze and oil checks, and then they grew up and flew away.'

Tom said, 'I'm not sure you're supposed to give chickens antifreeze anyway.'

'No, but . . .' said Minnie. 'Nothing. Goodnight.'

Dad didn't come out even at closing time. Mam decided to try to cheer him up with a fish supper from Mr Chipz. She bought me a cheese pie without asking. Marie had rice instead of chips because she's watching her figure. Minnie had bean sprouts with peas because she's so unusual. And we got Dad a huge haddock.

When we got back, Dad said he wasn't hungry. Then I said, 'We've got you a huge haddock.' And he was persuaded.

When we were all sitting down, Dad said, 'I've got

something to tell you and it's this: the Snowdonia Oasis Auto Marvel is in trouble.'

Everyone started asking what kind of trouble, but he held his fork up and we all went quiet again.

'Today we've lost a valuable customer. Over the last year, we've lost nearly all our most valuable customers. And today we had a call from our petrol supplier. Normally they just put petrol in the tanks and collect the money once it's all sold. The problem is, we take an unusually long time to sell their petrol. They don't think it's worth coming up here any more. They say the only way they'll give us petrol is if we pay up front. Now, you can't have a garage with no petrol, so what I want to know is, what is Team Hughes going to do about that?'

Everyone in Team Hughes had a different idea.

Marie's idea was to sell up and move to London so she could get famous and we could all be part of her entourage.

I said, 'We can't sell the garage. This is where we live! That's the whole point.'

'Besides,' said Dad, 'we wouldn't get that much for it. Not enough to move to London.'

Mam's idea was that we turn the Snowdonia Oasis into something more than a garage. 'If you look at our two competitors,' she said, 'they're both more than garages. First, there's the filling station on the A496 – and that's more than a garage because it's a Little

Chef. And the other one is on the Blaenau bypass and that's more than a garage too, because it's an Asda.'

'But you can't just turn into an Asda,' said Dad.

'We could open a cafe. Or a bed and breakfast. We could call it the Mountain View'.

Dad wasn't convinced. 'The mountain view in question is a bit grey, isn't it? It's not pretty.'

I said, 'It's not pretty. It's unique. Our mountain is inside out.'

'That's true,' said Dad, 'but I'm not sure it's an advantage.'

Minnie's idea was an insurance job. That's when you burn the garage down, say it was an accident and then make a claim on the insurance. No one thought that was a good idea.

'You can't burn the garage down,' said Mam.

'It's easier than you think,' said Minnie, and she went into worrying detail about how to set fire to your own house. 'We're off to a head start with all this petrol lying about. All we'd need is some trained rats. You let them run under the floorboards with burning rags tied to their tails.' Honestly, she did make it sound very easy. She even offered to go through the insurance policies and work out how much we'd get. But Dad put his foot down.

'We are not going to burn the Oasis down,' he said. 'This is our home and Team Hughes is going to fight to keep that home. That's the whole point. Am I right?'

'Not just keep it,' said Mam. 'We're going to make it better than ever. We're going to make it grow.'

'Grow into what, though?' said Marie.

'We are going to make the Snowdonia Oasis Auto,' said Mam, and she was glowing when she said it, 'into the premier indoor attraction in Manod.'

And everyone clapped. And Dad gave me some of his haddock.

6 April

Cars today:
CARBON BLACK BMW M5 — went up
the mountain road!
RED NISSAN X-TRAIL — went up the
mountain road!
TWO WHITE COMBI VANS — went up
the mountain road!

Weather — cloudy. And rainy

Note: COWABUNGA!

You can learn a lot about life by watching the Turtles.

For instance, in 'Enter the Shredder' the Mouser Robots completely destroy the Turtles' sewer-lair – where they've lived for fifteen years – and then kidnap their revered master, Splinter. Do the Turtles sit there wondering how to pay for petrol? No. They go and look for him. They burrow through collapsed sewers. They track the Mouser Robots by following the trail of destruction. They fight the Purple Dragon street gang and finally rescue Splinter so everything ends up back the way it was, the way it's supposed to be.

If the Turtles can cope with a completely wrecked home and a kidnapped master, then Team Hughes can raise the money for a tank of petrol.

Dad bought an old Mini Cooper S (top speed 90 mph) at the police auction in Harlech. It needed loads of work doing to it. But it had all its original features. For instance, the knob of the gearstick was made of leather and the indicator arm had a little light on the end that flashed when you were signalling, like a tiny Lightsaber. Dad said it was just the kind of thing that went down well on eBay.

Mam had the brilliant idea of keeping the computer in the shop, so that people can have Internet access for a pound for half an hour. Mr Morgan uses it to email his son, who is in Australia. This causes friction with Marie, who does her coursework on the computer. So, in a way, it's good that only Mr Morgan's used it so far.

Also, Mam started shopping in Save–A–Packet instead of Asda. She bought the loose cornflakes. You could get a bag the size of a sleeping bag for the same price as one box of Easy Porridge. Bargain!

It turns out that the reason they don't put the ingredients on the cornflake tub in Save–A–Packet is because there are no ingredients in the cornflakes. When you put milk on them, they sort of disappear. Instead of a bowl of cornflakes, it looks like a bowl of lumpy yellow milk.

No one complained. Team Hughes was working together.

We didn't even complain when Mam cancelled our TV subscription channels. It was a pity about Cartoon Network. But we still had the Welsh-language cartoon channel, which was free. It had all the Welsh cartoons – Super Ted, Will Cwac Cwac – and all your favourites translated into Welsh. It was a nice change hearing Michelangelo say, *'Dwy'n hoffi partio!'* instead of, 'I like to party!'

While we were eating our lumpy yellow milk, Mam said, 'The Bala Lake Sea Scouts are having a car-boot sale today at Bala Marina. Can we go there and raise the money for petrol? What do you say?'

Marie said, 'You mean, you want us to sell some of our stuff?'

'Nothing too special. Just things you've got bored with or grown out of. How about it?'

I said, 'Would my Legotechnic do?'

'Dylan,' said Mam, 'Legotechnic would be perfect. Good boy.'

Minnie said, 'What about all your football stuff . . . your shin pads, and all those replica tops? It's not like you're going to be able to play an actual game for years.'

I said, 'Well . . .'

And then she said, 'Or what about your PlayStation 2? You've got no one to play that with either.'

'You can play that on your own. That's the point.'

Mam said, 'Just the Lego, Dylan. Thank you.'

*

So I got a bag of Lego. Marie got some old clothes and CDs. Minnie got her 'Country Vet' kit, the one with the real thermometer. Mam said, 'That's lovely, but I thought you needed that. I thought you were going to be a vet when you grow up.'

Minnie said, 'I've got other ideas now.' And she winked at me.

We haven't got a car as such, but we have got a tow truck – a 1997 Wrangler (top speed 110 mph), 59,000 on the clock, a special edition with chrome bumpers. We were just getting into it when Mrs Egerton's tiny Copen tootled on to the forecourt and Tom got out with this huge bag.

'Show Mrs Hughes,' said Nice Tom's mam.

He showed us what was in the bag. Turtles stuff. Tons of it: lunch boxes, the strap–on shell, the Sewer Scooter, you name it.

His mam said, 'He wants to sell it. To help you out.'

Tom didn't really look like he wanted to sell it. He looked like he wanted to cry. Our mam said, 'That's kind, but there's no need. It's our garage. We'll sort it out.'

'No, no. He loves his job here. Tell them, Tom.'

Tom said, 'I love my job here.'

'He'd much rather have his job than a silly lunch box he should've grown out of years ago. Tell them, Tom.'

Tom said, 'I'd much rather have my job than an original Turtles lunch box from the very first series with the special pizza-slice holder inside.'

'Go on, get in,' said his mam. So he did, and off we went. Tom said he hadn't brought the best Turtles stuff, not the super-poseable models or the Turtle Lair with extra sewage piping. It was just what he could spare. But the minute he put it all out on the trestle table behind the car, we were surrounded by people wanting to buy it. And Tom was surprisingly hard about the price. Someone wanted to buy the strap-on shell for five pounds. He made them pay twenty-five. 'It's highly collectable,' he said. 'And still in its box. They go for forty on eBay.' He got thirty for the Sewer Scooter. It all went in the first half-hour, apart from the lunch box.

We had a few problems with the Legotechnic, namely that Max kept trying to eat it. And then he kept trying to throw it at people. So it was a relief when Big Evans came and bought it all. He's a friend of my dad's. His daughter is in my class. Her name is Terrible Evans. It's not just me who calls her that, by the way. Everyone does. She's got two pigtails. That sounds nice and girly, but actually they make her look like a Viking.

'Is that Legotechnic?' said Big. 'She's into all that. Costs a packet in the shops. How much do you want then?'

I said, 'Twenty-five quid.'

Terrible said, 'It's not worth it, Dad. He's trying to rip you off.'

'I'm sure he's not. I'm sure he's just trying to raise a little money, like the rest of us.' He started talking to Mam about how he was thinking of going up to London to work on the New Barrier.

'We'll give you a tenner,' said Terrible.

'Fifteen,' I said.

Big gave us twenty. Which was nice of him.

Terrible is the only girl in school who likes the Turtles. She's got a Turtles pencil case and she sometimes wears socks with a pizza-slice pattern. And now she was looking at the Michelangelo lunch box. Tom opened it so she could see the special pizza-slice holder. You could see she wanted it. Girls and lunch boxes. With boys it's football teams. With girls it's lunch boxes. The girls with the Tracy Beaker lunch boxes all sit together, but they never sit with the girls with the Bratz lunch boxes. And neither of them will sit with that girl with the Will Cwac Cwac lunch box.

Tom said, 'It's from when they were first out, look. So it's collectable. I'll take fifteen for it. The Michelangelo ones are the most popular.'

She looked at it and said, 'Michelangelo's a pillock.' That's how terrible Terrible is. She can't even cope with someone liking a different Turtle.

In the end Tom got twelve for it. He'd made nearly

a hundred quid altogether. He looked so happy, it made me wish I'd brought my PS2 and sold that.

Marie sold all the clothes she'd brought. Minnie sold the country vet thing and Mam sold everything, including a set of patio furniture we got years ago when Dad was planning to build a patio. Altogether we made nearly £300. Mam was really proud of us. She gave us a pound each and told us to go and buy ourselves something from the stalls while she packed up. We had to take Max with us.

The field was mostly full of boring estates and hatchbacks, a couple of people carriers and one funny electric car. Every car had a table next to it, most of them covered in old lamps and kettles and packs of old Yu-Gi-Oh! cards. Except the one next to the electric car, which was covered in leaflets about solar power.

Minnie said, 'This'd be a great place to do a robbery. Just jump in one of the cars and drive off.'

'Yeah,' said Marie. 'Brilliant if you've got the urge to steal two old desk lamps and a book about the Queen.' She didn't want anything from the car-boot sale, so she walked up to the High Street and got herself a tube of Tanfastic, which is fake sun tan that you rub on your legs. It's very convincing if it's done right.

Minnie found this immense *Dictionary of Crime*

and Criminals with a pull-out chart of 'Master Criminals' inside.

Tom came back with something in a big shoebox. I asked him if it was Turtles stuff. He shook his head and a weird little scratchy noise came from inside the box. I thought it was best not to ask.

I chose a little ball with a bell inside it for Max.

When we got back to the Wrangler, Mam wasn't there. We found her standing by this silver Montego Estate (I'm constantly impressed by the ample boot capacity of the Montego, by the way), staring at a huge metal box with taps and dials and knobs all over it. It looked like a fiendish machine from Shredder's lair.

'What the shell?!?' said Tom.

'A Gaggia,' said Mam. 'It's for making coffee with.' She was biting her lip.

'What's wrong with a kettle?' said Marie.

'You're right. You're right. Of course you're right. Let's go,' said Mam.

We were all getting back into the Wrangler when Mam suddenly strode off across the field towards the Montego. The next thing we knew, two massive blokes were putting the big metal box in the back of our truck. Mam said, 'A hundred quid! ONE hundred! It's exactly what we need.' All the way back home, she talked about all the different kinds of coffee we'd be able to make and sell with the Gaggia. 'The Oasis

Auto Marvel is on its way,' she said. 'We'll sell the best cup of coffee between Snowdon and the sea. Wait till your dad sees this!'

When he saw it, Dad said, 'A hundred quid!' He sounded just as surprised about the price as Mam, but less happy. 'A hundred quid!' he kept saying.

Mam said, 'All it needs is filter papers. And coffee. Oh. And a plug.'

'A plug,' said Dad. 'A hundred quid – and it hasn't even got a plug! How do you know it even works?'

'If it doesn't work,' said Mam, 'you can fix it.' Which is true, see. He can fix anything.

Dad went off to his workshop and shut the door.

'You've got no vision!' shouted Mam. And she went into the house and she shut that door.

We all stood on the forecourt for a while. There was another scratchy sound from inside Tom's box. He looked at it like he'd forgotten about it and said, 'I got a present for Mr Hughes. Shall I give it to him now, d'you think?'

'Why not?' said Minnie. 'Might cheer him up.'

Inside the workshop, Dad's legs were sticking out from under the Mini.

Tom said, 'Mr Hughes?'

Dad grunted.

'Mr Hughes, Minnie said you were worried

because your chickens had flown the nest and you hadn't counted your eggs. So I got you this . . .'

Dad slid out from under the car and stared at Tom.

'It's a present,' said Tom, handing him the box.

Dad lifted the lid of the box and looked inside. And looked and looked, like he couldn't believe what he was seeing.

'It is chickens,' he said. 'Two chickens.'

'And a starter pack of chicken feed,' said Tom, bringing the packet out from behind his back.

Dad put the box down on the floor and gently tipped the chickens out. They ran straight back into the box and huddled together in the corner.

'I thought you could have free-range hens. And sell free-range eggs,' said Tom.

'We could. We could,' said Dad. 'A few chickens round the place will give us a bit of atmosphere.'

But the chickens weren't really into ranging. Tom had bought them from this man who rescued chickens from factory farms, so they'd always lived in tiny little cages. And now they were too agoraphobic to come out.

'Sorry about that, Mr Hughes,' said Tom.

'No problem. I'm sure they'll come out when they're ready. What shall we call them?'

Everyone looked at Minnie – what with her being the genius.

Minnie looked at the box. 'How can we give them

names before we've had a proper look at them?' she said. 'We'll have to wait till they emerge.'

We took the box outside and waited by the car vac for the chickens to emerge. They must have been even more agoraphobic than we first thought, because they never did emerge. Mam did, though. She emerged from the house at about two hundred miles per hour, plonked Max on my knee and disappeared into the workshop. We could hear her shouting but we couldn't make out any words except every now and then Dad yelling, 'A hundred quid!'

This went on for a very long time. The sky got dark. We got hungry. I was thinking, Maybe if I'd sold the PS2, we'd've made more money and they wouldn't be having this fight.

I looked in my pocket in case I had any chocolate, and I found the little ball I had bought for Max. I sat him on the floor and rolled it at him. He laughed, but it was the jingly noise, not the beauty of a ball in motion, that interested him. All the same, I carried on doing it. Once or twice he did sort of poke it with his foot, like a nearly kick.

Minnie said, 'Bit early to start working on his ball skills, isn't it?'

I said, 'If I have to wait seven years for my next game of football, I'm going to make sure it's a good one.'

*

That's when it happened. A set of headlights suddenly lit up the forecourt. Our shadows chased across the petrol pumps and the Alta Gaz. Max jumped up into my arms out of fright. A Nissan X-Trail (top speed 110 mph), a BMW M5 (top speed an amazing 161 mph!) and two Toyota HiAce vans swept on to the forecourt out of nowhere. Me and Minnie and Tom just stared as they rolled up to the mountain gate. The driver of the BMW wound down his window (he was a very clean man, by the way) and he said, 'If you could open the gate for us, we'd be very grateful. Thank you.'

We all ran over to open the gate. The man said, 'Thank you,' and the vehicles started to move through the gate and head off up the mountain.

Tom said, 'What the shell?!?'

Max kept shouting, 'Car! Car! Car!' which is sort of what I was thinking too – except I was also thinking, Those tyres are no good for off-roading.

The door of the workshop opened and Mam and Dad came out. They weren't shouting at each other any more. They were staring, like the rest of us. Even Marie came out in the end. 'Unexpected traffic on the mountain road,' she said. 'Probably the biggest thing that's ever happened in the whole history of Manod.'

We couldn't stop looking. Even one of the chickens stuck its head out of the box after a while.

'Where are they going?' said Tom.

Dad said, 'Nowhere. I mean, that's where the mountain road goes, isn't it? Nowhere.'

'Unless the Sellwood ladies have suddenly decided to have lots of friends over,' said Mam.

But the cars kept going well past the Sellwoods' place. We could see the smudges of headlights every now and then as they worked their way up the twisty road. Then suddenly a streak of light punched into the clouds, right up near the top. Everyone went, 'Wow!' all together. The light stayed there, sticking and spreading out, like a frozen firework.

Minnie said, 'Like some strange alien searchlight scanning the skies for a long-lost mother ship!'

I said, 'That's the Nissan. It's got safari lights mounted on the roof rack. And a heated glove compartment so you can keep your takeaway warm.'

And Tom said, 'Cowabunga!'

7 April

Cars today:
BLUE LEXUS – Mr Choi (didn't stop)
CARBON BLACK BMW M5 – the shiny man
(would have bought coffee)

Weather – rain

Note: THE BEST BITS ARE BETWEEN THE
LINES

In other words, they still hadn't come down the mountain!

Nice Tom is supposed to come to work at eight o'clock. When I went out to get the milk at seven o'clock, he was already there on the doorstep, staring up at the mountain. He said, 'They didn't come down then?'

I said, 'No, they didn't.'

'I wonder what they're doing up there.'

Minnie, by the way, had lots of ideas about what they were doing. 'They're most likely a criminal organization setting up an impregnable mountain headquarters from where they can take over the world.'

'Like Shredder?' said Tom.

'A bit like Shredder,' she said, 'but people, not giant intelligent mutated rats.' By now she'd put the chart of famous criminals up on her wall. Bonnie and Clyde were on there and Al Capone and Vincenzo Perugia (the one who stole the *Mona Lisa*). She spent ages looking at their faces. 'Some people say there's a criminal type, you know. That all criminals have a certain look. What d'you think?' She pointed to a picture of Toto Riina (the head of the Mafia) and said, 'Don't you think he looks a bit like Tom?'

'Tom is not a criminal. He's just frustrated.'

'What about her? I think she looks a bit like me.' She pointed to Anne Bonny, the pirate queen. She looked absolutely nothing like Minnie.

After breakfast (lumpy yellow milk again), me and Tom went and stood by the car vac and did some more staring up at the mountain. The big shoebox with the chickens in it was still there. Every now and then we'd hear a scratching from inside.

I said, 'Minnie says we can't give them names until they come out, right. But what if they won't come out until they've got names?'

'How d'you mean, Dylan?' said Tom.

'Well, if they had names, we could call them. We can't call them if they haven't got names, can we?'

'I wouldn't know how to think up names though,' said Tom. 'I haven't got the skills.'

'Well, you bought them, Tom, so we should call them Donatello and Leonardo, like the Turtles.'

Tom smiled, and it was the most immense smile I'd ever seen in my life. It totally rearranged his face and he looked like a completely different person. 'Only one thing,' he said. 'It could be Michelangelo, not Leonardo. Michelangelo is the party dude.'

So we called, 'Michelangelo . . . Donatello . . .' and the minute we said it, this tiny, feathery black head peeped out of the box.

Tom went, 'Yes! Look at that!' The feathery head went back in again, obviously.

I started calling them quietly again. In case you don't know, by the way, Donatello is the clever Turtle. Raphael is the angry Turtle. Leonardo is the grown-up Turtle and Michelangelo is the party dude. Everyone usually likes Michelangelo to start with. He's the one who eats lots of pizza and says, 'I like to party!' (*Dwy'n hoffi partio!*) Most people think he says it too often. Like about ten times in each episode, which means that if you were watching it on Cartoon Network, he might say it like fifty times before breakfast. So they tend to move on from Michelangelo. But not Tom. Because he's so loyal.

All the way to school that morning, I just kept looking up at the mountain behind me, in case the cars came back down. They didn't. And the longer they didn't, the more amazing it was.

'Told you,' said Minnie. 'International criminal

organization. They're probably setting up their satellite tracking station as we speak.'

I said, 'The police wouldn't let them.'

'Bought them off,' said Minnie.

Our policeman is Sergeant Hunter. We only really see him once a year, when he comes over from Blaenau to do cycling proficiency with Year Six. He didn't seem the type that you could buy off. But then, as Minnie pointed out, 'If an international criminal organization wanted to build a satellite tracking station, what could Sergeant Hunter do about it?'

Our school is twinned with a school in Malawi called Gumbi. We saved up and bought their school a computer and a modem so we could all swap emails once a week. We're supposed to pick one person and write them an email about life in Manod. We were each given a photograph of someone to write to. Mine was a boy called George. The photo showed him holding a football with a whole bunch of mates, under a sign that said 'Welcome to Gumbi'. So that's two differences between Gumbi and Manod. Gumbi's got boys and Gumbi's got a sign.

This is Minnie's email to Gumbi (it was to a girl named Nelly):

Dear Nelly,

We live in a small town at the bottom of a big mountain. In the old days, there was a famous quarry at the top of the mountain. The men who worked up there had to get up at five in the morning to walk to the quarry. They put little white stones all along the path so that they could see their way in the dark. A hundred years ago there were four thousand men working up there. Four thousand men walking up the mountain road past the Misses Sellwood's place. It's amazing to think of it. When they got there, they mostly made slate for roofs. They used to bring the slate out and cut it into tiles out in the open. There were different kinds of tiles such as Empress, Duchess, Countess and Wide Ladies. In the winter it was so cold they called it the North Pole and they had to cut the tiles in special underground shelters called *caban crwn.* That's why they got sick. Because when they cut the slate indoors, the dust went straight into their lungs. They were mostly dead before they were fifty. That doesn't sound that young, but it means that hardly anyone in Manod has a grandad.

Nowadays Manod has the lowest crime rate in the United Kingdom, but back then it was more interesting. An infamous and bloody murder was done in one of the *caban* in 1898. What happened was, Thomas Jones and Mary Bruton (aged 33) were walking back over the top when . . .

And Ms Stannard had deleted all the rest. So it must have been horrible. The email ended with Minnie saying, 'Let us know all about Gumbi. Especially any infamous and bloody murders.'

So that's what Minnie wrote. And this is what I wrote:

We saw a BMW, a Nissan and two combi vans go up the mountain road.

That's all I could think about.

Ms Stannard said, 'It's a bit thin, Dylan. Not very interesting.'

'How can you say that? They went up and didn't come down. That means they stayed up there all night. Where did they sleep? There's no houses up there, except the old one by the mine. Did they go down the mine? What are they doing up there? They could have an underground lair . . .'

'Why don't you say all that?'

'I just did.'

'I meant in your letter.'

'Well, it's sort of between the lines.'

'Well,' she said, smiling, 'let's sort of put it on top of the lines then, shall we?'

So I wrote:

We saw a BMW, a Nissan and two vans go up the mountain road and they haven't come down again yet.

Ms Stannard said it was still quite sparse and asked me to try and add to it for homework. 'I know you've got new chickens. You could write about them.'

Ms Stannard said perhaps I'd better take the email home with me and finish it there. 'Maybe you'll find something a bit more interesting to write about.'

She was right about that anyway.

When we got back to the garage, the chickens were on the grass by the 'OPEN' sign. Mam had found an old rabbit hutch for them to shelter in, so they mostly stayed in there. Sometimes they'd come out, but they always looked nervous. When they walked, they put one foot down, then stood still and looked round, like they were in a minefield. Whenever anyone opened the shop door, they ran inside. Minnie said it was because they liked the fluorescent lights.

We tried to chase them out again, but every time we opened the door, the 'pong ping' noise frightened them and they ran off and hid behind the battery carousel. We were coaxing them out again for about the fifteenth time when suddenly the door went 'pong ping' behind us. We looked up and there he was, the clean man from the BMW.

'Oh,' said Minnie.

'Would you mind holding the door open a moment?' said Mam.

He looked a bit bewildered, but he did it. And Minnie chased the chickens right past him.

'Sorry about that,' said Mam, all calm, as if well-dressed strangers were always coming into her shop to help get the chickens out. 'What can we do for you?'

He was wearing the whitest shirt I'd ever seen. It was nearly luminous in fact. He was wearing it under a blue suit with his cuffs sticking out so you could see that they had little shiny cufflinks. His shoes were shiny too. He was the shiniest person I'd ever seen. Even his car was shiny, which is inexplicable considering it'd just come down the mountain road.

'Just petrol, please,' said the shiny man.

I said, 'I'll get it,' really quickly, because I was desperate to have a proper look at the car. It was only when I got out in the rain that I realized it might have been more interesting to get a proper look at the man. Anyway, in case you really want to know, the car had black and grey nappa-leather seats, satellite navigation, full communications pack and about forty thousand miles on the clock. I know you probably think it was nosy of me to look at the mileage, but it's all part of market research. The 5-Series BMW sometimes develops oil-consumption problems after the first fifty thousand miles. So it would be good for Dad to know the mileage.

I'd just finished filling the tank when Donatello jumped on the bonnet and started scraping away at the paintwork. I shooed her off before she had a chance to scratch it, but she did do her business before she left. I thought I'd better wipe it off, so I went back in to get some tissues.

Inside, the man was just giving Mam his credit card. 'I notice you have a Gaggia,' he was saying. 'Could I trouble you for a double espresso?'

Mam was great, of course. 'Not at present,' she said, 'though very possibly in the very near future.'

And I said, 'If you're still around in the very near future, that is.' See that? Market research again. Trying to find out how long he was planning to stay.

'We just need some filters. And some coffee. And some cups,' explained Mam. 'We do do dry cleaning.'

'I'll bear that in mind,' said the man.

'And we can get you discount tyres if you like,' I said.

'I've got tyres, thank you.'

I said, 'Yes, I noticed. Ceat Tornadoes. You'd get a better ride with Pirelli P7s. I just thought I'd mention it. That mountain road can be a bit rough.'

'Yes. Well, thank you very much . . .'

Then I remembered to say, 'Oh – welcome to

Manod, highest rainfall in the UK,' which is what Dad always says.

'I suppose everyone has to be good at something,' said the man, and I realized that somehow I'd said the wrong thing. When Dad said that thing about the rainfall, he made it sound good.

I couldn't figure out what I'd said different until Minnie said, 'Highest rainfall and lowest crime rate. The two facts may not be unconnected.' Then the man laughed. She is a brainbox.

Mam said, 'If there's anything you need, just let us know and we'll do our best. We do photocopying, Internet access, newspapers on request. And petrol, of course.'

'You've already given me petrol. That's why I gave you the credit card.'

'Of course it is, sorry.' She was a bit flustered because, behind the counter, Max was pulling at her skirt.

She picked him up. 'Oh,' said the man. Mam looked up and knew what it was right away. He'd seen Max's eyes. They are huge. You could fall into them. Mam smiled. The man said, 'Madonna and child.'

Madonna? I looked on the paper rack. Did he want a magazine about Madonna? Or a poster? Or a CD? We didn't have any.

Mam handed him his card back, saying, 'Thank

you very much, Mr . . .' She looked at the card to see his name.

He said, 'Lester.'

'Oh. Thank you very much, Lester.'

As he was going out of the door, I remembered Donatello's business on the bonnet. I grabbed the tissues and ran out after him. He was just opening the driver's-side door when I shouted to him to wait.

'The hens are free-range,' I said, wiping the muck off the bonnet. 'We sell the eggs if you're interested.'

'Not at the moment.' He got in his car.

'Just as well.' I picked the hen up. 'They haven't actually laid any yet. Have you, Donatello?'

The man had just shut his door. But when I said that, he opened it again and stared at me.

'Sorry,' I said.

'What did you say?' he said.

'Oh. I was talking to the hen, not you.'

'And the hen is called . . . ?'

'Donatello.'

He kept looking at me.

I shrugged. 'The other one's Michelangelo. I know they're boys' names and hens are girls but . . .'

'Whose idea was it to call them that?'

'Oh. Well. Mine, really. I don't like Donatello as much as Michelangelo. I know a lot of people hate Michelangelo, but I think that's stupid. He's legend.

They're all great, aren't they? Michelangelo, Raphael, Leonardo and Donatello.'

'Yes, they are,' he said.

'In their different ways,' I said.

'In their different ways,' he agreed. 'I have to go now, but I'd like to carry on this conversation another time.'

Then he pulled the door shut with the satisfying *thunk* you only get with a real class marque.

When I went inside, the others were all sort of holding their breath.

'What did he say?' asked Mam.

'He was just asking what the hens were called.'

'Well, that was friendly then,' said Mam. 'Go and get Dad. Quick.'

Minnie ran off to the workshop while me and Marie started arranging the collapsible camping chairs (Car Boot Crazy at the Dynamo Blaenau Football Club ground – £1 each) in a circle round the telly.

When Dad came in, Mam said, 'Right then, sit down. We've got something to show you.' And she turned on the telly, and on came the CCTV tape of Lester's visit. CCTV tape is not like normal telly. There's no sound and the picture is very jumpy, so we didn't see the door open. It was just – bing! – there's

Lester in the shop – bing! – he's by the drinks cabinet – bing! – he's looking at the newspapers.

Mam said, 'He's having a good look round. He wants to buy something, look. He just can't find anything he wants.'

'Who is it?' said Dad.

'That,' said Mam, 'is a new customer.'

I said, 'It's him from up the mountain.'

Dad went right up to the screen 'Why are his shoes all shining like that?'

'Because they've been polished.'

'You mean they really were that shiny? I thought it was something wrong with the tape.'

'They really were that shiny.'

'Whatever he's doing up that mountain,' said Dad, 'it's not looking after sheep.'

We were still glued to the CCTV. Mam said, 'Look, that's when he noticed the coffee machine. He'd have bought a coffee if it was working. See? What did I tell you. That Gaggia is going to pull them in.'

Dad said, 'Did he order any papers?'

'No.'

'Then he's not staying. A man with shoes like that reads the paper every day. If he was staying, he'd've ordered the papers.' He was starting to sound grumpy again, like he did when the Ramanans left. 'Come on,' he said. 'Homework.' But as soon as he said it, the door went 'pong ping' again. We all turned round, and who had come in? Only Lester. He looked pretty surprised to see a circle of camping stools around the telly. He'd have been even more surprised if he'd known we were watching him, but Mam quickly flicked it to forecourt live feed, so the only thing on the screen was his car and the back of the Jet Wash. Now I think about it, that might have looked even weirder.

'You said something about getting papers,' he said.

'Yes,' said Mam.

'I'd like the *FT* if you can get it.'

Mam looked a bit blank, but Dad said, 'Oh. No problem. *FT*. How long would you like it for? Just a day. Couple of days? Weeks?'

'Well,' came the answer, 'until further notice, I suppose.'

'Right. Until further notice it is,' said Dad.

Then the man said goodbye to everyone. Then he looked at me and he said a separate goodbye.

We waited until we heard the engine start up. Then Mam said, 'What's an *FT*?'

'An *FT*,' said Dad, 'is . . . beside the point. Mrs Porty will know. The point is, the point is . . . we have a new customer! A brand-new regular customer. Until further notice!'

'Thanks to the Gaggia,' said Mam.

'What d'you mean, thanks to the Gaggia? He bought a newspaper, not a coffee.'

'But he would have bought a coffee if we'd had any.'

'If we'd had any! He might've bought a racehorse if we'd had some. Shall we start a little stables just in case?'

'The Gaggia set the tone, didn't it? It's classy, that's what. He saw the Gaggia and he thought, These are the kind of people I can do business with. Frothy-coffee people. Not greasy-spoon people.'

Dad looked at her. Then he looked at the Gaggia and he said, 'Yes. It was. All thanks to the Gaggia.'

So we knew that row was over, which was nice.

Then we all watched the CCTV tape one more time for luck.

8 April

Cars today:
LAND ROVER — Mr Morgan
BLUE MONTEGO ESTATE — Mrs Porty
(came with the papers and was tempted by
the coffee. Said she would come back for
one later)
FIAT MULTIPLA — Mr Arthur from the
newspaper (full tank, latte)
TWENTY-ONE WHITE COMBI VANS!!!
RED FORD KA — Ms Stannard (stopped
for chocolate and ended up buying a hot
chocolate)
BLUE LEXUS — Mr Choi (stopped for petrol,
didn't want coffee)
GREEN DAIHATSU COPEN — Mrs Egerton
(came in to look at the coffee machine, said
she didn't like the look of it, asked for a
cup of tea. We don't do teas. Tom did one
for her just this once)
VAUXHALL ASTRA ESTATE 1.9 CDTi —
Mr Davis (first visit to shop — potential new
customer?)

Weather — wet locally. Sunny on higher ground

Note: SOMETIMES SUNSHINE IS NEARER
THAN YOU THINK

That same evening Dad came back from the Cash and
Carry with coffee, filters, paper cups, shoe polish

(because 'that man does not keep his shoes like that without polishing them') and a plug for the Gaggia.

Mam came back from the Snowdonia Mountain Rescue Charity Shop with a book called *Coffee Cavalcade* (20p), which told you how to make all kinds of different coffee and – geniusly – a BMW M5 *Owner's Manual*. 'Not that we want his lovely car to pack up,' she said, 'but it's as well to be prepared.'

Dad took that for himself and gave the coffee book to Tom, saying, 'Get reading that then. Your career in catering is about to begin.'

Tom said thanks a lot and rang his mam to tell her about it.

FT, by the way, is short for the *Financial Times*.

Next morning we waited ages, but the shiny man didn't come. Only Mr Arthur from the paper in his Fiat Multipla (top speed 109 mph). Which was interesting for me. I've always wanted to see a Fiat Multipla up close because I know it's got three seats in the front, which is unusual. Also, with its snubbed bonnet and widely spaced lamps, it actually looks like a turtle!

Mr Arthur is the editor of the *Manod Month*, our local newspaper. It used to be called the *Manod Week*, but there isn't enough news in Manod to fill a newspaper every week.

'That's because most news is crime,' said Minnie, 'and Manod is sadly lacking in crime.'

'Don't know about sadly,' said Dad.

'You'd like more crime, wouldn't you, Mr Arthur? Something to write about.'

'I was going to write about these visitors,' said Mr Arthur, 'but there's nothing to write. Except they're here. And everyone knows that already. I'm going to have to write about you, Dylan.'

At first I thought he was joking. But he really did want to write about me.

'Being the only boy left in Manod,' he said. 'Having no one to play footy with. That must be interesting.'

I wasn't sure it was that interesting actually.

Dad said, 'I play footy with him,' which wasn't strictly true. 'If you're looking for something to write about, why not the absence of a sign for Manod on the A496?'

'The sign is not a news priority, Mr Hughes,' said Mr Arthur. 'Everyone who wants to know about the sign already knows. A boy who has no one to play footy with though, that's a story.'

I said, 'I'll be able to play with Max, soon as he's old enough. He's nearly one.'

'So that'll be six years till you get a game.' He wrote something in his notebook. 'Well, there's my headline. Now I'll get my photo.'

He pulled out his camera and straight away, like magic, Marie was standing next to me. 'You can't take a picture with him looking like that,' she said. 'Hasn't even brushed his hair. When they have their photo taken for the newspapers, they spend hours in make-up and choosing clothes and—'

'Yeah, but I've got to be in Traswynydd by lunchtime.'

'It won't take long,' said Marie. 'Tom will fix you a coffee, won't you, Tom?'

'Oh yes,' said Tom. 'What would you like? Cappuccino, espresso . . .'

'Honestly, no. I've got a funeral to get to, see.'

'Americano, mocha, mochaccino . . .'

'Really, Tom. Thanks all the same'

'Please,' pleaded Marie. 'At least let me brush his hair.'

'All right. I'll have a coffee, thanks. A normal coffee with milk in.'

'Latte it is then,' said Tom.

'And I'll have an espresso, Tom,' said Dad.

Marie dragged me inside and up to the bedroom she shares with Minnie, and then she started brushing her own hair.

'I thought I was the one whose hair needed brushing?'

'I'm going to be in the picture too, aren't I? You want your sister in the picture, don't you?' She brushed her hair for about a hundred years and then she started brushing her face with this little thing of blusher. Every now and then she'd look at me and say, 'Hurry up then.'

I was quite interested in looking round the girls' room. I'm not normally allowed in there, see. One wall was nearly covered in tiny pictures. 'They're from the "Be Lovely" page in *Closer* magazine,' she said. 'There's a beauty tip there for every part of the body – eyes, teeth, fingernails, toenails – every detail of the female body.' It was quite interesting, when you were close up. But when you stepped back it was even more interesting, because she'd arranged all these cuttings into the shape of a woman, there on the wall. Presentation skills, see, that's what she's got.

When she'd finished, she made me take her photo with a Polaroid camera.

'What for?'

'So I can see how I look.'

'Look in the mirror.'

'You look different in photos,' she said. 'The camera adds five pounds.'

When we got back down, Marie said, 'Sorry to have kept you waiting, Mr Arthur,' and did him a smile the size of a Mercedes radiator.

'That's all right,' said Mr Arthur. 'Worth every minute.' He took a picture.

'Do another one now,' said Marie. 'Side on.'

She stood side on with her hand on her hip. In the end, she made him take about a million pictures of her standing in various poses until he said, 'I've really got to run. The funeral will be over.'

Marie wanted to know when it would be in the paper and made him promise to send her copies of the prints. He sent her a really nice one of her with her hair and teeth shining, about a week later. It completely made up for the fact that he'd cut her off the picture on the front page of the paper. It was just me standing by a petrol pump with a football under my arm and the heading 'The loneliest boy in Wales'. By the way, the Fiat Multipla does have three seats in the front row. Disappointingly, the driver's seat is in the normal place. If it had been in the middle, that would have been completely beastie.

Tom had made Mr Arthur his latte and Dad his espresso. He thought the machine was broken because it only made a thimbleful of espresso. Tom kept pressing the button until he'd filled a mug, and Dad drank it. He was quite jumpy after that. He told me and Minnie to go to school.

'But we want to see the shiny man.'

'Yeah, the shiny man, where is he? Has he fled the country? Yeah, he's probably fled the country. And left us with a pink newspaper and two ton of coffee.' He was speaking really fast. It was a bit concerning really.

Mam said, 'Dad, the coffee is making you edgy. Go and have a drink of water.'

'No, no, no, no. I'm going to take the paper up to him. Customer service, that's what it's all about. Dylan, get in the car.'

'But you told me to go to school.'

'No, I want you to come with me. He's taken to you. We'll take him up his paper and a cappuccino. That's what customer relations is all about, isn't it? Going the extra mile.'

Minnie said she was coming too.

Mam told Dad that it was daft to go all the way up the mountain with one cup of coffee. It didn't make economic sense, and anyway it would be cold when he got there. When Dad replied, he was talking so fast no one understood a word. He just went outside and climbed into the Mini Cooper. Minnie said, 'Can I get in the front since the car is named after me?'

Dad said, 'Yes.'

I said, 'But it's oldest in the front. I should be in the front.'

Dad said, 'Yes,' again. His mind wasn't on it.

I shoved past Minnie and strapped myself into the front seat. The interior was surprisingly luxurious with lots of faux walnut and the smell of leather. It was also surprisingly small. I felt like an egg in an egg box. I said, 'Are you sure we should be going up the mountain in this? I mean, how big is this engine?'

'If you don't like it,' said Dad, 'get in the back.'

I didn't. But I should have. Every time there was a hole in the road, we bounced out of it like a football. One time we spun around completely. Dad seemed to be pure delighted with this. 'It's just like *The Italian Job*!' he yelled.

I said, 'What's "The Italian Job"?', trying to start a conversation that would take my mind off the possibility that we might eventually bounce off the mountain completely.

'You know *The Italian Job*. A group of criminals does a big robbery in Milan. Or is it Turin? One of those places, anyway. And they get away by stopping all the traffic. They cause this big traffic jam and they get away in Mini Coopers because the Mini can drive down steps and through underpasses and drainpipes and everything. Brilliant.'

Minnie leaned forward – which was pretty brave of her. 'How much did they get away with?' she said.

'Millions. It was bullion. They nicked bullion.'

'Gold bullion?'

'A big pile of it. Tons of it.'

'And they got away with it?'

'Yeah. Well, sort of. You'd have to see it. Michael Caine was in it.'

'Oh,' said Minnie, disappointed, 'it was a film. I thought you meant it was a proper robbery.'

*

You can't often see the top of the mountain from Manod because the top is usually covered in cloud. And so is the middle. So is the bottom a lot of the time. Sometimes the cloud in Manod is so low, you have to walk through it to get to the upstairs toilet. I know it sounds exciting, driving through cloud, but it's actually like driving through lots of dirty grey dishcloths. We were driving through grey so long, we began to feel we were turning grey ourselves.

A little white lamb suddenly jumped out in front of the car. Dad braked and parped the horn, and the lamb ran off. Typically, it ran off straight ahead, down the middle of the road, so we had to stay behind it. As Minnie said in her letter to Gumbi, 'We drove at lamb speed through the murky air of Planet Dishcloth for what seemed a lifetime, until all at once we were out, above the cloud, on the upper slopes of Manod Mountain.'

And guess what? It was sunny! It had been raining more or less non-stop in Manod since February, so driving into the sun was like – well, imagine if you opened a cupboard in your kitchen and found a beach. Dad wound down the windows. The daft lamb ran back into the cloud. After all that grey, the green of the grass and the white of the lambs seemed like the brightest colours you'd ever seen. Even the slate didn't look grey anymore. It was blue-black and silvery, like an old Mercedes with a new wax finish.

Out of the back window all you could see was this dirty, thick duvet of cloud stuffed into the valley, with Blaenau Mountain sticking up out of it in the distance.

The road ahead was just like a dribble of tarmac with grass growing down the middle of it, like a really long Mohican. You could see the old shepherd's hut off to the left. 'He's got to be in there,' said Dad. 'There's nowhere else.' He wasn't talking so fast now.

As we got nearer we could see two men in orange jackets. One of them was on a quad bike. I was just getting excited when Dad stopped the car.

'What?'

'Look.' There was a barbed wire fence going straight across the road and over the hillside. 'They've fenced off the whole top of the mountain.'

We all got out of the car and looked over the fence. The man on the quad bike drove over. It seemed to take ages for him to get to us, and then he didn't get off his bike or take off his hard hat. He said, 'Can I help you?' in a voice that said he wouldn't help you if you were hanging off a cliff.

'Nice morning,' said Dad. 'We've brought Lester his paper.'

'And his coffee,' I said, holding it up.

'Pass them over. I'll see he gets them.'

'Oh, but . . . the coffee will go cold.'

'I'll see he gets it.'

'This fence . . .' said Minnie.

'It's a temporary structure. We apologize for the inconvenience. It will be removed once we've secured the site.'

'What site's that then?' said Dad.

'Our site,' said the man in orange. Then he put the *FT* on his seat and the cappuccino into a handy drinks holder just under the handlebars, and was gone.

Minnie said, 'Well, there's a criminal headquarters if ever I saw one.'

She was pointing at two shapes next to the old hut. You couldn't see them at all at first because they were the same colour as the grass and the stones. But if you kept looking, you could make out two domes, one on each side of the hut. They were like big tents, but not flappy or flimsy at all. They were made of something hard, like two big shells.

We watched the man in the hard hat tootle up to one of the domes on his quad bike and then go inside. I said, 'The Technodrome!' because that's what it looked like. In case you don't know, the Technodrome is the headquarters of the Turtles' arch enemy, Arko Saki, known as the Shredder. It's a big, round, heavily armed metal ball with rooms inside. It's like a building that rolls. Only this one probably didn't roll. Dad and Minnie didn't know what the Technodrome was, so they didn't say anything about it. Dad was just looking back down the valley and then up at the sky.

After a while Minnie started fretting about going to school.

'Yes,' said Dad. 'Seems funny though, to be somewhere nice and sunny and then drive off into the rain on purpose.' He still didn't move. 'Do you know, there are places in the world where the weather's like this all the time? Sunny and bright.'

I said, 'Like Gumbi. It hardly ever rains there.'

'Or like here,' said Minnie. 'It looks like it's always sunny up here. Look how dry the grass is.'

'Oh, yeah,' said Dad. 'That's cheered me up no end.'

Which surprised me a bit, him saying that, because why did he need cheering up?

So we drove back down through Planet Dishcloth, saying nothing, just quietly turning grey. Then suddenly, up ahead of us, two great lights appeared in the mist. Something big was driving towards us up the cinder road. Dad flashed his headlights and beeped the horn. The lights stopped moving and so did we.

'Wonder who that is,' said Dad. 'I hope he's going to back up.'

Nothing happened.

Then Dad said, 'Dylan, go and tell them it's easier for them to back downhill than it is for me to back uphill. Go on.'

I stepped out of the car. It really was like a different planet out there. I couldn't see my hand in front of my face, but I could hear the engine of the vehicle churning over and even feel the warmth of the engine in the wet air, like the hot-air blower in the customer toilet. I walked four or five paces before I saw it: the front end of a van, jutting out of the mist like a massive present sticking out of tissue paper. I couldn't see the whole van, but I could tell it was the same kind as we had seen the other day. It had 'F a V' written on the door.

I shouted, 'Hello?'

I could hear a window being wound down, and out of the mist a voice shouted, 'Hello?'

I couldn't see a face.

'Dad says it's easier for you to back downhill than it is for us to back uphill.'

'Tell Dad he's wrong.'

I thought about this for a minute. Then I said, 'Are you sure? He's not usually wrong.'

'Maybe he's losing his touch, eh?'

And that was it. I could hear the window going up again.

Dad was cross. He kept muttering, 'Can't see a blind thing,' as he bumped up on to the grass. The engine of the van coughed and the big yellow eyes lurched forward. It passed us in the mist. Once it had gone by, Dad went to put the Mini in gear again. but then he stopped. Another pair of big yellow eyes was going by: a second van was rumbling past, kicking up big sods of earth and even stones.

'Hell's milk teeth,' said Minnie.

Then another one went by. Followed by a fourth, then a fifth, a sixth, a seventh . . .

There were twenty-one. Plus the two that were already up there. That's twenty-three big vans on the top of Manod Mountain. When we were sure the last one had gone, we headed back down to town. But me and Minnie spent the whole time looking out of the back window at the mist. It was full of tail lights.

When we got back to the shop, the forecourt was jammed with cars. We could hardly get in at the shop door, it was that full. Everyone in Manod had seen the vans go up the High Street and then turn left up the mountain. Everyone knew that something was going on, and everyone thought we must know what it was.

Mrs Porty was at the counter saying, 'I hear it's a telephone mast, which is a terrible thing because everyone knows they spread radiation and though there are no people up there, there are badgers.'

Mam was holding Max. She looked tired and cross. 'I'm afraid I can't help you, Mrs Porty,' she was saying.

'Well, I heard,' said Mr Morgan, 'that it was going to be a bunker for the government in case there was a big attack. They're going to helicopter them all up on to the recreation ground and they'll have police cars waiting by to take them up the mountain. The vans were taking food up there, tinned food like, and dry goods. And they'll be comfy in there for a year and up.'

'Like Baxter Stockman,' said Tom. Everyone looked at him. 'He was the one who made Mouser Robots that could eat through metal. People thought he just had a few of them. Then April O'Neil found an underground cave and it was completely full of them, hundreds of them, just lying there waiting.' Everyone still looked at him. He said, 'In the Turtles.'

'Oh,' said everyone. 'Right.'

Then Big Evans said, 'Well, I heard it was good news.'

It went quiet for a bit.

'I heard that all these vans and what-have-you, they've gone up there to reopen the quarry. There's going to be work in Manod. That's what I heard. What do you think?'

'That would be very nice,' said Mam.

Mr Choi said, 'We had some young people in, the other night, come down from Blaenau they had, looking for a musical rave. Could that be it? Could it be unruly youths?'

You could see that Mam had had enough of this. She was going to chuck everyone out, which would have been a great selling opportunity missed. So it was good that Dad came in and shouted out, 'We've just been up there, so you could ask us.'

Everyone started talking at once.

Dad put his hands up in the air and said, 'Before we start, who would like a coffee? And what kind?'

Everything went quiet for a minute. Then Tom's mother asked for a skinny latte decaf. Everyone stared at her. They didn't know that Tom had been reading *Coffee Cavalcade* to her down the phone.

Mr Morgan coughed and asked for one too.

'Skinny latte decaf?'

'Coffee.'

'Coming up.'

Mam took the orders. Dad made the coffees. I passed them round. And that was great teamwork. I looked across at Mam to see if she was cheering up. Dad had given her a big frothy mochaccino with a flake in it. The steam was swirling all around him like a genie.

'Toxic waste,' said Mrs Porty, 'that's what I heard.'

'Oh, I wouldn't say so,' said Dad. 'They've got a barbed-wire fence round the old quarry. They're very big on security. I can't see that would be a worry with toxic waste. Who'd want to steal toxic waste?'

There was more talking and the door went 'pong ping'. Everyone looked round. It was Mr Davis, the butcher. Everyone was too surprised to speak. He has not been in our shop for eleven years; I don't know why. In fact he didn't actually come in now, he just stuck his head round the door and snarled, 'I know what's going on up there, don't think I don't.'

Tom's mam said, 'Perhaps you wouldn't mind telling us then, Mr Davis?'

He said, 'And I know you're all in on it. Don't think I don't. You all wee in the same welly, I know that.'

Then he was gone.

Everyone looked at Dad. He shrugged. 'Never weed in a welly in my life.' Everyone laughed.

And then the phone rang and everyone went quiet again. Dad answered it. Everyone leaned forward, trying to hear. You could tell it was a man. And Dad was being very polite to him, saying things like, 'No trouble, honestly. No, really. Of course.' We could tell it was him. When Dad put the phone down, everyone started asking questions at once. Dad shushed them. 'He said thank you for the papers and coffee. That he's quite happy to come and collect them himself, so there's no need to take them up in future.'

'See,' said Mrs Porty, 'something to hide. This is exactly what happened in Llechwedd with the wind farm.'

'But . . .' said Dad. Everyone went quiet again. '. . . if it's no trouble, and if Dylan wants to come up tomorrow, he's got something up there the boy might be interested in.'

Every single person looked at me.

Ms Stannard looked really puzzled. She said, 'I don't think I've ever known you be interested in anything, Dylan.'

'What is it you're interested in, Dylan?' asked Mrs Porty.

I shrugged. 'I talked to him about hens,' I said.

'Hens?'

'Hens.'

9 April

Cars today:
All of them. Every single car in Manod and
the outlying farms.

Weather – sunny intervals. Well, one sunny
interval. Apart from that, rain

Note: EGGS ARE SO VERSATILE

I remember this day because it was so random. No one
normally takes any notice of me at all, but this day
everyone in Manod was looking at me. When I left for
school, Big Evans was on the forecourt talking to Dad
about his noisy gearbox.

'Course I may not need a gearbox if it's right about
the quarry,' he said. And he winked at me! 'You going
to find out for us then, young Dylan? You going to see
what's going on up there?'

'Can't,' I said. 'School.'

Dad said, 'School can wait a bit, can't it?'

'Not really.'

'School's important. But it might be a bit rude not
to go up, seeing as he did ask and seeing as he is a
guest in this town?'

I just said, 'Got to go,' and went.

*

Mr Morgan passed me in the High Street in his Land Rover. He slowed right down and leaned out of the window. 'Been up yet, young Dylan?' he asked.

I said, 'No. Got school.'

'Fair enough. No pressure,' he said. I thought at first he must be talking about his tyres, but when we passed Mr Chipz, Mr Choi was opening up for the day and he asked me if I'd been up yet too.

'Can't. It's school.'

'Whenever you're ready. No pressure.'

When we got to the school gates, more or less everyone was asking me. It was like everyone in Manod had gone completely random. It was a relief to get inside the school.

Or it would have been a relief if Ms Stannard hadn't said, 'Oh. You're early, Dylan Hughes.'

'No, I'm not.'

'Earlier than expected. I thought you were going up the mountain.'

'Couldn't,' I said.

'Why not?'

'Well . . . school.' I really think she should have known that, to be quite honest.

'Oh.' She looked at me for a long time, like she was trying to puzzle something out. Then she said, 'Did you finish your letter to our friends in Gumbi?'

Which obviously I hadn't because of all the excitement about the new customer.

'Right then. As you seem to be finding it hard to think of things to write about, I suggest you go to the top of the mountain, see what's going on up there, and write about that.'

'What? Just go, miss? Up the mountain? By myself?'

'I'm sure your father will be only too happy to help you with your homework. I'll text him.'

Dad got me from school and we went up the mountain. When we came through the cloud and into the sunshine, Dad stopped the car for a minute, got up and walked around in the bright blue air for a while. He tried to get me to join him, but I stayed in the car.

Then we drove right up to the wire and Dad flashed the men with his headlights. The men on the quad bikes came trundling over. I thought they were going to chase us away again, but Dad said, 'We've got—'

And the one in the hard hat said, 'I know what you've got.' He unhooked the wire for us and we drove through. We passed a long, low shed with about six men standing around inside, and some more men sort of jogging towards it.

'That was the canteen when this was a mine,' said Dad. He stopped the car. And I saw why the men were jogging. They were chasing a football. One of them trapped it, turned and then booted it back. The wind caught it and it came spinning towards us. I dived out of the car just in time to chest it down. I looked up. All the men had their hands in the air, shouting, 'Over here! Over here!' I thought, if I do a good job here, they might ask me to join in. I was just lining up the shot when something happened. All the men put their hands down and walked off towards the shed. I looked behind me. Lester was walking towards us. He said good morning. Dad said, 'Morning. How was the *FT*?'

'Yes. Thanks for getting it.'

'And the petrol? The petrol was good, I hope.'

'The petrol,' said Lester, looking a bit bewildered, 'was fine. The petrol was fine. I have something I think might interest you.' Then he noticed that I had the football. 'You can leave that out here on the grass,' he said.

So that was it. I didn't even get a kick. We followed Lester towards the old quarry. Dad kept nudging me and hissing at me to look interested and be polite. 'We're going to go inside the mountain. I haven't been inside since I was your age. We used to come up here and play games and smoke ciggies. Then they put these cages over the entrance. This is going to be good.' It would have been a lot better if we'd had a kick-around.

Walking into the mountain, I couldn't help think-ing about Baxter Stockman and his cavernous lair full of Mouser Robots. I grabbed hold of Dad's hand. But as it turned out, there were no robots and it wasn't cavernous. It was quite cosy really, like a tunnel, with soft yellow lights on the walls and a nice warm breeze blowing from somewhere. Randomly, there were narrow railway tracks on the floor.

All around were piles of big wooden boxes. Two men in fluorescent orange jackets picked one of the boxes up and set it on top of a set of wheels. Then one stood at the front and one at the back, and they trundled the box along the track, down into the mountain. Lester watched them until they were just two bobbing orange dots, then he smiled at us and said, 'Over here.'

One wooden box was leaning against the wall with a big light shining on it. He made us stand right in front of the box. You couldn't see the orange dots now, but you could still hear the wheels grumbling off down the track. Lester lifted the lid off the crate and then stood back.

The inside of the wooden box was even more unexpected than the inside of the mountain. It wasn't dry goods and it wasn't toxic waste.

It was a picture, a picture of a woman trying to read a book. The woman's face was in colour, but her clothes were in black and white and the top of her head was missing. The most random thing though was that one of her boobies was sticking out of her dress, like you sometimes see on the front of the papers. I looked at Dad. Lester looked at both of us, then he said, '*The Manchester Madonna*.'

'Right,' I said and looked at Dad again. It didn't look like Madonna to me.

'By Michelangelo,' said Lester.

'Right.'

'You've perhaps not seen it before. It's not as well known as some of the others. An interesting connection with your own little feathered Michelangelo, of course – this is in tempera.'

'Right.'

'So it was made of eggs.'

'This was made of eggs?' said Dad.

This had to be the most random thing ever. I was beginning to think that Lester was mad like mad Baxter Stockman. I decided to avoid eye contact and look at the woman in the picture instead. Far away I could just about hear shouting. The men outside must have started playing footy again.

Lester was still talking. 'Yes, yes. The rest of us make omelettes. Michelangelo makes a masterpiece. I think this justifies your affection for him.'

Dad said, 'When you say, made of eggs . . . ?'

'I'm sure Dylan will explain in more detail,' said Lester, 'but basically, whereas modern painters use paints in which the pigment is dissolved in oil,

Michelangelo and his contemporaries dissolved the pigment in egg white. It's called tempera.'

'Right.'

I know it sounds daft now, but it was only when he said that that I realized it was a painting. It looked so real, even though it didn't look like a photograph. I didn't know what it was.

'As you can see, the painting is unfinished. The Madonna's clothes . . .' Madonna again. '. . . are blocked out in black, but one assumes they were going to be painted blue. Somehow it adds to the drama. As if the master was in such a hurry to capture the perfection of this girl's face, he couldn't wait for the paint to arrive. He knew that if he waited one morning, her beauty might have begun to fade. Isn't that what Art is about? Rescuing Beauty from the ravages of Time. To save one moment from eternal silence.'

'Definitely.'

'According to Pliny, of course, that's how art began. A girl called Dibutade was saying goodbye to her lover. He was going to war. She put a candle beside him and traced his outline from the shadow cast against the wall. She wanted him to stay, you see. I imagine the Maestro looking at this girl with the same feeling. He didn't have the right paints, but he felt he had to capture that moment. I imagine him waiting for a consignment of lapis lazuli which never arrived. Lapis is a precious stone. They would have crushed it into powder, dissolved it in the egg and then applied it here as a wash. You see. It's amazing that the drapery has real gravity even though all we have is the shading.'

'Amazing,' said Dad. 'But then eggs are amazing, aren't they?'

I didn't look up from the painting. She was definitely nothing like Madonna, even when she was young. There were some boys in the picture, too – two little and two big. The little ones were messing about, trying to stop her reading. One of the bigger boys seemed to be holding an old sock and they were both staring at it really closely, like it was a clue or something. You could make out the outlines of two other people in the background, waiting to be coloured in like in a colouring book or like they were just materializing on a teleporter platform. The thing is, even though the rest of the picture was mad, even though the top of the woman's head was missing, her face looked real. It looked warm.

'A painting like this,' said Dad, 'obviously it puts omelette right in the shade, unless you were really hungry. But while we are talking about eggs, I just want to say that we can do you an egg sandwich, scrambled eggs, omelette, anything you like.'

That's how immense my dad is. Even when we were stuck in this weird Technodrome thing with a mad inventor and a picture made of eggs, he never lost focus. He was still thinking about the Snowdonia Oasis Auto Marvel.

Lester said, 'Actually I never eat eggs.'

'Right then. But what about all these men up here? Are they up here for long? Because we do outside catering. Or we could do. We'd like to.'

'I don't want to keep you,' said Lester. 'I'm sure Dylan has to get to school.'

'Well, not really. I mean, this is educational, when you think about it, isn't it? We could tell Ms Stannard that—'

'No,' said Lester, a bit too quick. 'No. I'm afraid I have to ask you to be discreet about this. I'd rather you didn't . . . talk . . . to anyone about this. To no one at all. I shouldn't have mentioned it really.'

Dad promised we'd keep it to ourselves. 'Not that it's easy to keep secrets in a town like this. But we'll do our best.'

'Thank you.'

'So, what is the secret?'

'I'm sorry?'

'What is it you're doing up here?'

'Probably the less we say about that the better, really. Thank you for coming.'

Dad didn't say anything until we were back in Planet Dishcloth. But I could see he was thinking about it, trying to figure it all out. After a while he said, 'That was completely –' he looked out of the window into the cloud, trying to find the right word – 'incomprehensible.'

'Do you think we might be talking about different Michelangelos?'

'I think we might.'

At Manod Old Primary we have 'Wet Play', which means you're allowed to stay in class at playtime if it's raining, which, let's face it, it is. There's giant Connect Four, giant draughts, and an art table. The girls usually crowd around the art table and pretend to be making hand-print robins or something while they talk to each other. I usually put my coat on and go and play penalties, with the slate man as goalie. No one else ever goes into the playground at playtime. Until today. They were all sheltering by the old bike shed. Then as soon as I came through the gate, they rushed me. Hundreds of them. Like some big nightmare game of tig and everyone was on except me. I tried to run away but there was nowhere to run to. They all crowded round me going, 'What's up there? What did you see? What did he say to you? What're they doing?'

Ms Stannard saw what was going on and came trotting over, blowing her whistle.

'Get back, you girls!' she shouted, shooing them away. 'Put the poor boy down.' Then she pulled me out of the middle of the crowd and I think she said,

'He's mine!' She took me into the foyer, shut the door and said, 'Now. So what is it? What's up there? What did you see? What did he say to you? What're they doing?'

'I can't really tell you, miss.'

'Excuse me?'

'He asked me to be discreet, miss.'

'Discreet about what?'

'I'm not sure, miss.'

'Were they wearing strange suits, like for chemicals?'

'No, nothing like that.'

'Were they building something? A mast perhaps or . . .'

'No, miss. There's no digging going on or anything.'

'What did you do up there?'

'He showed me a picture, miss.'

'A picture of what?'

'A woman, miss.'

She looked more serious now. 'What sort of woman?'

'I don't know, miss. She seemed nice enough. He asked me not to say too much about it.'

'He showed you a picture of a woman and told you not to tell anyone?'

'He said to be discreet.'

'You must have some idea what sort of woman she was. Was it Charlotte Church?'

'No. She was wearing a kind of sheet, miss. It didn't entirely cover her, to be honest, and there were some boys with her.'

'So he showed you a picture of a woman in a state of undress and he said . . .'

Suddenly I remembered something useful. I said, 'Miss, do you know Michelangelo?'

'Not the Turtles, Dylan, not now.'

'But, miss . . .'

'That's enough. If you can't tell us anything, then you have no excuse for being late. I'm going to deduct two merits from your score.'

She'll have a job. I haven't got any merits.

When it was home time, things were even worse. I was walking up the High Street with Minnie.

'Minnie,' I said, 'is Madonna from Manchester?'

'No.'

'Is there another Madonna – not the famous one? Or maybe there's another Michelangelo – not the party dude.'

'Dylan, look behind you.'

I did. The whole school was following us up the High Street. Kids. Their mothers. Ms Stannard. Even George the Lollipop Man. They were all walking behind us like a big human tailback.

And when we got to the garage, it was gridlock. Every last car in Manod was on the forecourt or on the verge outside. Anyone passing would think there was a car-boot sale. Except there was no one around. Everyone was in the shop. When me and Minnie walked in, it went mental. Everyone was tugging at me and asking the same question. I couldn't see where Minnie had gone. It was quite frightening until Mam shouted, 'Excuse me! There is a baby here. Could we have a bit of calm, please.'

They all went quiet. Dad took Max off Mam and then he said, 'Dylan and I went up the mountain today and I have to say we were made to feel very welcome. But the man up there – Lester, his name is – he has asked us to be discreet about what we saw.'

Now everyone started shouting again. Max started to cry. Everyone stopped shouting and apologized.

'I'd like to be more forthcoming,' said Dad, 'but I'm not sure I can be.'

'It all sounds very strange to me,' said Ms Stannard. 'He showed little Dylan pictures of a lightly clad lady and asked him not to tell anyone. Not even his teacher. It's improper.'

'Lightly clad lady?' said Mr Morgan.

'I heard it was Madonna.'

'Pictures of Madonna?' asked Marie, suddenly interested.

Suddenly, from the corner where the computer was, Minnie said, 'Is this it?'

Everyone crowded round the monitor. And there she was again, the woman in Lester's picture. She didn't look as warm on the computer as she did in real life.

'Oh!' said Ms Stannard. '*That* Michelangelo!'

'Oh!' said Marie. '*That* Madonna.'

It turns out that Madonna is another name for Jesus's mother, and *The Manchester Madonna* is a famous painting of her by a famous old painter. The painting comes from the National Gallery. Minnie kept Googling around to try and find out more.

'So what's it doing up in the quarry?' said Mrs Porty.

'I said all along,' said Minnie. 'An international criminal organization.'

'Oh,' said Mrs Porty. 'I knew there was something not right about that one. His shoes are too shiny.'

Cars today:
WHITE MONTEGO — Big Evans (full tank of petrol, box of fudge)

Weather — wet

Note: HOME IS WHERE THE ART IS

This is the day Big Evans left and Terrible Evans poked me in the eye.

It turned out that the cars that went up the mountain were nothing to do with robberies and nothing to do with opening the quarry. Newspaper Arthur found out the whole story and put it in the *Month*:

Home Is Where the Art Is!

The town of Manod is playing host to some of the most distinguished visitors in its history. King Charles, John the Baptist and St George are all 'hanging around' nearby at the moment.

Readers will recall that the extensive floods in London last year created chaos in the financial sector. The Royal Family had to move to Balmoral permanently as Buckingham Palace could no longer be insured. Arsenal Football Club moved to Milton Keynes for a similar reason. The House of Commons decamped to

Birmingham. The entire collection of paintings in the National Gallery of Art were moved to 'a secret and secure location'. It turns out that this is the town of Manod.

Of course this information is supposed to be top secret. Publishing it in the *Manod Month* shouldn't compromise that secrecy as no one reads it anyway.

As Dad said, we should all be proud that Manod is a 'secret and secure' location. And it's an honour to have all those works of art in the town.

'It won't put spuds in the oven,' said Big Evans.

'No,' said Dad, 'it's not spuds. It's art. It's good. It's different. We can't put things back the way they were. We've got to go forward.'

'I am going forward,' said Big. 'I'm going forward all the way to London.'

'That's a shame. Just when things are really looking up in this town.'

'When I look up,' said Big, 'all I see is clouds.'

He filled up with petrol and asked for a box of fudge. We have these boxes of fudge with 'Souvenir of Manod' on the lid in fancy writing and a picture of the mountain. We hadn't sold one since . . . well, ever, really. They were all a bit dusty so I wiped one with a chamois leather before giving it to him. Dad said,

'Since you're in a spending mood, you wouldn't want to buy a Mini Cooper S, would you?'

'No. Thanks all the same. I'd best be off.'

He stood there for a while looking at the picture. Then he looked at the mountain. Like he was playing 'Spot the Difference'. Which wouldn't have taken long, by the way, because the mountain in the picture is green and covered in sheep and daisies, whereas the actual mountain is just a big blank smudge of grey, as if someone has come along and rubbed it out with an immense eraser.

Dad went off to get Big his change and Big said, very quietly, just to me, 'Keep an eye on my little girl for me, will you?'

'Who?'

He looked at me funny, and then I realized he was talking about Terrible Evans. I'd never really thought of her as a little girl before. I said, 'Oh. Yeah. Sure.'

'Thanks.'

'How do you mean, though? Look after her?'

'In school. Keep an eye on her. She's going to miss her dad.'

'Oh.'

During Wet Play, I offered to have a game of Connect Four with Terrible. I said, 'Are you OK?'

She said, 'I go first. I'm blue. You're red.'

'Yeah. But are you OK?'

She stared at me.

'Cos your dad's gone off, hasn't he?'

She beckoned me closer to the Connect Four frame with her finger and, when I was right up to it, she poked me in the eye.

21 April

Cars today:
BEIGE LUTON VAN – Brake Brothers
LAND ROVER – Mr Morgan and Sian

Weather – damp, then wet

Note: – THAI FOOD COMES TO MANOD

I don't normally notice vans that much, but I remember this one. I remember everything about this day. Dad had been to the Cash and Carry early. He normally comes back with some bread, some milk, and maybe something for the sweet counter if we're running out. Today he had fifty cup-a-soups and fifty Pot Noodles (twenty chicken and sweetcorn, twenty barbecue beef and ten chicken satay). The chicken satay was a completely new flavour. 'I've never eaten Thai before,' said Tom. 'I bet no one in this valley has.'

Mam was a bit nervous. She said, 'If we haven't got money for petrol, should we really be buying Pot Noodles?'

'You were the one who said we had to have a vision,' said Dad. 'There's at least a dozen men up there. That's a dozen potential customers. Cup-a-soup, shoe polish, photocopying. They'll be buying stuff quicker than we can ring it up.'

'Yeah, but . . .'

'Mr Morgan says he's going to buy the Mini Cooper for his daughter. That'll cover the petrol. And the Pot Noodles have got a longer shelf life than nuclear waste. Don't worry about it. We are on our way!'

Inside the shop, me and Minnie built a tower of Pot Noodle cartons, almost as tall as her. I thought she'd be disappointed that it was just paintings and not criminal masterminds up at the quarry. But she wasn't. She said, 'Art and criminals go together like fish and chips. Half the paintings in that gallery have been nicked. During wars, soldiers steal them. It's called booty. Some of those paintings are worth a fortune. Someone's bound to try and nick them.'

'Yeah, but not from here. They're up a mountain and down a quarry.'

'Doesn't matter. You know who nicks them mostly? The Mafia.'

'The Mafia? Why?'

'They use them instead of money. If one Mafia boss has to pay another Mafia boss say twenty million pounds, instead of sending a cheque or the cash, he sends a painting. Then it doesn't go through the bank account, see. Harder to detect, isn't it?'

'A painting's not worth twenty million.'

'Some of them are. That's why they're hiding them in the quarry.'

'Twenty million though?'

'A few years back a man in a white Vauxhall Nova stole a da Vinci worth fifty million from a castle in Scotland.'

'I bet he's not driving a Nova now.'

'He dumped it in a nearby forest and continued his escape in a black BMW 5-Series – just like Lester's. It might have been Lester. He looks a bit fly.'

' Surely if he had fifty million, he'd've upgraded to the 6-Series.'

'Dylan, when you were speaking to Lester, that time with the chickens, what did he ask you?'

'Nothing. Just what they were called.'

'Is that all?'

'He wanted to know who gave them their names. I told him it was me. Why?'

'Thinking.' I like it when Minnie does her thinking. She usually comes up with something.

The tower of Pot Noodles sort of stuck out a bit to one side but it still stayed standing.

When Mam saw the size of the Leaning Tower of Pot Noodle, she started to fret again. 'How much did you spend?'

'You've got to speculate to accumulate,' said Dad.

'I don't want to accumulate. I want to pay the mortgage.'

'Put yourself in the position of a man who's just driven a big van down the mountain road. He's tired. He's tense. He's got to get out to open the gate. He smells coffee. He thinks, just a coffee. He follows his nose into the shop and once inside . . .'

'Chicken Satay Pot Noodle,' said Tom. 'Who could walk past that?'

'But what if he doesn't stop? What if he comes down off the mountain and thinks, I can't wait to get my foot down? What if he comes down thinking, Why would I stop at the garage when I could drive on to Asda and buy myself an all-day breakfast, the newspapers, some nice fruit and veg?'

'Or a bag,' said Marie. 'They've got these lovely shoulder bags with, like, flowers on them. In Asda.'

'And pizzas,' said Tom. 'Fresh pizzas. You can even choose your own topping. You can have bacon-and-bean pizzas even.'

'I'll tell you why he won't go to Asda . . . customer relations.' He looked at me. 'Lester has taken to Dylan. Therefore we have customer relations.'

Nice Tom said, 'Why though? Why has he taken to Dylan?'

'Yeah,' said Marie. 'It's got to be a misunderstanding.'

'No, it hasn't,' said Mam. 'It's perfectly understandable. Anyone would take to him. People take to him all the time. He's lovely.'

'Unless you need an oil change,' said Dad.

'No,' said Minnie. 'Actually, it *is* a misunderstanding.'

Everyone looked at her.

'Dylan told Lester it was his idea to call the chickens Michelangelo and Donatello. Lester has never heard of the Turtles. He thinks Dylan named his hens after great painters of the Italian Renaissance. He thinks Dylan is interested in art.'

Dad stared at me and then at the tower of Pot Noodles. Mam was already looking at the tower of Pot Noodles.

Minnie was still talking. 'If Lester talks to Dylan again, he'll realize he's made an embarrassing mistake. And then we'll have bad customer relations.'

Dad whispered, 'Why did no one mention this before?' It was the same whisper he used when he found out about the motor-oil/antifreeze mix-up.

'I've only just worked it out,' said Minnie.

'How come he's never heard of the Turtles?' said Tom. 'Is he thick or what?'

There's no denying Mam was upset about this, and it led to a bit more shouting between her and Dad, so me and Minnie slipped out to school. We were just passing the Spar when Dad came running up behind us.

He'd obviously thought of something. He always thinks of something.

'Dylan, I'd like a word with you,' he said.

We went and sat by the mural, just under the panel of Elvis Arriving at Sun Studios for the First Time, and Dad told me all about Luther Blissett. I'd never heard of him. Dad said, 'He used to play for Watford in the 1980s.'

'That's before I was born.'

'I know. I know. Well, he was playing at Watford at the same time as John Barnes. You have heard of John Barnes.'

I said, 'Scored an inspirational individual goal against Brazil in 1984.'

'Exactly.'

'Well, Barnes and Blissett both used to play up front for Watford. OK? So Watford's got two strikers and one of them is John Barnes. John Barnes – who scored against Brazil, who was PFA Player of the Year 1988, who played for England seventy-nine times, who wrote the *Anfield Rap*. And Luther Blissett – natural goal-scorer and good bloke. So AC Milan – one of the richest and greatest clubs in Europe – decides to buy one of them. Which one?'

'John Barnes.'

'They bought Luther Blissett.'

'Why?'

'By mistake. They knew that Watford had two strikers and they bought the wrong one.'

'But . . . how?'

'Doesn't matter. The point is, Blissett goes from Watford to Milan in one very, very big move. And maybe it's a mistake, but he's there. All he's got to do is raise his game and no one will ever know.'

'And he does it?'

'Well, not really, to be honest. Scored five in the season, and they sold him back to Watford. But the point is, he was there. And everyone loved him and he came back a better player. He scored a hat-trick for England and he's still Watford's greatest-ever goal-scorer.'

'So?'

'So it's not about being the greatest ever. It's about being the best you can be.'

'What is?'

'This.'

'This what?'

'This situation with the paintings and everything.'

'Oh. Well, they did say I could have a game actually. If I came back up . . .'

'I'm not talking about football.'

'Yes you are. You're talking about John Barnes and Luther Blissett.'

'I'm talking about you. I'm saying, Lester thinks you're some kind of John Barnes genius, and we all know you're just, well, you're just Dylan. But that's all right. You have to take it as an opportunity. Lester thinks you're clever. All you've got to do is pretend you are clever.'

'Actually, I tried that in school. It doesn't work. Wouldn't it be better if we tell him that Minnie's the clever one, not me? That he's made a mistake?'

'Lester doesn't look like the type of person who likes being told he's made a mistake.'

I was beginning to think that he didn't have a plan after all. Then he said, 'OK, so this is the plan. Minnie is clever, right. She tries to teach you all about Michelangelo and that lot. And when the time comes, she goes with you. So what she can't teach you, she can whisper to you.'

Brilliant!

Minnie found the whole thing exciting. 'This is a scam,' she said. 'This makes us con men. We are perpetrating a fraud.' She could hardly stand still, she was that excited.

I said, 'I'm not perpetrating a fraud. I'm being polite.'

'Whatever.' We sat at the IT table, looking up Michelangelo on Wikipedia. It told you where he was born and when – which I couldn't remember at all. And it showed you pictures of his works of art. His most famous is the Sistine Chapel in Rome. It's an actual chapel and he painted scenes from the Bible all over the walls. He did all the painting himself because he didn't think anyone else was good enough to help him. He did it all lying on his back on top of a high scaffold. He fell off a couple of times. The Pope was annoyed that he took so long doing it. Go on, ask me anything. I can still remember it all now.

That's what I said to Dad when I got home. 'Go on, ask me anything. Anything about Michelangelo.'

He was sitting on one of the discount garden chairs, next to the counter. He said, 'Where was he born?'

'Actually, he doesn't know that,' said Minnie. 'But you can ask him anything else. Ask him about the Sistine—'

'OK . . .' But he never did ask me. Because while he was thinking what to say, a beige van turned up. It was an ordinary Luton van, but it had pictures on the side – pictures of men in bow ties and chef's hats, holding pans, and the steam from the pans turned into curly writing that said 'Brake Brothers' Larder Fresh Food'. The driver parked up and came and put his head round the door of the shop. Disappointingly he wasn't wearing a bow tie or a chef's hat. The door said 'pong ping' and the man said, 'This is Manod, isn't it? Only there's no sign on the A496.'

'Signs are not a funding priority,' said Dad bitterly. 'How can I help you?'

'I'm looking for Mountain Road?' He said it as though it was the name of a road, like Waterloo Road. But it was obvious what he meant. So it was a bit bizarre that Dad didn't answer. He seemed to freeze.

The man said, 'Doesn't ring a bell? Mountain Road?'

Dad stayed frozen.

Minnie said, 'It's just here, through the gate.'

The man left. Dad watched him open the gate, jump in, drive through, jump out and close the gate again, and all that time Dad didn't move or speak.

It turned out that the Brake Brothers sell frozen food to pubs and cafes. And not ordinary frozen food either. 'Cajun chicken wings, chilli con carne, steak and ale pie,' said Dad.

'How,' he said to Mam, 'how, how, how did we ever think they wouldn't have arranged their food? What insane hope was it that made us think they might need us?'

'You mustn't blame yourself,' said Mam.

'I'm not blaming myself. I'm blaming you,' said Dad.

'I know how to make chilli con carne if anyone wants some,' said Tom.

'That's the point,' said Dad. 'Why would you make it when they can bring you a frozen one? They've got a vanload from Brake Brothers, so what do they need? Nothing. Why would they buy our cup-a-soup when they've got buckets of Scotch broth and minestrone? Why would they look at our Pot Noodle when they can have chicken tikka masala? They're not going to want to shop here at all.'

'Nice though, chicken tikka masala,' said Tom.

Later that afternoon, Mr Morgan brought his daughter down to look at the Mini Cooper. Dad let me help him give it a wash-and-wax and scrub the tyres. It looked like a brand-new car. He'd painted it racing red. Mr Morgan's daughter is called Sian. She said the car was lovely but she didn't like the colour. 'Well, it's racing red,' said Dad. 'Like in the film. You know, *The Italian Job*.'

'No, I don't know. It's just a bit aggressive for me.'

'What?' said Dad. 'How can a colour be aggress-ive?'

'Yes,' said Mr Morgan, 'how can a colour be aggressive?'

'It's colour psychology, isn't it? Red. Like in bullfighting. A little red car racing round these lanes, that's like a red rag to a bull to some male drivers. I'd be leaving myself open to burn-ups and road rage and all sorts of things. Why d'you think it's called racing red, Da?'

Mr Morgan said, 'She's doing psychology at university, see. She knows about these things.'

'It was just supposed to look like in *The Italian*

Job,' said Dad. 'It's the one where they rob a bank in Italy and use Minis as getaway cars.'

'Well, it sounds like a very aggressive film,' said Sian.

So we didn't sell the Mini. And it looks like we're not going to sell the Pot Noodles either.

25 April

Cars today:
FORD SCORPIO — Sergeant Hunter
JAGUAR XJ 4.2 V8 SOVEREIGN (registration
IN5UR3) — Barry and Tone from the Insurance

Weather — damp, turning wet later

Note: SOMETIMES YOUR FRIENDS ARE
ENEMIES IN DISGUISE

Another lesson that the Turtles can teach us is that anyone can make a mistake. For instance, in 'Notes from the Underground', three rock-eating monsters chase the Turtles down a tunnel where they find an underground city. There's a mysterious Entity living there who rescues them from the monsters so — understandably — the Turtles think he's on their side. But really he's got a plan of his own, which is to keep the Turtles in the underground city forever. They have to fight their way out when he attacks them with intelligent magma.

So it's not surprising if a person mixes up motor oil and antifreeze sometimes. Or, if a person wakes up in the night and hears noises coming from the work-shop, and looks out of the window and sees a light on, it's not surprising if that person just thinks that his dad is outside, spraying the Mini Cooper a different colour from racing red. That would be an easy mistake to make and the person might not even know it was a mistake until he came down the next morning and found his dad talking to Police Sergeant Hunter about how someone had stolen the Mini.

Sergeant Hunter looked at me and said, 'Did you hear anything, young Dylan?'

'Yes.'

'What?'

I told him all about the light being on and the door being open.

'What time was this?'

'It was quarter past three. And about ten minutes later I heard the engine start up.'

Dad was amazed. He said, 'And you didn't say anything?'

'I thought it was you, doing a respray.'

'Why would I start the engine up if I was doing a respray?'

'I don't know. Maybe if the paint was wet, you could take it for a drive and that would help it dry quicker.'

Dad rolled his eyes. We went to school.

Minnie was pure delighted that someone had finally done a crime in Manod. 'Crimes usually come in waves,' she said. 'This is only the beginning.' All the way to school she kept staring into people's faces, trying to see if they were the criminal type. 'The thieves may well still be among us,' she said.

As soon as she got to school, she started telling everyone about it. By the time lessons started, every kid in the school was in our class listening to her talking about how an armed gang had come up to the garage in the middle of the night and stolen our souped-up turbo Mini Cooper, probably to do a bank job. 'Mostly, cars are stolen to order for use in other, more serious crimes, as getaway vehicles,' she said. 'Our Mini is probably burnt out on a bypass in Birmingham now.' Then she went on to tell everyone how I'd looked out of the window and mistaken these armed master criminals for my dad. Everyone laughed. I wondered why Ms Stannard wasn't chasing everyone back to their own classrooms, then I noticed that she was sitting on one of the desks, listening too. 'Carry on, Minnie,' she said. 'This is an excellent exercise in speaking and listening skills.' Minnie even wrote her email to Gumbi about the robbery. In the afternoon, I got an email from George:

Dear Dylan, Thank you for your last email, which was quite dull. Is it true that you mistook a gang of armed robbers for your father and gave them the keys to his car? He must have been cross. Please write and tell me more funny stories about your life in Manod. Don't be dull again!

Your friend, George.

At lunchtime, Terrible Evans pointed straight at me across the dinner hall and started to laugh very, very loud and very, very long. I couldn't wait to get home. At least there everyone already knew the details.

But when we got home, there was a Jaguar 4.2 (top speed 155 mph!!! 0–60 in 6.3 seconds) on the forecourt. I knew it wasn't ours. There were two men in the shop wearing suits. One had a mobile phone tucked into his top pocket and the other one had a big droopy moustache like a walrus.

'Hello, junior,' they said when I walked in. 'I believe you saw the whole thing?'

'Well . . .'

'I'm Barry by the way,' said the one with the moustache. 'And this is Tone.'

'As in Ring Tone,' said Tone, and he made his phone ring for a joke. 'We're from the insurance company.'

They spoke in turns, like they were on *Blue Peter*.

'We just want to know what you saw,' said Barry. 'Take your time.' He got out a notebook.

I said, 'Well, it wasn't much, really. I just woke up and heard a noise and there was a light on and that's it.'

'Time?'

'Three fifteen.'

They both wrote down the time and said thank

you. Minnie asked them if they thought it was the beginning of a crime wave.

'Let's hope not,' said Barry. 'We're looking into this because it's so unusual. Manod has the lowest crime rate in the UK. Normally. We wondered what was different this time.' When he said this, he looked straight at Dad.

Dad said, 'I locked the workshop before I went to bed. They forced the door. You can see that if you just go and look at it.'

Barry looked at me and said, 'Can you remember what woke you up? Did you hear wood being splintered or anything of that sort?'

I thought about this hard before saying, 'No. No, I didn't.'

'We're just looking for clues, you see,' said Tone, 'to why this happened.'

'When it's never happened before,' said Barry.

Clues. I thought really hard. Maybe if I could remember a clue, that would make up for not stopping them doing the robbery.

'You didn't hear voices? Another car pull up? We're wondering how they got up here, you see.'

'Nothing like that,' I said.

'There's no one been round the garage lately who's a bit unsavoury? A bit of a criminal type?'

As soon as he said that word, I looked at Minnie.

She looked like she might be about to say, 'Tom.' I jumped in and said, 'No. Definitely not.'

'Definitely not?'

'Definitely not.'

He looked at Dad. 'And the car itself, just to be sure, was a Mini Cooper S, in racing red.'

'That's it.'

I said, 'With faux walnut interior, leather knob on the gearstick and alloy trims.' They looked at me. 'Dad put alloy trims on the wheels. They looked immense. He was trying to sell it, you see, to Mr Morgan's daughter, to get money for petrol. That's why he wanted to make it look smart. But she didn't like the colour. Isn't that right, Dad?'

Dad nodded. The two men were looking quite pleased, so maybe what I'd said was a good clue.

'Any questions?' said Barry.

I said, 'Is it true that the Jaguar's got height sensors that lower the ride by fifteen millimetres at speeds over a hundred mph, improving aerodynamic efficiency, vehicle stability and fuel economy during high-speed cruising?'

'We don't know,' said Tone.

'It's illegal to go over a hundred mph.'

'And we never do anything illegal.'

They thanked me anyway and told me to ring if I thought of anything else. Barry gave me a pen with his phone number on the side in gold writing. What a nice man!

After they'd gone, Dad went into the workshop, even though everyone in Manod knew there was no car in there to work on. When Mam took a cup of tea out to him, he wouldn't let her in. He still hadn't come out when I went out to chase the hens back into their rabbit hutch. I was about to go in when the door of the workshop opened and Dad stood there, looking at me.

I said, 'Night, then.'

He said, 'Night, son.'

It didn't look like he was going to say any more. So I said, 'Dad, I'm really sorry I didn't realize they were robbers.'

He still didn't say anything.

'If I had a wish, I'd wish to find the car, Dad.'

He stared at me and he said, 'Want a game of penalties?'

How random is that?! I couldn't have been more surprised if he'd asked me to do an oil change. I mean, he does play penalties with me sometimes, but only if I've asked him about a gazillion times. He went in goal for the first ten. Then I went in for the next ten, then we swapped back and then back again and we kept going until we couldn't see the ball any more, just a pale smudge in the dark. It was completely hectic and I won 83 to 77. Then we sat on the step for a while, looking at the moon moving through the clouds. He said, 'You know, if you go anywhere on a train, you should always take a zebra with you.'

'What?'

'It's about probabilities. You know insurance companies? They make their money by working out how likely it is that something is going to happen. For instance, everyone has to pay car insurance because it's quite likely that one day you'll crash your car. Say it's a hundred to one. But if you go on a train, the chance is slimmer. Like a million to one. But the chances of a zebra being hurt on a train are almost non-existent. Zebras are almost never hurt on trains. So if you go on a train, take a zebra and you won't get hurt. Understand?'

'Not really.'

'What I'm saying is, look after yourself. OK?'

It seemed like a bit of a roundabout way of saying it. But it was definitely a one-for-the-scrapbook night.

The penalties were so surprising that I wasn't as surprised as you'd think when I came down next morning and found that Mam was already up and that Dad had gone away.

26 April

Cars today:
JAGUAR 4.2 – Barry and Tone

Weather – heavy rain

Note: EXTREME FOOTBALL

This morning sticks in my mind mostly because of the breakfast. We were in the shop before school when Barry and Tone pulled up in their Jaguar 4.2. They wanted to speak to Dad. Mam came down and said, 'I'm afraid Mr Hughes has gone away on business.' Then she took Max and went back to bed.

We all looked at each other. Dad had never gone away on business before. And Mam had never gone back to bed before.

I said, 'What're we going to do?'

'I'll tell you what we're going to do,' said Marie. 'We're going to have a decent breakfast instead of that stuff that makes the milk go yellow.' And she took one of the satay Pot Noodles and squirted boiling water into it from the Gaggia.

I didn't think this was right in the circumstances, but it did smell good. 'What's it like?' I said.

'Like a mixture of hot peanut butter and string. It's good.'

Minnie said, 'Maybe we should all have one, to get our brains going. We need to make a plan.'

'Does Pot Noodle really get your brains going?'

Minnie read a list of all the chemicals and E-numbers from the side of the carton and said, 'If that lot doesn't make you think, nothing will.'

So I had one. And when Tom came, he had one too. Through a mouthful of noodles, he said, 'Where's Mr Hughes gone then?'

'He's gone away on business,' said Marie, 'because this garage isn't making enough money. Which is completely Dylan's fault. Because he let the robbers stroll off with the Mini.'

Like I didn't know that.

'I wonder what kind of business he's gone on?' said Tom.

'It doesn't matter what, or whose fault it is,' said Marie. 'The point is, the garage isn't making enough money. If we want Dad to come back, we have to get the garage to make more money.'

When you put it like that, it sounded simple.

'We could turn to crime,' said Minnie.

'Not me,' said Tom.

'Oh, come on, Tom. Just because it went wrong once, doesn't mean you can't do it. Try, try and try again. And we'd be helping you this time.'

'Yeah, but I'm reformed now, see.'

'Right then,' said Minnie. 'We've had it.'

'Have we?' said Tom. He looked worried. 'If it's going to make things difficult, maybe I could do just one crime.'

'No need,' said Marie. 'Think about it. The men are still up the mountain. They still have to drive over the forecourt. They're still a potential market. All we have to do is figure out what to sell them. Any suggestions?'

No one had any suggestions.

I just sat there wishing I'd stopped the robbers. Or that I could find the car. Or even just a clue.

Tom said, 'I could sell my boxed set of poseable Turtle action figures. They're highly collectable.'

'It's very good of you,' said Marie, 'but you've already sold enough Turtle stuff, Tom. Thanks all the same.'

Tom said, 'Phew.'

'We couldn't have a party, I don't suppose?' Marie went on. 'It'd be nice to have a party. I've often thought about it. Dad's workshop would make a great party room. We could have music and dancing, and I'm sure people from school would come.'

'And that would generate income how?' asked Minnie.

'All right,' snapped Marie. 'It was just a thought.'

Then Minnie said, 'Cakes.'

Everyone gasped. The fact is, she is a genius. As Tom said, 'I love cakes. And so does everyone, really.'

'We know they've got cajun chicken wings,' said

Minnie, 'but have they got cake? Probably not. We can make the cakes ourselves, so no overheads.'

'Yeah, but what kind of cakes, though?' said Tom. 'Because ginger cake's not nice, for instance.'

'We'll do like a menu, so they can order and we don't have to bake a thing unless they want to buy it. And this is the master stroke. We'll invent cakes. Special cakes specially designed for men who work up a mountain with works of art.'

So that's how Picasso Pie was invented. And Titian Tart and Tintoretto Turnover. And Crispy Choc Constables. All morning Minnie kept coming up with more names of painters and Marie kept matching them with cakes. Even Tom helped. They sat down at the computer, giggling and laughing and playing with the fonts and colours. I didn't know the names of any painters. Or cakes. Or fonts. So I left them to it.

'Next time one of them comes down,' said Marie, 'we'll give him the menu.'

It was good to see Team Hughes working again. Even if the captain was away. And the team manager was in bed. And I was stuck on the bench.

Mam stayed in her room most of the morning because she was missing Dad, which was understandable. I remembered how much the Pot Noodles had cheered us up, so I looked in *Coffee Cavalcade* and decided to make her a mochaccino – a mixture of coffee and chocolate and milk. We didn't have any actual hot chocolate left, so I crumbled a Flake into the mixture and took it up to her room. She seemed to like it.

I said, 'How long will he be there?'

'Who?'

'Dad.'

'Oh. Dad. What about him?'

'How long will he be away?'

'Where?'

'Away on business. You said he was away on business.'

'Oh. I don't know. A while.' She carried on looking out of the window.

'What kind of business is he away on?'

'Hmm?'

'Has he gone to work on the New Barrier?'

'Hmm.'

'Well,' I said, 'can't stand here chatting all day.'

Actually I could have, because there was nothing else to do. But Mam didn't try and stop me, so I went.

Donatello had laid an egg!

On top of one of the butane canisters. It had a feather stuck to it and it was still warm. Immense! But also pointless. I was going to run and tell the others – but then I thought, How much difference does one egg make, really? And then I thought how sad it was that this hen had gone to all this trouble to lay an egg that wasn't going to make any difference. Just like I wasn't going to make any difference. And then it came to me. Something that Dad said: customer relations is about going the extra mile.

Why should we wait until one of them comes down to give them the menu? I could take the menu up to them. All right, we didn't have a car. But our grandads all walked up that mountain to go to work. I could do the same.

I ran into the shop. The menus were piled up next to the printer. They looked completely legend: yellow letters on a blue background. There was no sign of the girls. Tom was in the back. I took a menu and a cagoule, and I went. I was going to climb the mountain. I was going to do my bit to make the garage pay. I took my match ball, in case there was any chance of a game.

It was good, walking up. I'd only ever been up in a car before, which is why I hadn't noticed the white stones until now. Every couple of minutes you'd pass one. It was like one of those puzzles where you look at a picture for ages trying to see the hidden face, and then suddenly you can see it, and then you can't stop seeing it. It was just like that. Once I'd spotted a few of the stones, I could see a whole line of them leading up into the clouds like a piece of string. When I'd been walking for ages, I looked back and realized I hadn't gone that far. I could still read the writing on the Oasis Auto Marvel sign. I nearly gave up then, but I thought about the four thousand grandads who did the walk every morning and I thought, It can't be that far if they did it before they even started work for the day. I dropped the ball and started to dribble it up the path. I kept thinking how good it would be when there was someone who could kick it back to me.

I don't remember walking into the cloud. I just remember that suddenly it was colder and wetter than before and I couldn't really see any more, and the stones beneath my feet were slippy. I picked up the ball and thought about turning back, but then I saw another white stone up ahead. I walked over to it and from there I could see the next one, and from there I could see the next one and then the next one, and on and on. Then I saw something else. It was about the size of a house but it had hair growing out of it – thick, spiky hair. I stayed quiet. So did the hairy thing. So did everything. It was like the whole world had gone quiet. Or vanished. There was just me, two white stones (one ahead and one behind) and this big hairy Thing. I took a step backwards. I slipped. I lost my grip on the ball. It went rolling off down the mountain. You could hear the crunch of the pebbles for ages after it had disappeared. The Thing must've heard it. But it didn't move. As I straightened up, the cloud around the Thing sort of unswirled for a moment.

It was a big block of slate, a huge block of slate with moss growing all over the top of it. One side of it was smooth as a windscreen when you touched it. I wondered what it was doing there. Maybe it was the last big piece of slate that they had cut. Maybe the mine closed before they had time to split it into Wide Ladies or whatever. When you looked closer, you could see that there were arrow markings and bits of writing on it, like instructions maybe for when they would turn it into slates. And there were little drawings, too, cut into it but so lightly that it felt like if you just wiped your hand over them, they'd disappear. It was a row of faces, all looking up towards the corner of the rock. I couldn't see what they were looking at, unless they were all really, really interested in moss. So it wasn't a big hairy thing, it was just a rock, which was good. Though I'd lost my football, which was not good. But I still had the menu, which was the point.

Walking out of the cloud and into the sunshine was completely mint. Now I know how a car feels when the car wash stops and the hot air blower starts. I could feel myself drying out. I could see everything getting brighter and clearer. The slate was blue. The moss looked like it was made of gold, and men's voices up ahead were the best sound ever, like a party where everyone is waiting for you to arrive. Then, as I got nearer, a ball came rolling towards me down the hill. I looked up. Two men in overalls were standing by the canteen, yelling. A third man was running towards me, chasing the ball. He nearly had it, but it hit a rock, bounced up and came curving down towards me. I got right under it, chested it on to my right foot and volleyed it. It dropped dead, right at his feet. He trapped it, shouted, 'Nice one!' and waited for me to catch up with him. When I did, he said my favourite sentence: 'Fancy a game?'

It was a game for the scrapbook. We played five-a-side, but the ground was so rocky and bumpy it was like there were a hundred invisible players on the pitch. You'd lay off a nice long pass to someone and suddenly the ball would turn round and come back at you, or it would veer off to the left all of a sudden and you'd have to go after it again. It was extreme football. It felt like we were playing against the mountain. It was completely hectic and we lost 5–3. I hit one ball that would have been a textbook goal if it had just gone in. I did Team Hughes proud.

Afterwards, one of them got me a can of Sprite and we all sat on a rock and watched the sun go down. The moment it dipped behind Blaenau Mountain, all the cloud in the valley turned hazard-light red, as if someone had thrown a switch. And a voice behind me said, 'Pure Turner. Almost makes it worth being in Wales, a sunset like that.' It was Lester.

I looked around. He was very surprised to see me. 'How on earth did you get up here?' he said.

One of the men explained that I'd walked up.

'You walked all the way up here?' He made it sound like I'd walked to the moon.

'We wondered if you'd like some cakes?'

'What?'

'I've got a list here . . .' I passed him the menu, but he passed it to the man who had asked me if I wanted a game. 'We have our own caterers. We don't need anything.'

The football man said, 'If he's walked all this way, though . . .'

Lester was already shoving me towards the Technodrome, saying, 'I know what you really came up for.'

The man shouted after me, 'I'll pin this up on the canteen wall, then.'

'Yes, yes,' said Lester, not looking back and not slowing down.

I didn't mind. I was interested to see inside the dome, and if he asked me about Michelangelo again, that was fine. I'd know the answer. Probably.

The dome was disappointing inside. It was full of computers and phones and chairs, like a proper HQ, but it didn't have a massive screen on the wall showing you satellite pictures of your enemies or any Mouser Robots or a secret store of mutagen, just a man in a white shirt talking on the phone. In the corner there was an easel with a painting on it and a light shining on the painting. Lester said to the man, 'This is the boy I was telling you about. The one with the eye. He's walked up here, would you believe. Walked. Like Raphael. Did you know that Raphael walked from Urbino to Rome to see Michelangelo's drawings?'

The one with the eye. I was starting to like the sound of that. I walked over to the painting. I imagined myself saying, 'Ah yes, the Sistine Chapel,' or, 'No one celebrates the beauty of the human form like Michelangelo,' but when I got there, I froze. This picture was different. Whatever it was of, it wasn't the human form. And I had a nasty feeling it wasn't Michelangelo either. It was a whole picture of nothing but fruit and stuff – and some nuts. They looked really real, but they were just, well, shopping. It might have been an advert, except who would do an advert for nuts?

Lester was on the phone, talking to Tom. 'Yes, he's up here now. He's walked the whole way. I can't let him walk down. It'll be dark and I can't really spare a driver to take him down. Could you possibly come and collect him? You could? Marvellous.'

I thought, yes, and make it quick. I mean, nuts? What are you supposed to say about nuts?

Lester came and stood behind me and started

telling me about how even though the National Gallery was closed owing to insurance problems, they had decided to show one painting a week in a special room there. 'Things are quite difficult in London at the moment, so the idea is to send paintings that are uplifting or morale boosting. What do you think? Will this do the trick?'

I was trying to imagine how difficult things would have to be before you could be uplifted by a nut. Not even a real nut. A picture of a nut. Then I remembered that Dad was in London and I wondered if he was having a difficult time. I sort of forgot Lester was there for a minute. I must have looked a bit weird, because he asked me if I was feeling all right. I didn't want to tell him about Dad, but I didn't know what else to say. Luckily, just then the man from the football game came in. 'You should take a look at this,' he said, and he handed Lester the cake menu.

Lester started reading, then he started smiling, and then he started laughing. 'Did you do this?' he asked.

This was my chance. I could say, 'No, it was my sister,' and then it would all come out about her being the clever one and it all being a big mix-up. But before I could say a word, Lester said, 'Too modest. Who else could it be?' Then he said, 'Well, I think we'll take some of these cakes, shall we?'

'Will you? Will you really? That's brilliant!'

'Yes, why not?' He looked at the menu again. 'Who

would ever have thought it? You really live and breathe art, don't you?'

'Well,' I said, 'I try, you know.'

He pointed to the picture and said, 'The Meléndez. You probably already know the story.'

What should I say now? If I said no, I might sound daft. If I said yes, he might test me on it. So I kept staring at the picture.

He said, 'Oh, sorry. Sorry. You haven't seen it in the flesh before. This must be a special moment for you.'

And he backed off and sat at his desk, and I was trapped. If I stopped looking at the picture, he was bound to start asking me questions. So I had to carry on looking at it. I just stood there, looking and looking. The nuts didn't get any more interesting but I did start to need the toilet. I tried to hold on. I tried to not think about it. But I ended up bouncing up and down on my toes.

When Tom came in, Lester shushed him and pointed to me. 'Been like that for half an hour,' he said. 'His powers of concentration are completely extraordinary. I've never seen anything like him.' Then he said to me, 'Dylan, are you ready to pronounce judgement?'

I said, 'I need a wee,' and ran outside.

When I came back in, Lester was still talking about

me. 'Utterly absorbed. Even forgot his own bladder while he was standing there.'

'Nice picture this, though,' said Tom. He was staring at it, quite closely, as if he was trying to pick the best nut.

'Yes, poor Meléndez. He was quite brilliant, as you can see, but because of the politics of the time, he was flung out of court. He wanted to paint great pictures – battle scenes and so on – but of course such things are expensive. You need lots of paint and lots of time. Because he'd argued with the king, he couldn't find a patron to pay for him to do the work. So that was it. He was stuck. He just painted whatever was to hand, usually food. Still lifes.'

'I'd rather look at this than a battle any day,' said Tom.

I nearly said, you should try spending half an hour looking at it, mate. You'd wish it was a battle then. He was still looking at the picture, like he really liked it.

'Do you know the story of Proust and the still lifes?' said Lester.

I wasn't going to get caught again this time. I said, 'No.'

'Well, a friend came to see Proust, a middle-aged man, who said that he was bored with his life, that he needed excitement and beauty. Proust told him to go and look at some still lifes like this one. And they would teach him that there was beauty in the most boring places – in the pots and pans in his own kitchen.'

Tom was still staring at the picture, 'Are they oranges?' he said.

'Yes. Oranges and a melon and, of course, walnuts. We can speculate about what's in the boxes but I imagine—'

'I've never seen oranges with the twiggy bit sticking out of the top before. I mean, I knew they grew on trees, but I've never seen, you know, the attachment.'

'Right,' said Lester. 'And they look perfectly ripe. Just right to eat, but you can also somehow tell that that won't last long. As I said before, a moment of beauty rescued from decay.' He looked across at me. 'Well, perhaps you should paint a picture, Dylan. A picture that would show us the hidden beauty of Manod.'

I was so shocked I forgot to be polite. I blurted out, 'Manod's beauty's not hidden. Manod's lovely. Anyone can see that!'

'Actually, not everyone can see that. It takes someone special to see the beauty in a place like this.'

'No it doesn't! Anyone can see it! Tell him, Tom.'

'Oh yes, Manod's one shell of a town.'

Tom didn't really want to go. He wanted to carry on looking at the nuts. I walked out, climbed into the Wrangler and banged on the horn until he came.

*

All the way down the mountain I kept thinking, How could anyone be so wrong about Manod? Even as I was thinking about it, we turned the bend and you could see the town snuggled up in the valley. The wet slate roofs were shining blue and there were little spindles of blue smoke rising up from all the chimneys. I said, 'How could he say such a thing? How could he even think it?' but what I was thinking was, Poor Dad. I mean, what's a picture of nuts compared to an inside-out mountain?' Then I saw my ball – the one I'd dropped earlier – stuck in between two big rocks. Tom let me out to collect it.

Mam came out to open the gate. She didn't look too happy. Before we'd even parked, she was going, 'Where do you think you've been?' and so on. When we got into the shop, the girls even joined in. I waited till they'd all finished, then I told them about the cake order.

'Immense!' said Marie.

'Legend,' said Minnie.

'How many?' said Marie.

'Which kind?' said Minnie.

Admittedly I probably should have known the answer to the last two questions. But it was all right in the end because on Monday a van came down, and when Tom opened the gate for it, the driver gave him a proper written order!

I said, 'Let's see it then.'

He gave me the paper and said, 'I was talking to the driver. He's taking that picture off to London.'

'Right.' The paper was an order for a dozen Crispy Choc Constables and a Picasso Pie. As I said at the time, 'Cowabunga!'

Tom just stood there, watching the van go off down the valley.

Lester was in the passenger seat. He gave us a wave. Tom said, 'It's gone now. Gone to London. We'll never see it again, most likely.'

'What's that then, Tom?'

'The picture, Dylan.'

'The one with the nuts?'

'It was the oranges that really got me.'

'Right.'

'Everything's always changing, isn't it? Even the mountain is changing. Every second of every day, we get a minute older.'

I thought about this for a while. Then I said, 'I'm not sure that's quite exactly right, Tom. But I know what you mean.'

6 May

Cars today:
BLUE LEXUS — Mr Choi

Weather — sunny intervals

Note: PAINTINGS ARE LIKE MUTAGEN

This is the day that Mr Choi finally offered Tom a job. Even though it wasn't the job he wanted, it was still good.

Picasso Pie was easy to make. It was just apple pie with a big pastry nose and one pastry eye sticking out of the pie. Anyone can stew apples. Marie can make pastry and Max was happy playing with the spare bits. In fact, one of the bits of pastry he played with, we used as the eye.

It was a lot harder with the Crispy Choc Constables. Save-A-Packet doesn't sell chocolate chips, so we had to use chocolate buttons from the shop. They taste nice, but when you put them in the cake mix they don't look right. They look like eyes, staring at you. Minnie suggested picking them out of the mixture and breaking them into smaller pieces. No one suggested letting Max help with this bit. He just sort of did it. He was very good at bashing up the chocolate buttons but less good at giving them back. Also, it was during this bit that he tasted the cake mix, and after that he was like a shark that has tasted blood. We tried to keep him away from the bowl, but he screamed and screamed. So we had to placate him with a big spoonful. While he was eating it, our guard was down and he painted himself with cake mix. It seemed like a waste to wash it off, so we let him sit there and lick himself clean. He didn't get that clean, though he did stay happy.

When we put the broken buttons back in, it still didn't look right. As Minnie said, 'The ratio of chocolate to cake mix has changed in the chocolate's favour.' The finished cakes looked like bits of chocolate buttons stuck together with a tiny mortar of cake.

Mam was unhappy with the state of Max's hands. And of the kitchen. And with the amount of chocolate buttons we had used. 'Please stop eating the food from the shop,' she said. 'That's our stock. You might as well sit down and eat money.'

Minnie said, 'It's OK, Mam. We've decided to outsource the cake-making part of the business anyway.' This means we asked Tom's mam to bake the cakes for us. She said she was delighted to do it. All we had to do was collect the orders and get her the ingredients. 'I can bake anything you like,' she said, 'but I've never heard of a Titian Tart.'

'We made the name up. You can put whatever you like in them,' said Minnie. 'Use your imagination.'

'Well, I haven't had do that too often recently, but I'll give it a go.'

The men up the mountain ordered cakes every day, and different cakes every time. Sometimes there were some left over, so we sold them in the shop. We were soon selling more cakes than anything else. And we were getting more visitors than usual too, because of what Tom did to the window.

Tom kept talking about the nut painting and how he was never going to see it again because it had gone to London. Then, on the Saturday morning, we found him in the window of the shop, changing everything round. He'd been down to Save-A-Packet and he'd bought great big bags of stuff: soap powder, raisins, cornflakes, pumpkin seeds, peanuts, everything. And now he'd moved all the antifreeze and screen-wash out of the window and replaced them with big piles of all this random shopping. He'd made like a carpet of soap powder and put a pile of raisins in one corner, next to a big pile of cornflakes. Then he'd put little empty milk and juice cartons round the whole lot and some bits from a barbecue set. 'I thought to myself, I can't paint, but that doesn't mean I can't make a still life to look at, does it?'

'No, that's true.'

Minnie said, 'Did you ever think of just stealing the original still life and looking at that?'

'No, I didn't. Because I'm reformed.'

Everyone who saw Tom's window liked it, but Mr Choi was the first one to actually copy it. He said, 'This is good. You did this? You can do one for me?'

Obviously Tom didn't normally talk to Mr Choi or go in his shop because of Mr Choi having ruined Tom's life by giving the job to the red-headed girl. But then Mr Choi said, 'I'll give you a tenner.' So that won Tom over.

Mr Choi's window was empty except for a big blue glass fish and a pie advert. Tom took them out and put a great big basket tipped on its side, spilling lovely new potatoes and onions all over the place. And in among the potatoes he put bits of fishing line, and some floats and a net, and it made you hungry just looking at it. He was doing this first thing on the Monday morning, so everyone stopped to watch him on the way to school.

After he'd dropped his girls off, Mr Elsie the chemist knocked on Mr Choi's window and asked Tom if he wouldn't mind doing the same in his shop window after he'd finished. Mr Elsie's window used to have this big cardboard foot, advertising corn plasters. When Tom went over there, he found all kinds of old,

old-fashioned bottles in the back of the shop and he put them in the window with a picture of an old man with a mortar and pestle. Mr Elsie gave Tom ten quid too.

The window of the Snowdonia Mountain Rescue Charity Shop, that was a mess – big piles of old clothes and books. They couldn't pay Tom but they said he could choose something from the shop, so he picked one of those wind-up torches, and on the Tuesday he went in there and dressed up this old mannequin as a climber – bobble hat, boots, everything. He gave him a book to read and put a nice cardigan on him and he put a steam iron in his free hand. The steam iron is a bit random, but it was such a bargain that it went that afternoon.

The window of Mrs Porty's newsagent's used to be all notices and adverts. Then she got Tom in. He cleared the space and put a shelf in the window, with all the boiled sweet jars on it. That doesn't sound like much, but it's the best one really. When the sun shone on them, they looked like jars of different-coloured raindrops or jewels or something.

The Spar even. They've taken that big green Spar sign down and swapped it for a great big photograph of Manod Mountain. It looks bizarre – but in a good way, because the real mountain sticks up behind the picture of itself.

The new windows were even in the paper, look:

back to Terrible. 'In case someone would like one as a souvenir,' she said.

Because her dad had asked me to keep an eye on her, I sat next to Terrible in art. We were supposed to be doing paintings of Our Town to send to Gumbi. I was painting the mountain, and so was she. I suggested that we paint half each and make one big painting instead of two little ones. She didn't say anything, but she shoved her picture next to mine. I said, 'D'you fancy a kick-around during playtime?'

'Why are you asking me?'

I wasn't sure whether to tell her about her dad or not, so I just sort of shrugged.

'Is it because I've got short hair?'

'No, it's because I really want a kick-around.'

'Because I've got short hair I'm supposed to like lads' games, is that it?' And she shoved me in the chest and I fell off my chair. That time Ms Stannard definitely saw what happened, but all she did was tell everyone to hold up their paintings.

Most people had painted the mountain, except Jade Porty, who had painted her own house, and Minnie, who had painted the bus shelter. 'Does anyone notice anything about them?' said Ms Stannard. 'What do they have in common?'

'They're not dry, miss.'

'Anything else? No one? They're ALL GREY! All of them are completely grey. We're supposed to be bringing good cheer to our friends in Gumbi, not making them suicidal. If they see these paintings, they'll get up a collection for *us*. Paint something colourful, please.'

Terrible painted a picture of a little boy being punched, with bright red blood spurting out of him. It didn't look much like me, but I am the only boy in town. I stayed calm, but at home time I went round the backs instead of up the High Street.

If you go round the backs, you get a really good view of the mountain. That's when I saw the Misses Sellwood's car heading for town a lot faster than usual. When I got on to the Blaenau Road (B5565), everyone was walking quite quickly, trying to get home before they arrived, but the car came round the corner and everyone jumped into the shop doorways, waiting for it to pass. But it didn't pass. It pulled in to the kerb and the driver wound the window down. And it wasn't Miss Sellwood at all, it was the Brake Brothers man.

'Kid,' he said, 'you're from the garage, aren't you? Have they got a tow truck up there, d'you know?'

'Certainly have,' I said. '1997 Wrangler, fifty-nine thousand on the clock.' I think he was impressed.

I was telling him about the special-edition chrome bumpers when I noticed that the bumper of the Misses Sellwood's Rover was badly dinted and that Miss Elsa herself was sitting in the passenger seat.

I said, 'I see you've got Miss Sellwood.'

Miss Sellwood said, 'Are we at the Spar?'

'No, Miss Elsa, just by the pub.'

'Oh, I don't want to go to the pub.'

The man said, 'Do you know this woman?'

'Yes, she's Miss Sellwood.'

'Do you know she's completely blind? She was driving, and she is completely blind. She came straight down at me and never slowed up. I near killed her. She near killed me. I had to swerve to avoid her.'

I said, 'Are you all right, Miss Sellwood?'

'Right as rain, thank you, Dylan. But Edna is bad with her nerves. So I had to come down to get her prescription.'

'That's dangerous though, Miss Sellwood. You should have asked Mam to come and get you.'

'I didn't want to put her to no trouble. Anyway, this nice young man is taking care of me now. And he's doing a very good job, I must say.'

'You're all right then?'

'She's fine,' said the man. He was a bit sharp with me, actually. 'And her car's fine. Whereas I have tipped my van.'

'Oh. When you say tipped, is that tipped over?'

'Right on its side. That's why I need the tow truck.'

'Righto. No problem.' But I wasn't going to let it rest there. This was a classic opportunity for a bit of market research. I said, 'So did the food tip out at all?' quite casual.

And it had! He'd lost the whole load of food and admitted that the men on the mountain were waiting for it. They would be starving. This was it – our chance to become a catering force!

On the Hughes Family team sheet that afternoon we had: Tom driving the tow truck; me making the whole thing happen through the magic of market research; Minnie as brains; Marie operating the lifting gear; and Mam – well, Mam didn't seem that interested, really. I suppose Max was keeping her busy.

Minnie had the brilliant idea of taking all the Pot Noodles up with us, as it was such a good opportunity. When she asked, Mam just said, 'If you like . . .' and carried on looking out of the window.

Obviously it was a disadvantage having no captain, but it also made us determined to do him proud.

Some people are sometimes surprised that Marie is so good with machinery. The thing is, Dad has to read lots of magazines about cars for his work, and there's nearly always a beautiful woman on the front. So from when she was still quite small, Marie got the idea that beautiful women are supposed to be interested in cars. And she is beautiful. Plus Dad was always encouraging us to learn about engines anyway. Even me. Until the mix-up about the difference between antifreeze and oil and Ms Stannard's Fiesta, which could have happened to anyone. So that's how Marie became good with machines. Like Donatello (the Turtle).

As we drove up the mountain we were all singing:

Splinter taught them to be ninja teens (He's a radical rat!)
Leonardo leads, Donatello does machines (That's a fact!)
Raphael is cool but crude (Gimme a break!)
Michelangelo is a party dude (Party!)

Miss Sellwood tried to join in the song.

When we got up the mountain, there were cardboard boxes all over the side of the road. The rain had made them soft and floppy and most of them had burst. You could see the little packets of frozen food inside. The big beige van was wedged sideways into a ditch at the edge of the road so the undercarriage was showing. Lester was walking up and down, looking worried.

Minnie said, 'We are so going to sell Pot Noodle.'

'Hey!' Marie shouted and jumped out of the truck. 'It's sunny up here. How come it's sunny? How long does it take to get a tan?' She took off her jumper and rolled up her sleeves.

Tom was fastening the lifting gear to the van's front axle. Lester went over and said, 'How bad is it, do you think?'

'Well, you definitely won't be able to refreeze any

of the chicken. Stuff like lasagne takes longer to defrost, so you might be lucky there.'

'I was talking about the van,' said Lester, 'not the food.'

'Oh. Right. Well, you're best off talking to Marie. I'm not really a mechanic. I just help out about the place.' He waved to Marie, who was now in the driver's seat.

The chains tightened. The exhaust gave a big puff of smoke and suddenly the van started to move upwards very slowly, like when you really don't want to get out of bed. Then, when it was mostly up, we all took a step back and it suddenly plonked on to its wheels and stood there in the road again, as if nothing had happened.

Tom started to undo the chains. Marie got back out of the cab. She said to the driver, 'You might as well give it a go. You could have got away with it. The ground's dead soft and you weren't going fast.'

And she was right. It started first time. The driver looked very happy. He said, 'I'm going right back to Birmingham to report that old woman. I'll come back when they've locked her up.'

'Oh, don't do that,' said Marie. 'She only comes out of a Wednesday. All you have to do is pick a different day. Tell him, Lester.'

Lester went to say something, but the driver just turned the van round and headed off down the mountain, scrunching a big box of frozen chicken wings down into the mud as he went. The van had a surprisingly tight turning circle, for a vehicle with such a long wheelbase.

Miss Sellwood didn't seem to mind being talked about.

'The whole thing is very exciting,' she said. 'I haven't seen the mountain so crowded since the war. Did you know they brought all the paintings from the National Gallery and put them in the quarry to stop Hitler dropping bombs on them?'

'Yes, I did,' said Lester. 'We're doing it all again now.'

'Oh, but you needn't,' said Miss Elsa. 'Hitler's dead now.'

Lester tried to explain about the problems with the floods and the insurance. But Miss Elsa was too happy remembering the war. She said, 'Were you up here then? The last time? Do you remember the night we had a dance out by the big boulder?'

'No. I wasn't born, I'm afraid,' said Lester.

'What a shame. It was a lovely night. You're interested in art though, I hope?'

'Yes. That's my job.'

'Our father loved to paint,' said Miss Elsa. 'Painted all the time. You should come and take a look at his pictures. You'd appreciate them more than most. More than me, anyway. I'm blind, you know.'

'Yes,' said Lester. 'Yes, I think that point has been made.'

Marie and Minnie got the boxes of Pot Noodle out of the van and carried them to Lester's car.

Marie was saying, 'It's not exactly Delia, but it'll fill a hole while you're waiting.'

'How very generous. Pot Noodle?' said Lester. Only he pronounced it like '*Pot* Noodle' so you could tell he'd never heard of it before. Marie explained that all you had to do was add water – 'boiling water, that is' – and that there was a choice of flavours. The man who'd asked me to play football that day came over and said, 'Thanks very much. You've saved our lives.' Then he gave me a big wink and said, 'Pity you couldn't save our bacon.'

'Oh. Yes,' mumbled Lester. 'Indeed. What do we owe you?'

I was thinking, Fifty-three Pot Noodle at £1.75 a pop, that's . . .

But Marie said, 'No, no. We're neighbours. We're just being hospitable.'

'Oh. Well. Thank you very much.'

When she got back in the Wrangler, Tom said, 'Fifty-three Pot Noodle at one pound seventy-five a pop, that's . . .'

'Ninety-two pounds seventy-five,' said Minnie.

'A lot of money,' said Tom.

'I know it seems daft, turning the money down,' said Marie, 'but I had a feeling it's what Dad would've done. And if Dad would've done it, it must be right.'

It's funny, but that's exactly what I was thinking. We sang all the way down the mountain. 'Team Hughes always sticks together no matter what.' Like the Turtles TV theme. Not the original, the remake.

We were right about it being right!

We were just closing up when Ms Stannard came in for chocolate. She always comes in for chocolate at closing time. Marie says it's because she's probably spent the whole evening trying not to think about chocolate so that she won't eat any, but at the last minute her nerve goes and she jumps in her car and races up to the garage.

She was trying to get Mam to help her choose between Revels and Minstrels when Lester came in. Ms Stannard gave him this big smile and asked him which he preferred, Revels or Minstrels.

'I've never really thought about it,' said Lester.

'How disappointing. Still, now that you're in Manod you'll have lots of time to think about things you haven't thought about.'

'Yesssssssssssssssss,' said Lester really slowly. 'Yessssss.' Then he looked at Mam. 'I just wanted to say thank you for all you did today. I wondered if there was anything we could do in return.'

This was it. Our big chance. We all looked at Mam. She could name her price. She said, 'Oh, it's all right. Glad to see the back of the Pot Noodles, to be honest.'

Lester looked a bit surprised. 'Well – I was wondering – a lot of the men have been complaining about the bread we get from our supplier, and it struck me that perhaps you . . .'

'Yes.' That was me, not Mam. 'Yes, we can get bread. And what about milk?'

'Of course. Yes. Milk. Thank you.'

'How many?'

'Well, there are twelve of us up there so . . .'

'Six litres of milk, ten sliced loaves. White or brown?'

'Five of each, I imagine.'

'Great. And the cakes?'

'Well, the cakes seem to be very popular.'

'Great.'

I looked at Mam. She still didn't seem to be taking that much interest, even though I was being so brilliant.

Then Minnie was brilliant too. 'Are they all happy with the *Financial Times*?' she said. I'd never have thought of that one.

'Oh. No. No, they're not. What do you suggest? The *Mirror*?'

'Five *Mirror*s. Maybe a couple of *Guardian*s?'

'Yes, that sounds about right.'

'I'll put them on your tab. And the *Manod Month* keeps you in touch with what's going on, round and about,' said Minnie.

Lester said, 'Is anything going on, round and about?' and then he made a little 'ha ha' noise. Nobody joined in. 'Well,' he said. 'Thank you again. If you're sure there's nothing else I can do, I'll go.'

That's when Ms Stannard said, 'You could show the children the paintings.'

Lester frowned. 'Children?'

'I'm the teacher here. It'd be lovely to show them the paintings . . .'

'I'm afraid that wouldn't be possible. We have security issues and health and safety and, really, you're not supposed to know the paintings are here.'

He gave me a bit of a look.

'They'll never have an opportunity like this again,' said Ms Stannard.

'I'm afraid they're not having that opportunity now either.'

'They're in desperate need of visual stimulation. Do you know, I had an art lesson recently and they painted everything grey. The yellow ochre, the crimson lake, the magenta – all untouched.'

'I wish I could help,' said Lester.

'When they boarded off the boating lake, the council sent us an artist to paint a mural on the fence. I suggested Arthurian scenes. Or something to do with the geology. Do you know what they voted for? Scenes from the life of Elvis Presley. Up to and including the King's encounter with Mr Davis in Home and Bargain. Go and look at it. No appreciation of art round here.'

'If they don't appreciate it, it seems a shame to drag them up a mountain to look at it.'

'I'll let you sleep on it. You can give me a ring when you've really thought it over.' And she wrote her number on the front of his *Financial Times* and walked out.

Lester looked at Mam. 'It really won't be possible,' he said.

She just sort of shrugged and said, 'Fine. Whatever.' Which isn't the kind of thing she normally says.

That night I decided to give Mam a surprise. 'No need to cook,' I said. 'Look what I got.' I'd managed to save a whole pack of lemon and coriander chicken fillets. They were sealed, so it was fine. There was enough for Tom to stay and eat too. We microwaved them and had them with baguettes and sat around trying to work out how much money we were going to make from all this new business. It was a lot. Compared to what we normally made it was, anyway.

'We could make a lot more if we stole one of those paintings,' said Minnie, looking at Tom.

'You couldn't steal them,' said Tom. 'There's men on quad bikes and everything up there.'

'There's always a way,' said Minnie. 'Like when an as yet unidentified thief stole a priceless Bruegel from the Belvedere in Vienna. D'you know what he did? He posed as an expert and told them the frame had woodworm. Then he said he had just the thing for woodworm, which was wasps. Special wasps that ate the woodworm. So they paid him – they actually paid him money – and he built like a tent around the painting to keep the wasps in. Then he went for his tea break and never came back. They didn't take the tent down for hours because they were scared of the wasps. And when they did . . . no painting. He'd gone off with it. Perfect crime.'

'See, I could never do that,' said Tom. 'I'm frightened of wasps. I—'

'There were no wasps. That's the whole point,' said Minnie.

'Then what did he need a tent for?'

'One hundred and fifty-seven,' said Marie. 'That's what we made today.'

I said, 'Dad's going to be amazed. The way things

are going, we'll be making so much money he'll be able to stop working on the New Barrier and come home. Won't he, Mam?'

She said, 'I'd better get Max ready for bed. Clear the table when you've finished.' She said it in a faraway voice, like she was thinking about Dad coming home and really cherishing the thought.

Cars today:
MINIBUS — Gwynedd Education Committee

Weather — damp

Note: LESTER'S NOT HIS REAL NAME

This minibus is the one that comes every morning to collect Marie and take her to Blaenau High School. It is actually quite beastie for a minibus. Mountain Rescue used to use it, so it has snow chains and bull bars and four-wheel drive and an exhaust that sounded like a helicopter.

It stopped at the garage because Ms Stannard had got her way – sort of. Lester was going to let her take a school party up to the quarry, but it had to be on a Saturday because the men were doing essential maintenance in the week. I mean, who is going to turn up on a Saturday? When it pulled on to the forecourt, it turned out that the answer to the question was: everyone. The whole school was on this bus, except me and Minnie. Then Minnie got on.

I said, 'What about Mam? She'll be on her own.' Marie had gone to Blaenau.

Minnie said, 'Conwy Car Boot Madness.'

So we got on the minibus. Mam hadn't had time to make our breakfast. Or sandwiches. And we'd sold all the Pot Noodle. So we made do with a couple of Mars bars each from the sweet rack in the shop.

One good thing about being the only boy in the school is that no one wants to sit with you. So I could eat my chocolate in peace, though I did notice Terrible Evans glaring at me over the back of her seat, like she could smell the chocolate.

The minibus couldn't take the corners on the mountain road. Twice we had to get out while the driver edged it round a big boulder. Then we pulled out of the clouds, and the others were so amazed by the sunshine that they all clapped. Except Terrible Evans, obviously.

Lester met us at the top. You could tell he didn't really want us down his quarry. First thing he said was, 'It's such a beautiful day, it seems a shame to take them underground when they are surrounded by such natural beauty.'

I said, 'Yeah,' thinking I might still get a game out of this.

Ms Stannard said, 'It's not a shame at all. Lead the way, Lester.'

We all followed him in through the quarry entrance. There was the warm breeze and the little railway track, just like last time. He explained that the track was once used by wagons bringing slate to the surface. Now specially adapted trailers carried the paintings down to the secure chamber. He showed them one of the trailers.

'You can pull it back and forth if you like, see how it works.'

'Can we ride on it?' said Jade Porty.

'No.'

'And the paintings,' said Ms Stannard, 'where are they?'

'In the secure chamber, directly below us. I'm afraid we're not covered for people going down there without hard hats, and as we don't have any hard hats—'

'Nonsense,' said Ms Stannard. 'The quarry's been closed for forty years. Anything that was going to fall down has fallen down long since. You worry too much, Lester.'

And she took herself off down the track. Everyone followed her. Even Lester.

The track led down and down. It kept doubling back on itself like the big flume at Plas Madoc. You could feel yourself getting deeper and deeper. It was funny to think that you were almost down the mountain but on the inside. I couldn't concentrate on the feeling though, because Terrible Evans kept coming up behind me and trying to get her hand in my pocket.

Suddenly we came round one last corner and, instead of more tunnel, there was a room. I don't mean a room like a bedroom. This was like the inside of the biggest room you've ever been in, which in my case is the National Exhibition Centre in Birmingham the time we went to the Motor Show. It was that big. It was lit by these great big floodlights on stands. And it was full of hundreds and hundreds of rows and rows of wooden boxes. Hundreds of them. Hundreds and hundreds, leaning against these big metal shelves.

'There it is,' said Lester. 'The entire National Gallery collection.' He looked over and gave me a little smile when he said that. Then he strolled down to the rows of boxes and pointed to the first one.

'Early medieval altar pieces and so on . . . up as far as Giotto.'

He moved on to the next row.

'Early Renaissance Italian and the North European school – Bosch, Bruegel and so on . . . please feel free to look.'

'Feast your eyes, children,' said Ms Stannard. 'Some of the highest achievements of civilization are here before us, under our mountain. Imagine that.'

Some of the girls followed her down the first row. It was just boxes. A lot of boxes, but just boxes.

Lester was on another row now. 'High Renaissance Italian up as far as Raphael . . .'

Ms Stannard stopped him. 'Am I right in thinking,' she said, 'that they are all boxed?'

'Yes. Oh yes, of course. These are valuable works

of art. We have to take extreme care. We check the humidity, the temperature, the dust content . . .'

'Yes, but . . . can we look at any of the paintings?'

'Oh no. My word, no. Do you mean, take them out of their boxes? No, no, no, no.' He made it sound like they might run away. 'Well, I hope that's given you some sense of what we're about here. Perhaps you'd like to follow me back up . . .'

Ms Stannard wasn't going to budge though. 'Children, take a look at the ceiling,' she said.

We all looked up. It was steep and pointy, like a massive rock tent or the roof of a house, and it was covered in marks and shiny wet. And while I was look-ing up at it, Terrible Evans gave me a rabbit punch in the kidneys. I doubled over and she took my other Mars bar.

'This is not a natural cave,' said Ms Stannard. 'It was cut from the living rock by your grandfathers and their fathers before them. They used their bare hands, chisels and hammers. And, a bit later, small explosive charges. It took the best part of a hundred years to carve it out. Look, it's like a secret cathedral. And strangely enough, it's called a gallery. And now this one is filled with art, so it's an art gallery.'

I was trying not to notice, but Terrible was now chewing my Mars bar behind my back, right next to my ear.

'You might say,' said Ms Stannard, 'that this is their work of art.'

'No, no,' said Lester. 'It's very impressive, but it's a work of engineering. Excavation. Whatever. Not art.'

'Well, you say that, Lester,' said Ms Stannard, 'but who are you to say? You think these wooden boxes are works of art.'

'No. They contain works of art. Great works of art. The greatest, actually.'

Ms Stannard kept on at him. 'How can something be a work of art if no one can see it? It's only a work of art when someone's looking at it. At least we're looking at this ceiling.'

And just as she said that, Terrible thumped me in the kidneys again.

I'd had enough. I turned on her. She grinned and ran off, back up the tunnel. I went after her. I chased her up the steep passageway. I could hear her footsteps ahead of me and the boomy voices of Lester and Ms Stannard arguing behind me.

Suddenly the footsteps ahead stopped. I started running quicker, thinking I'd get her now. Then I stopped. There was a scream. A terrible scream, blasting past me down the tunnel. They must have heard it in the big cave, because the boomy voices stopped and the next thing I heard was a hundred footsteps hurrying up the tunnel.

The scream came again. And before I had time to think, I was running towards it. I got to the top. It was coming from that little room off the main entrance, the one where we'd looked at the picture of the Madonna. I pushed the door open and Terrible turned to face me. 'Sorry,' she gasped. She could barely catch her breath. 'Sorry. I thought it was real.'

She was pointing to the corner where the Madonna had been and I nearly screamed too. There was another picture, of a different woman, an ugly woman. But when I say ugly, I don't mean not nice-looking. I mean, her face should have been certificate eighteen. She had great big nostrils, pointing out at you like a pair of truck exhausts, and as for her eyes, well, I've seen bigger on a potato. Her skin was all wrinkly like an old balloon, especially her neck, which was like a turkey's. Her clothes were old-fashioned, like from history. She had this random thing on her head. I suppose it was a hat, but it looked more like half a couch. The worst thing was, she was coming out of her dress at the top. If the painter had painted her a minute later, well, you don't want to think about that.

The others had caught up with me by now. They were crowding in through the door. Minnie came over and stood next to me.

'It isn't real, is it?' said Terrible. 'Is it a photograph or what?'

'It's a painting,' said Minnie, and then she said very, very quietly to me, 'and it's not by Michelangelo.'

I whispered, 'Thanks.'

Lester had come in now. 'If you could just step back a little please.' He was obviously worried that someone might breathe on his painting. 'Step back, please. Everyone.

'I'm sorry you've been distressed,' he went on. 'But do feel free to leave. As I said, I'm only too happy to have the paintings to myself.'

But Terrible was trying to bring her heartbeat down. 'That's a painting? Why would anyone want to paint that? Why?'

'What a good question,' said Ms Stannard. 'Lester, what's the answer?'

She was talking to him now like he was in Year Six. And the best thing was, he replied!

'Well,' he said, and he really should have kept his mouth shut, 'there are several schools of thought on the matter. Some see it as a simple comic grotesquerie. Some as a satirical comment on the foolishness of old women who dress in a way that is inappropriate to their years.'

He was staring at Ms Stannard when he said this. She glared back at him.

'Shouldn't be allowed,' said Jade Porty.

'I imagine that's what the artist is trying to say,' said Lester.

'No, I mean the picture shouldn't be allowed,' said Jade. 'It's upsetting. Very upsetting. It upsets me completely. If I looked like that, I'd hide myself, not go getting my portrait painted and shoving it in other people's faces. There is no need for that, no need at all. It's not necessary, that isn't. No wonder you're putting it down a mine. Are they all like that?'

I'd never seen anyone so revved up. And all the time she was saying this stuff, the girls behind her were nodding their heads and agreeing with her.

'It's interesting. Dylan and I were talking just the other day about Michelangelo.' When he said that, everyone looked at me. They looked at me funny, like he'd said, 'The other day Dylan and I fell down a sewer and were turned into Ninjas by a talking rat.' Lester kept going. 'We were saying that art is about beauty. And of course until Michelangelo – in the Middle Ages, for instance – artists mostly saw beauty as a temptation to sin. Michelangelo was almost the first to celebrate human beauty for its own sake. And yet here we have someone doing just the opposite. Looking at ugliness. It's quite radical . . .'

I said, 'Dude.' I couldn't help myself. You hear the word 'radical' and you say 'dude'. It's normal behaviour. Unfortunately, it also reminded him that I was there.

'Dylan,' he said, 'step forward and take a closer look. Tell us what you think.'

I walked over to the picture just to try and kill time. It was about life-size in a neat wooden frame, so it was like looking in a mirror. I wondered if the woman in the picture ever looked in a mirror. Maybe they didn't have them then. Maybe she didn't even know what she looked like till she saw the painting. I said to myself, Dylan, there's only four things you know about painting – the names of four painters. It's not Michelangelo because Minnie said so. Donatello does machines, which this isn't. Raphael is cool, which this definitely isn't. So that leaves Leonardo. So that's what I said. I said, 'Leonardo?'

I could hear Minnie sucking her teeth. I could feel everyone else holding their breath, waiting to see if I'd said the wrong thing or not.

Lester said, 'Remarkable.'

And everyone started breathing again, including me.

Lester was saying, 'Of course, it's not actually by Leonardo. In fact it's Dutch, but the influence is clearly there, in the brushwork, of course. And also in the subject matter. The picture bears an uncanny resemblance to a sketch in one of Leonardo's notebooks. Leonardo, as you know, was as fascinated by ugly faces as he was by beautiful ones. He made hundreds of drawings of them. Whether from life or from his imagination, we don't know. But he never made one the main subject of a painting as this man did. His name is Massys, by the way. Quentin Massys. My namesake.'

'I thought your name was Lester,' said Ms Stannard.

'Actually, Lester is my surname. My first name is Quentin.'

'Oh,' said Ms Stannard. 'I see.'

And then he started to talk about how amazing and unexpected it was that this Dutch painter had worked so closely with Leonardo all those years ago. But none of us was listening. We were all standing there thinking, Quentin?!

He said, 'It's as though Massys is saying, "Yes, there is beauty in humanity, but not everyone is beautiful. There is ugliness too."'

'You've either got it,' said Jade Porty, 'or you haven't.'

She definitely thinks she has, which shows how much she knows.

Lester said, 'Well, I hope you've all found this entertaining and educational. I wish you all a safe journey down the mountain.'

Everyone started to go, but Terrible waited for a bit. Then she said, 'You're wrong about that picture, mister.'

'Am I really?' said Lester.

'He painted it so everyone would feel good. You're just not thinking about it right.'

'Aren't I indeed?'

'He's painted someone so ugly that anyone looking at it would think, "I'm not so bad after all." When you first see it, it's horrible. But if you just keep looking, it makes you feel great. I feel like a million dollars now.'

Lester opened his mouth, but he said nothing. You could see she'd given him something to think about.

When we got outside, Terrible was sitting on a rock, eating my Mars bar, and the funny thing was, she did look good. Not a million dollars, but maybe half a million, or even three-quarters. The picture had been mutagenish again. It had changed her just like the shop windows had been changed. She caught me looking at her, smiled, and threw the rest of the Mars bar at me.

Back on the bus, Ms Stannard came and sat by me. What is the point of being the only boy in the school if you don't get a seat to yourself? She said, 'Dylan Hughes, I believe you've been hiding your light under a bushel. I believe you're a lot cleverer than you let on. Leonardo. Who would have thought?'

Even though I knew it was another misunderstanding, I did start looking out of the window, wondering if it could be true. If you could get cleverer. Like the Turtles were not clever when they were just turtles, were they? They were amphibians. But then Splinter came along and they learned to be good with machines and got a Sewer Sledge and everything. Maybe sometimes a person can turn into something else.

A caterpillar doesn't know it's going to be a butterfly. A tadpole doesn't know it's going to be a frog. And when those pet turtles were flushed down a toilet, they didn't know they were going to turn out to be Ninja Heroes – or even mutants.

16 May

Cars today:
RED TOYOTA PRIUS T4 AUTOMATIC —
Dr Ramanan (fill up, oil check, cup-a-soup)
ANOTHER RED TOYOTA PRIUS T4 AUTOMATIC
— some people I don't know (petrol,
cappuccinos)
A BLUE TOYOTA PRIUS T4 AUTOMATIC —
a random person (petrol, a box of fudge)
SILVER SKODA OCTAVIA — the Ellis brothers
FORD SCORPIO — sergeant Hunter
BLUE LEXUS — Mr Choi (petrol)
RED FORD KA — Ms Stannard (petrol)

Weather — rain (including rainbows)

Note: THERE'S NO SUCH THING AS BAD
WEATHER

Friday 23 May is our busiest weekday since the log-book began. We actually ran out of cup-a-soups. We even sold a box of Manod fudge. And this was all down to Mam because she was the one who bought the umbrellas.

What happened was this: when we came back from our school trip to see the wooden boxes, Mam was in the shop. Which was a surprise because we thought she was going to Conwy Car Boot Madness. That's a massive car-boot sale beside the harbour in Conwy.

Mam never misses it. But that day she just shrugged and looked out of the window at the rain. She said, 'Oh, guess what? It's raining.'

On the Monday, when we told her there was no cereal left for breakfast, she did the same.

'Looks like it's Mars bars again,' I said.

'That is so unhealthy,' said Marie. 'You can kill yourselves if you like. I'm going to sort out a proper breakfast for myself.' She had a Bounty, because they've got real coconut in them, which is very good for you.

I stuck to Mars bars and took Mars bars for lunch as well. I took an extra one because I knew that Terrible Evans would probably nick one. But she didn't. She came and sat next to me and started chatting about the Turtles. 'Did you know,' she said, 'that in the original comic, Splinter wasn't a mutant rat?'

'No. I didn't.'

'In the telly series, Splinter is a rat who used to be a human. But in the comics he's a rat who was always a rat. On telly he used to be Hamato Yoshi, who mutated into a rat because of mutagen. In the comics, he was Hamato Yoshi's pet. A pet rat. He's supposed to have learned martial arts by copying his master's routines. I mean, how mad is that?'

'Well, it's a bit mad, but so is four pizza-eating ninja turtles when you think about it.'

'Yeah, but it's just not credible, is it? A human who mutates into a rat is much more likely than a rat that learns martial arts, surely?'

'Well, maybe.'

It's possible that Terrible Evans was more interesting before she mutated.

She didn't hit anyone all day. During morning break she spoke to Jade Porty. During maths she put her hand up twice. After school she walked up to the garage with us, and she laughed at the hens, but not in a bad way. She stood and watched while we fed them. She said, 'Look at the way they walk – it's hilarious!' It is true that hens do walk funny, but I don't think our hens are funnier than any others. They sort of lift their legs very high up before putting them down. 'You know what they are?' said Terrible. 'Ninja chickens!'

While we were doing this, a van came down off the mountain. Lester hopped out of the passenger side to open the gate. We took him his *Financial Times* and waved him off.

'That's your picture,' said Minnie, 'the ugly-woman one. It's going to London.'

'I don't care,' said Terrible. 'I've got it all up here. It's all up here.' She pointed to her head.

I hadn't really thought about the vans going to London before. I watched this one disappear and wondered if Dad would go and see the picture.

Anyway, the point is, when we went indoors, there was no tea ready. I said to Mam, 'We're starving.'

She said, 'Eat then,' and carried on looking out of the window. 'Oh! Rain,' she said. 'There's a surprise.'

We were sick of Mars bars by this point, so we had soup – not cup-a-soup, proper soup out of a tin – and Quavers instead of bread. I offered some to Mam but she wasn't interested. Marie said, 'She's depressed. It puts you off your food. I wish I was depressed. I might get rid of these thighs.'

Minnie said, 'You haven't got thighs.'

'Everyone's got thighs.'

This went on for ages. I stopped listening because I'd had this idea: if a painting stopped Terrible Evans being terrible, then maybe a painting could stop Mam being depressed. All I had to do was get her to come up there with me.

It turned out that that was easy. I just went in to her and said, 'Mam, I've got to go up to the quarry on Thursday because of the cakes. Can you give me a lift?'

She didn't even look at me. She just went, 'Whatever.'

So the next Thursday I strapped Max into the Wrangler (top speed 90 mph), which was the only vehicle we had left, and we drove up the mountain. I had to hold on to Max because his baby seat was still in the Mini. Because Mam had never been up before, I thought she'd be surprised that it was sunny on top, but she didn't seem to notice.

The picture was still in its box. All the paintings were in boxes, but before taking one off to London Lester liked to open it up and make sure it was the right picture and that it wasn't damaged. Then he'd put it back in the box again. 'The whole thing should only really take about half an hour,' he said, 'but I like to do it on a Thursday so I have the whole weekend alone with the picture. I have it boxed up again on Sunday evening and then travel up to London with it on the Monday morning. I always accompany the Art. Just to be on the safe side.'

While Lester was talking, one of the men was undoing the box. It was surprisingly complicated. The box had a lid that fitted tight into the top. You lifted that off with a crowbar. 'The trick is finding the groove where the crowbar fits,' said the man. 'It's here, under the writing, look. Just under the "T" of National.' Inside, the box was stuffed with straw and there were these metal brackets to hold the picture in place. The top two had little catches on them so you could undo them and lift the picture out. I couldn't believe it. It was a picture of rain.

'Oh no,' I sighed.

'You don't like it?' said Lester. 'It's too late for your taste, I imagine.'

How can a picture be late? Late for what? I just said, 'Yeah.'

'I thought I'd play safe for a week. This is a very popular picture.' The painting by the way is called *The Umbrellas* and it's by Renoir. It's a picture of people standing out in the rain with their umbrellas up. Except there's a woman at the front with a big shopping basket. She looks a bit miserable, which could be because she's got no umbrella, or it could be because her shopping basket is possibly filling up with water. There's a beardy bloke behind her saying something. Probably, 'Do you want to buy an umbrella?' It looked like any day in Manod, really. Except most people in Manod don't have umbrellas.

Lester said, 'It's not entirely without interest. In it you can see Renoir moving away from straightforward Impressionism towards something more classical and sculptural. The woman at the front, for instance. And yet the play of light and shade across the umbrellas themselves is true to the original aims of—'

'It's lovely,' said Mam.

'The play of light and shade across the umbrellas? Yes, I think we can say he—'

'The people,' said Mam. 'They're out in the rain, but they're all smiling or getting on with things. Why are they so happy?'

167

The man who'd been helping with the box said, 'Maybe they're somewhere where it hardly ever rains. Maybe that's why he painted it? Because rain was a special occasion.'

'Interesting,' said Lester, 'but incorrect. He painted this picture over a long period. He began it in 1881 and didn't finish until 1886. I'm not saying it poured down continuously for five years, but I do think that we can assume a certain familiarity with rain over that period.'

'Rain's OK,' I said, 'if you've got an umbrella.'

'Exactly,' said Mam. 'It's umbrellas. You hardly see umbrellas any more, do you? Don't they look lovely? Like big flowers. And every one of them's got two people under it. Whispering, chatting, laughing. The umbrellas are like parties on sticks.'

And that was it. On Saturday morning, Mam took us all to the Pen-y-bont Car Boot Carnival (this year's beneficiary the mid-Snowdonia meals-on-wheels) and told us all to go and look for umbrellas. I got two of those little telescopic black ones that fit in your glove compartment, and a golf umbrella the size of a satellite tracking station with 'Gordon's Gin – the Gin That Thinks It's It' written all round it. Minnie found a whole bag full of kids' umbrellas with ducks and frogs on. Marie found a white one with a pearly handle which was more pretty than waterproof. Mam found a whole load too. And when she'd finished at the car boot, she took us to the Oxfam shop in Llanrwst, the Sue Ryder shop in Blaenau, and the Mountain Rescue shop in Manod, still looking for umbrellas. And when we got home, she went up into the loft and found three more there. Fifty umbrellas altogether.

She got Marie to paint some flowers and the words 'Manod Parapluies – Take One, They're Free' on three of the old plastic flower bins from the shop. She put a bin full of umbrellas on the forecourt next to the papers. She put the second one in the bus shelter, and the third one she filled with the frog and duck umbrellas and on Monday she asked Ms Stannard to put it in the playground.

'Umbrellas,' said Ms Stannard. 'There's a health-and-safety issue there. They could poke each other's eyes out.'

'I never thought of that,' said Mam.

'Then again, if you can't poke someone's eye out in primary school, when can you? Let's give it a go, Mrs Hughes.'

That lunchtime no one opted for Wet Play. Even though it was raining as hard as usual, everyone took an umbrella and played out. Actually there weren't enough umbrellas, but that was OK. People just shared, like in the picture. In the playground, it felt like you were inside a great big restless tent. Back in the classroom, the Connect Four and the big draughts stayed in their boxes.

Most people in our school get a lift to school, but the morning after the umbrellas came, everyone took an umbrella and walked. From up where we are, at the top, in the garage, it looked like a cup-final crowd moving down the street.

It looked so good, people would come up to the garage just to look down the street. And they bought coffee! In the end Newspaper Arthur came and wrote about it:

Whatever the Weather

There are many unusual sights in Snowdonia but few as colourful as the so-called Manod March. Every morning at 8.50 and every afternoon at 15.45 the streets are briefly ablaze with colour. And what's the reason? Umbrellas! Manodians have taken to doing the school run on foot, with umbrellas. 'There's no such thing as bad weather,' says resident Mrs Porty, 'there's only inappropriate clothing.' The massed umbrellas of Manod can be seen snaking up and down the whole length of the Blaenau Road like a psychedelic boa constrictor. When I say briefly, by the way, I mean it. Get there ten minutes too late and Manod is just another rainy, grey mountain town.

That's if you get there at all. There's no
sign for Manod on the A496 and the turn-
off itself is difficult to spot, concealed as
it is by the advertising billboard for
Diggermania (Harlech).

Psychedelic boa constrictor! How hectic is that then?
How many towns have a high street like a psychedelic
boa constrictor?

And this time he put a picture of Marie in. She
was smiling under the massive 'Gin That Thinks It's
It' umbrella. The caption said she was 'singing in the
rain', but she wasn't singing. She can't sing.

If you ask her now, Marie says it was her smile, not
the umbrellas, that did it. Whatever. The day after the
paper came out, Dr Ramanan turned up before
school, filled up with petrol and said he wanted to
watch the umbrellas. Then came Sergeant Hunter in
his Scorpio. 'Just making sure it doesn't constitute an
obstruction,' he said. Then another Toyota Prius and
a Skoda Octavia with the Ellis brothers in it! Even
though they now live in Conwy, their mam still reads
the *Month*, and they'd come back to see the umbrellas.
They had their Yu-Gi-Oh! cards with them, so we
played that on the bonnet of the Octavia until Dr
Ramanan shouted, 'It's starting!' and they all looked
down Blaenau Road. The Ellis boys got up on the roof
of their Skoda to see better. Me and Minnie should've

been gone by then, but we wanted to see it too. It was like a dance. One minute the streets were empty, the next minute there was the psycho whatsit boa constrictor. And then it was gone again as they all went round the corner into the school.

'We're late,' said Minnie.

'Yeah,' said Mam and she kissed us both goodbye, which is a thing she hadn't done for a while. 'I used to hate the rain,' she said. 'Imagine how terrible it would be if the rain stopped now. We'd have no umbrellas.'

We walked back towards the shop and – guess what? There was a rainbow! And not an ordinary rainbow like you'd see in a normal town – a double rainbow. One really bright one, with another, fainter one floating just above it. The colours on the fainter one were back to front. It's something to do with reflections. Sergeant Hunter said, 'Congratulations, Mrs Hughes', and it sounded like he thought she'd made the rainbow too.

26 May

Cars today:
CARBON BLACK BMW M5 — Mr Q. Lester
(new tyres and oil change!)
RED NISSAN X-TRAIL — man from the quarry
(came by to collect Lester)

Weather — fine persistent rain

Note: WHO REALLY RULES THE WORLD

We could see this day coming a mile off. The first time I saw Lester's tyres (6 April), I knew they wouldn't last on the mountain road. I even said so. Go back and look it up if you like.

We were just walking up from school when we saw the BMW coming, heading for the garage. Only it wasn't gliding along like a top-marque executive saloon. It was bouncing and wandering like a badly ridden quad bike. The tyres had gone.

When we got to the garage, Lester was walking up and down, really tense, like someone waiting for road-side assistance. Tom said, 'Would you like a macchiato with vanilla?'

'Thank you, no. I need to catch a train. I'm due in London.'

'What about with caramel?'

'No. Thank you.'

'Butterscotch?'

I could see Lester was getting annoyed, so I said, 'Marie can fix the tyres. She'll be home in about ten minutes.'

He looked at his watch. 'How long does it take her to change a tyre?'

'Well, I'm no tyre expert,' I said, 'but I think you've burst two, not one.'

'What!?!' He ran outside to check. Front passenger side and rear driver side both as flat as pancakes.

'And you've only got one spare,' I said. 'So we'll have to go into Harlech to Acres of Tyres.'

Lester sort of yelped, then he took out his phone and started texting like mad. I explained to him that since he needed two new tyres anyway, he should really consider switching to the Pirelli P7s, which are ideal for rough conditions and that, since it was off the road anyway, he should take the opportunity to have an oil change, which I promised not to do myself.

He wasn't really listening. He kept looking at his phone, like he was waiting for a reply to his text. Tom came out and said his mam might give him a lift. 'She'd need directions, though. I don't think she's ever been to London.'

'It's all right. One of the men's coming down to collect me. He'll be here shortly.'

'So,' said Tom, 'how's the painting?'

'What?'

'The painting with the oranges. I liked that painting.'

'Yes. Good, thank you,' said Lester and he looked up the mountain road.

I suddenly noticed that this was an ideal opportunity. I said, 'You know, while you're waiting, you could come for a walk through Manod and see all the Hidden Beauty.' I said it like that with capital letters, so he'd know I was still offended about him saying that Manod's beauty was hidden.

'Oh yes,' said Tom. 'You could start with my still life. That's what started everything. Come and have a look.'

He took Lester over to see his window display. It wasn't as colourful as it had been when he first did it. I think we might have mice, and there'd been some trouble between the chickens and the cornflakes.

Lester said, 'It's . . .' but then an incoming text beeped his phone. He said, 'Thank heavens,' and went over to the gate.

'It's what?' said Tom.

'What?' Lester was opening the gate. You could already see the big Nissan X-Trail powering over the rubble.

'The still life.'

'It's cornflakes, isn't it? And dried fruit?'

'Yes. I couldn't paint them, so I just bought them.'

'Very ingenious. Very modern,' said Lester. And

the X-Trail rumbled through the gate on a set of Pirelli Scorpion STs.

'The reason the beauty of Manod is hidden,' I said to myself, 'is that you won't look at it.'

Lester said, 'Must press on. I may still catch the train at Birmingham.'

'If you're going on a train,' I said, 'you should take a zebra with you. Always take a zebra with you if you're going on a train.'

'Why?'

'So you don't get hurt. Zebras almost never get hurt on trains.'

'I'm sorry?'

It was like the highest-rainfall thing. It didn't sound any good unless Dad was saying it.

I said, 'Nothing. Sorry. Safe journey.'

Mind you, you have to be impressed by those Pirelli Scorpion STs. Nothing's going to puncture them in a hurry.

As soon as Marie came home from school, Tom drove us all to Acres of Tyres in Harlech. Harlech's by the seaside and it's got a castle and a cinema and Diggermania, obviously, but the best thing it's got is definitely Acres of Tyres. The next time we had to do one of those letters-to-Gumbi things, I wrote about Acres of Tyres:

Dear George

Thank you for your letter telling us about the giraffes. We don't have giraffes in Wales, but we do have Acres of Tyres. Acres of Tyres is exactly what it says it is. It is acres and acres of tyres and you can walk around looking at them. It's immense. They've got massive tyres for trucks and tractors and tiny ones for Smart cars. They've even got a section of tyres for pushchairs and wheelchairs. Most people don't realize there are so many kinds of tyre. Even if you stand on top of something, all you can see is tyres, tyres, tyres. On the wall as you go in is a tyre from the Ferrari in which David Coulthard won the European Grand Prix. It's huge and it's got steel ribs sticking out of it. You can see where the rubber melted because the wheel was going so fast. Although it's only supposed to be a shop, it's really a whole day out. You need a whole day to appreciate it really.

There was a bit of an incident in the Meadow of Retreads, when a man in a bobble hat stepped out from behind the Tower of Radials and almost stood on my toe. It was Mr Davis, the butcher.

I said, 'Sorry,' even though it was his fault, not mine.

And he said, 'You will be,' which is exactly the kind of thing he always says. But then he said, 'We all will be. We'll all be sorry soon.' And he looked at Minnie and Marie and Tom.

Tom said, 'Why's that then, Mr Davis? And by the way, Mam and me had some of your sausages last night and they were tip-top.'

'Thank you, Tom,' said Mr Davis. 'You know what they've got hidden up in that quarry, I suppose.'

'Paintings,' said Tom. 'We've seen some of them.'

'Yes. The ones they want you to see.'

'Well. Yeah. The one I saw was mostly fruit. You'd've liked it, Mr Davis.'

'But what about the ones they don't want you to see?'

'Well,' said Tom, 'I didn't see them, so I can't say.' He looked at me.

'The paintings up there,' said Mr Davis, and he made his voice even quieter. 'are not just paintings. They're information. Information about who really rules the world.'

'Right,' said Tom. 'And who really does rule the world, Mr Davis?'

'If I knew that,' said Mr Davis, 'I wouldn't have spent my life up to my neck in scrag end somewhere in Snowdonia.' Then he moved in closer and whispered, 'Think about it. Paintings. A cave in Wales. What does that remind you of?'

'Slate?'

'King Arthur, isn't it? The Holy Grail.'

We all looked at each other. And then we looked at the tyres. We were lost for words. Except for Tom, who said, 'What's the Holy Grail?'

Minnie said, 'It's the cup that Jesus used at the Last Supper. It's got special powers. One of King Arthur's knights is supposed to have found it. And they're all supposed to be asleep in a cave.'

'In Manod?'

'Why not?' said Mr Davis.

'Because it's not a cave,' said Minnie. 'It's a quarry. It was first excavated in 1805, which is about thirteen hundred years too late for King Arthur, who, by the way, never worked down a quarry.'

Mr Davis looked at her, then he looked around as if he was worried that tyres might have ears. He said, 'Why would they go to all that trouble to hide a few paintings? And why is there no sign for Manod on the A496? Secrets, see. A quarry full of secrets. That's not paintings they've got up there. That's power.'

We managed to get a full set of Pirelli P7 retreads (including a spare) for Lester for less than the price of two new tyres. Bargain!

On the way home, Tom said, 'He's an amazing man, that Mr Davis. He sees things no one else sees. Like the time he saw the flying saucer outside the din- ner dance in Llechwedd. Hundreds of people at that dance, and he was the only one to spot the flying saucer.'

I said, 'And he saw Elvis. In Harlech Home and Bargain.'

'He's barking mad,' said Marie.

Minnie said, 'He told me that liver was alive. Mam sent me down to buy liver, and he said he didn't sell it. He said, liver is alive. He said, if you put it on a plate and come back ten minutes later, it will have moved.'

'And will it?' said Tom.

'I don't know,' said Minnie. 'He wouldn't sell me any. We had to have meatballs.'

'He's right about the paintings, though,' said Tom. 'That fruit picture, that wasn't normal. It made me feel funny. Maybe there is power in it.'

And as we turned up the Blaenau Road (B5565) I thought, Maybe Tom was right. Maybe the paintings weren't just paintings. Manod had changed a lot since the paintings arrived. Maybe the paintings were like mutagen, changing the town. Maybe we were living in Ninja Manod!!

Back in the workshop, Marie started work on the oil change. I definitely thought I'd be left on the bench for this job because of the mix-up with Ms Stannard's Fiesta. But no, Marie needed all hands. Minnie read the instructions out of the manual and kept an eye on

Max. Marie did all the technical things and I did all the fetching and carrying. When she sent me for oil, I made sure I read the can. When she asked me to get the car jack out of the boot, I discovered that there was a big wooden box in there, but I didn't mention it. I didn't want to distract anyone.

When she'd undone the engine drain, Marie told us that we had to leave it for forty-five minutes to make sure it was really empty. We were starving, but Marie didn't want to have to get cleaned up and then come back and get dirty again. Minnie suggested making her something she could suck through a straw. Marie wasn't convinced.

I said, 'Lester's left one of his paintings in the boot.'

'He hasn't.'

'He has.'

'We shouldn't. Should we?'

'No. Not with all this oil around.'

'Maybe we could take it into the house?'

'Then I'd have to get cleaned up,' said Marie. 'Which I don't want to do.' Then she put her hand over the box and went, 'Can you feel the power?'

And we all laughed. And in the end we laughed and talked for forty-five minutes and forgot all about the painting in the box. And we did it! We all worked together and we did it – a new set of tyres and an oil change. That's another lesson from the Turtles, see:

each separate Turtle is good, but put them all together into a team and they are unbeatable. As Splinter says in *Teenage Mutant Ninja Turtles, the Movie* (they're mean, green and on the screen): 'Together, there is nothing your four minds cannot accomplish. Help each other, draw upon one another, and always remember the true force that bonds you.'

And the true force that bonded us was the Snowdonia Oasis Auto Marvel. We were all trying to make it grow so that Dad could come back. After all, there was a whole fleet of heavy-duty vans on top of the mountain, any one of which could need a new tyre or an oil change any time. I explained this to Mam, and she seemed quite persuaded. I made her promise to tell Dad on the phone. 'Especially tell him that we did an oil change and it worked this time, and even more especially that I helped,' I said. 'Then he'll see how much things have changed here.'

That night something woke me up. I looked out of the window, and there was a light on in the workshop and the door was open. I thought, Dad's come home. I didn't even put my dressing gown or my slippers on. I was in the workshop before you could blink.

It wasn't Dad. It was the girls. They looked really surprised when I ran in.

'I thought you were Lester,' said Marie. 'I nearly died.'

'What are you doing?'

They were struggling with the wooden box.

'We couldn't sleep,' Marie said. 'What if the Holy Grail's in the box? So we just had to look.'

I said, 'You don't open it like that.' I got a jemmy and slipped it into the groove that was hidden under the letter 'T' of National, flipped it up, then undid the two screws, and it opened.

The girls were impressed.

Inside, it was packed in bubble wrap. We took it out and there was the picture, clamped in a kind of bracket inside. Except it wasn't a picture. It just looked like a block of gold.

It was Minnie who said, 'What if it *is* the Holy Grail?' but we were all thinking it. Maybe that's why it was hidden in the boot of the car instead of with the other pictures?

I unfastened the bracket, opened the hinge and lifted the gold block out. It wasn't a block of gold. It was wood, covered in gold. It had a little clasp on the spine. I undid it and it opened like a birthday card. The picture inside was gold and bright, bright blue – the same mad blue as the Misses Sellwood's hair. It glowed like a little lamp.

'Wow!' said Marie. 'What is it?' She shoved in next to me and made me drop the painting. Minnie caught the other end of it just in time or it would have fallen on the oily floor. That's when we decided to take it into the house.

We set it up on Marie's dressing table. It was pretty but random. We weren't even sure it was a painting. Not like the other paintings. It was more like a very short picture book, with just two pages. On the left page there was a king, kneeling down with three other men, all with big long beards, standing behind him. On the other page there were a lot of women with wings and a tall woman in a blue dress, holding a baby. She looks like she's about to chuck the baby over to the king. Some of the angels are looking up at her, sort of saying, 'Go on, chuck him!' And the king's got his hands up to catch him, but he doesn't look like he's going to make much effort, though he does have these big goalie hands. Minnie said it was the Madonna again. She didn't look anything like the other Madonna though. And if that's Jesus's mam, I feel sorry for Jesus, being chucked round like that.

We decided to keep the picture in the house because it was safer and cleaner. Minnie took her big chart of 'Wasps of Europe' (she bought it in case she ever decided to do a perfect crime using wasps) down off her wall and hung the picture up in its place. It looked like it had always been there. Which is why we forgot to put it back the next morning, and that's why, when Lester came to collect his car, he drove off without it.

30 May

Cars today:
SUBARU IMPREZA – two random lads
(filled up, bought a map)
MORGAN PLUS EIGHT – a rude stranger

Weather – extremely heavy rain

Note: A FATEFUL MOMENT

This is when Manod finally got a sign on the A496.

OK, so it wasn't like millions of cars came, but the main thing is – from a market-research point of view – neither of these cars comes from Manod. They're both strangers! As Dad says, 'There's no such thing as strangers; there's only customers you haven't met yet.'

Actually, the man in the Morgan probably won't come again and we don't want him to. On the good side, though, he wouldn't have found us if it hadn't been for the new sign. So that shows that the sign works.

It wasn't the council who put up the new sign, by the way, it was us. Minnie got the idea from the baby-chucking picture.

We all woke up late the day after we did the oil change and Mam made a legend breakfast – porridge, sausages, everything. Immense! Including eggs laid by

Donatello. She laid every day, but Michelangelo still hadn't laid a single one.

'Mr Lester paid cash,' she said, 'so this is a celebration breakfast.'

That's when we realized that if he'd paid, he must've been and gone. We all rushed to the window. We could just see the BMW slipping off into the clouds. He'd gone, but he'd left the picture.

'Looks like you made a good job of those tyres, Marie,' said Mam.

Marie said, 'Yeah. He should go to Kwik-Fit or somewhere to check the tracking, but he should be all right.' But her brain was thinking, Oh my God, he left the Holy Grail behind.

'Well,' said Minnie, 'I'll suck a mint imperial.'

'Why?' said Mam.

'No reason.'

We didn't want to get Mam involved.

On the way to school, Minnie said, 'He's bound to come looking for it, once he notices it's missing. And when he does we'll give it back, and if he doesn't, then it's finders keepers.'

This sounds OK in theory. In practice, it meant that she brought about ten million girls – including even Terrible Evans – back with her after school and they all swarmed upstairs to look at the picture. They all sat there on the bed, staring at the picture like it was a PlayStation.

Jade Porty said, 'Is it a girl or a man?'

'It's a man, obviously,' said Minnie.

'But he's plucked his eyebrows.'

'He's a man. But he's plucked his eyebrows. They did that in those days.'

'He's done something funny to his hair too. It looks like it's been welded.'

'He's got lovely hands though, hasn't he?' said Terrible.

'Yeah,' said Jade. 'Girl hands.'

Then there was a sound like a helicopter – which was Marie's school bus pulling up – and another ten million girls got off that and they went upstairs too. All the girls who normally got off in Llechwedd or in Manod town, they'd all come to see the picture.

Marie's friends were more interested in the women. The red-headed girl from Mr Chipz (and who invited her, by the way?) wanted to know why they all had such big heads.

Minnie explained that they didn't have big heads as such. 'Women used to shave their foreheads in those days. A high forehead was a sign of beauty.'

Terrible said, 'When were those days, anyway? The days when men plucked their eyebrows and women shaved their heads.'

Then Mam came up to see what was going on.

'What's going on?' she said, like she was about to throw them all out. Then she saw the picture and she went, 'Ooooh, look at that cloth. What is it? Damask? Doesn't it hang lovely then?'

Terrible Evans said, 'Mrs Hughes, don't they look good? They've got their heads shaved. Like me.'

Mam walked up to the picture to get a better look, and as she went by she passed me the baby. Didn't even look, passed him to me sideways like a rugby ball, like the Madonna in the picture, chucking babies around.

I took Max downstairs. Tom had already gone home. It was just me and Max. The boys. I sat him down and rolled his ball at him. He went to kick it at first, but then he grabbed it and hugged it like he'd just saved a penalty. I said, 'Good boy. Again? Give me the ball and let's do it again.' But he seemed to prefer just holding it.

Then I realized I could hear someone banging on the door of the shop. I looked out. It was Lester. Obviously he'd realized about the picture. I ran upstairs.

Marie ran down to let Lester into the kitchen while I put the picture back in its box. The box was under the bed. The bubble wrap was still in there. All we had to do was fasten the catches in the right order and make sure it was all the right way round. Easy. After all, we'd just done an oil change and fitted a whole new set of tyres. I did the catches and Minnie slid the lid back into place. We were like clockwork.

Mam said, 'Have I been missing something here? Where did you learn to do that?'

Marie told the other girls to wait five minutes before coming down, so that we could get rid of him. It might look a bit weird if there were two million girls in the same room as his painting.

Down in the kitchen, Marie was telling Lester how we'd found the box when we were looking for the car jack and we'd decided that it was a risk leaving it there, what with the oil and so on, so now it was in the house for safe keeping. 'How's the tyres then?'

'The tyres are fine. But the picture is here? You're sure?'

'Oh yeah. You've got the picture, haven't you, Dylan? What about the oil? I wasn't sure if you had a brand preference?'

But Lester wasn't thinking about oil. He just grabbed the picture off me and hugged it like Max had hugged the ball. He just stood there for a minute, enjoying breathing. Maybe he hadn't been breathing properly for a while. He said, 'I'm so sorry. I should never have left it in the car, of course. It should never have been in the car even, but . . . you acted with your usual good sense and kindness.' He smiled. 'I'm so grateful. Perhaps you'd like to look at it. It's the least I can do.'

And he started to undo the box. Only he wasn't that good at it. He couldn't find the little groove under the lid. I got a bread knife and did it for him.

He lifted the little gold book out of the box and opened it on the table. 'It's a diptych,' he said, 'a sort of tiny portable altar. It was made for Richard II.' Then he stopped.

Terrible Evans had just come in from upstairs. And Jade Porty. They smiled at him and stood behind our Marie, looking at the picture. He carried on. 'It's all gold leaf. We know who everyone is in the picture because everyone has their emblem – a sort of logo. For instance, the king holding the arrow is Edmund, who was killed by Danish archers. The king holding the ring is Edward the Confessor, who is supposed to have given his wedding ring to a beggar and the . . .'

He stopped again. Two of Marie's mates had come in now, and also the red-haired girl from Mr Chipz and Mam with Max. They all smiled at him. He smiled back and carried on.

'So you see, it's less like a painting and more like a puzzle.'

'Or a code,' said Minnie, looking at me.

'Or a code. Indeed,' said Lester. Then he stopped. The rest of Marie's mates had come in now. The ones at the back were standing on chairs.

'This is turning into quite the public lecture. Where were we? Well, King Richard is wearing a white deer. That's his emblem. And the angels are wearing it in his honour. It's on the back of the frame as well. Look.' And he went to close it, then stopped again. About another hundred females had come in. They all smiled. He smiled back, but looked at me. I smiled too.

'Well, perhaps I'd better . . .' He was going to put the picture back in the box, but all these millions of girls did a big disappointed 'Ooooh'. They sounded like the Kop after a missed penalty. He was too scared to stop then. He said, 'Well, what else can I tell you? Oh. Yes. The little pommel at the top of the banner here. It looks like a simple silver orb, but if you look closely you can see it contains another picture – of a castle on an island. Can you see? We only discovered that quite recently when the picture was cleaned. A hidden masterpiece. That could be an emblem of Manod, of course – something that looks quite small and insignificant but which hides something wonderful – namely, these paintings.'

He was at it again. Small and insignificant! He can change his own tyres next time.

'So there we have it. *The Wilton Diptych*. Painted towards the end of the fourteenth century, artist unknown. Goodnight.'

He grabbed the painting, snapped it shut and shot

out through the door before you could say, '0–60 in seven seconds.'

And this was a Fateful Moment, because in his hurry Lester forgot the wooden box the picture came in. And without that box, we'd never have been able to do our Great Art Robbery.

Anyway, the point is, in school the next day all the girls (which is everyone) were on about emblems, and during art Minnie said, Why didn't Manod have an emblem? And Ms Stannard said we should design one. And so they all spent ages painting clouds and sheep and mountains and stuff. And Ms Stannard was really cheery because . . . you know what? For once, all the paints got used, except the grey. The yellow ochre, the crimson lake, the Prussian blue, and forty shades of green. Only the grey was left untouched.

All I could think of was that picture of me in the newspaper, on my own, on the forecourt with a ball.

When Ms Stannard saw it she said, 'Football, football, football. What's football got to do with Manod?'

I said, 'Absolutely nothing, miss.' Which was definitely true.

'Now, girls,' said Ms Stannard, 'and Dylan, let's think about a motto to go with our pictures. When you drive into Blaenau, for instance, there's a sign which says . . . what?'

'It says, "Moving Forward into the Future,"' said

Minnie. 'Like there's a town somewhere that's drifting backwards into the Past.'

'Exactly. We can do better than that. At Harlech they have, "Harlech – a town to live in." As though there are some towns that you're not allowed to live in. Who can think of a slogan for Manod?'

I thought of 'No Ball Games', like it says on the bus shelter.

It was Minnie obviously who thought of:

Manod - Somewhere
Under the Rainbow

with a picture of a mountain with a rainbow on the top. Everyone loved it so much they decided to make it into a proper sign, on a big piece of wood with proper paint. And when it was finished they loved it even more, so Ms Stannard got someone from the Parish Council (Mr Elsie, the chemist) to come and look at it, and he said it was very impressive but not a funding priority. And Ms Stannard said we didn't need funds.

The next morning, we all got the bus up to the junction with the A496. Found the old signpost on the grass verge. Fixed the new sign to it with 'Better than Nails' and a piece of 4x2. Put it back in its hole and filled it in with bricks. Manod Elementary did some teamwork of its own!

The sign obviously worked, because we had two cars from out of town the very next day. One was the man in the Morgan. He stopped on the forecourt and looked at the gate and said, 'Is that it?'

I said, 'Is what it?'

'There was a sign back there, pointing down here. And now the road's stopped. What was the sign for?'

'The sign's for Manod. This is Manod.'

'Well, that's useful, isn't it? A sign inviting you into a dead end. I'm out for an afternoon motoring in the mountains. I was just getting ready to let rip.'

I said, 'You want the Blaenau Bypass, then. You can let rip there, all the way to Harlech.'

And he did.

Then these two lads came in an Impreza, filled up and went up the mountain road to do a bit of off-roading. The one on the passenger side said, 'You're the kid in the paper, aren't you? The last boy in Manod?'

'That's me.'

'You might not like it now, but you'll love it when you're older. You'll be the busiest lad in Manod then, eh?'

'I don't know.'

They were gone.

This is what Newspaper Arthur wrote about the sign, by the way:

Signs of Life

A new sign has appeared on the verge of the A496 near Blaenau, pointing to the Manod turn-off. The turn-off has been unmarked for several years. Those wanting to go to Manod will now find it easier to get there. Though they may have difficulty occupying themselves after arrival.

So Manod finally had a sign, which is what Dad always wanted. And it was all down to Minnie!

At night-time, if you look out of her bedroom window you can just about see a scarf of yellow light, out past the town. That's the A496. I said to her, 'Imagine that. When he comes home and he sees that sign, he'll be so impressed and everything, and he won't even know it's by you. Legend!'

4 June

Cars today:
CARBON BLACK BMW M5 — Mr Q. Lester
(two Titian Tarts and a Picasso Pie)
ROVER 3500 V8 — the Misses Sellwood
(delivering painting)

Weather — rain

Note: THE HANDSOME REWARD

Oh, the Handsome Reward. We spent ages guessing what Lester might give us for assisting in the recovery of his priceless painting.

'Imagine if he gave us one of the paintings to keep,' said Minnie.

'That nut one would be good,' said Tom.

'Cash would be better,' said Marie.

We were all wrong.

Lester came in himself this morning to collect the cake order and he said, 'I'm so very grateful for the care you took of *The Wilton Diptych*. To my mind, it is the most exquisite thing in the entire collection. Not that my mind counts, of course.' And then he gave us the reward. It was a book. A book! *The National Gallery Companion (Revised and Expanded)*. What kind of Handsome Reward is that? When you think about it, he was asking to have one of his pictures stolen.

'Actually,' he said, 'I wrote it myself.'

So he didn't even pay money for it! He wrote his name in the front for us, but he didn't say why.

We said thank you, but only because of customer relations.

'Perhaps you could go and look through it and pick out any that you like. My own choices don't seem to have struck much of a chord in London.'

'Oh, that's a shame,' said Mam.

'Yes, the comments book for *Grotesque Old Woman* was so strongly worded, it had to be shredded.'

Tom said, 'What about the pizza painting, though? How could anyone not like that?'

'Pizza painting?'

'The one with the pizza boxes and the nuts.'

'Ah. The Meléndez. No, I'm afraid not. Really the whole exercise is a most dreadful waste of time. People in general would far rather look at pictures of footballers or celebrities or some such. The paintings should simply be left here in peace.'

'With you.'

'Exactly.'

'They must've liked the umbrella painting, though,' said Mam.

'The Renoir met with deafening indifference – perhaps it was over-familiar,' said Lester.

'Well, we loved it here,' said Mam. 'Come and see.'

And she made Lester come and stand on the fore-court. 'Just step up there,' she said, pointing to the little wall by the 'OPEN' sign. He did as she told him. It was about ten to nine. 'Any minute now,' said Mam. And then out it came out on to the street: the psyche-delic boa constrictor. I have to say, it does look hectic. You should come and look at it. It's easy to find, now we've got the sign.

'I don't understand,' said Lester.

'This is me,' said Mam. 'I did this. I bought the umbrellas after seeing your painting. This didn't hap-pen before. This is my work of art, inspired by your work of art.'

'How extraordinary,' said Lester. Then he got into his car and drove off.

'I think that means he was impressed,' said Mam.

We would have gone straight off to school then if we hadn't heard a massive blast on the impressive horn of the BMW from somewhere up the mountain. So we knew he'd met the Misses Sellwood on their way down and we thought we'd better wait.

As I opened the gate to let them through, I said, 'Did you miss him?'

'Have we missed him?' said Miss Elsa. 'Oh dear. We saw him go by and we hurried after. We did so want to speak to him. What a pity. We've missed him, Edna.'

'We wanted to show him one of Father's paintings, see,' said Miss Edna. 'Here, help me out with it.'

There was no sign of a bump on the car, so Lester must have managed to avoid them. That's the beauty of power-assisted four-wheel drive. The painting was in the boot, wrapped in a tea towel with 'Souvenir of Caernarfon' written on it. We carried it into the shop. Marie was just getting ready to go to school herself. She said, 'Hello, girls,' to the Sellwoods, and they went all giggly. They love it when she calls them girls because they're not girls, they are old, old women. I mean really old. It's quite funny when Miss Elsa giggles because she doesn't make much of a sound, but she does shake. She's quite wobbly most of the time anyway, but when she giggles, she's just a blur. The bright blue hair makes her look like some kind of dancing lollipop.

Miss Edna said, 'This is one of our da's paintings.'

'Oh, lovely,' said Marie. 'Is it the one of the mountain? The one you were telling us about?'

Miss Elsa said, 'This is one of our da's paintings.'

'They know that,' said Miss Edna. 'I just told them that. They're asking if it's the one of the mountain. I told you they'd be more interested in the one of the mountain.'

'He painted one of the mountain,' said Miss Elsa.

'They know that.' Miss Edna was trying to get the tea towel off the painting. Her hands looked like big chunks of tangled-up string.

'Here. Let me,' said Marie, and she took the tea towel off.

We were probably thinking it would be a big grey painting, like the paintings we did in art. It wasn't. It wasn't a bit like that. It was a painting of a little girl, the prettiest girl any of us had ever seen, prettier than our Marie even, if you ask me.

'Look at that complexion,' said Marie. 'That's real skin tone for you. And her hair. That hair has got body. And lustre. And not a split end in sight. That outfit's lovely, too, isn't it?' The girl was dressed up like a gypsy or something. 'Who is it then? His old girlfriend?'

The Misses Sellwood giggled again. Edna said, 'They want to know who it is, Elsa.'

Elsa said, 'Tell them who it is.'

'Don't you recognize her?' said Miss Edna. 'That's our Elsa, look.' And she nudged Miss Elsa so that her old, wrinkly face was next to the round, glowy face of the girl, like a walnut next to a peach.

'It's me,' said Elsa. 'It's a picture of me when I was a little bit younger.' And she laughed so hard a sound came – a dry sound, like someone scrunching paper.

We all looked from the pretty little girl to the old

blind lady who stood at the counter, staring up into nowhere.

Time is obviously the strongest mutagen of them all.

Marie didn't say anything. She was staring at the picture. She looked at Elsa, then she looked back at the picture again, really quickly.

'She was lovely though, wasn't she?' said Miss Edna. 'That's why Da painted her and not me. She was lovely. Wouldn't you say, Marie?'

Minnie said what we were all thinking. 'You've changed a bit then, Miss Elsa.'

'Minnie!' hissed Mam and frowned.

'We all do, you know,' said Elsa. 'You'll change yourselves some day.' Her knobbly hands were gripping the counter for support. 'Pretty as you are.'

Marie said, 'Excuse me,' and, instead of going to school, she went up to her room and closed the door.

Lester's book wasn't that bad after all, by the way. Even though nearly all the pictures were of women with no clothes on. Great gangs of them, running round in the woods, or sleeping in fields, or being chased by men in armour. In one the woman was having a picnic with some men in bowler hats. Me and Mam and Minnie and Max sat down to look through it that night (Marie was still in her room). I was telling them how every time anyone saw a painting, the painting seemed to change them.

'They'd better not see some of these,' said Minnie. 'That'd be hectic. Everyone in Manod running round the woods in the nuddy.'

There was also a surprising number of pictures of people getting their heads cut off. As Mam said, 'Don't even think about that.'

There was one of a man and a woman and a little dog, all standing next to each other, with a little mirror on the wall behind them. The mirror was so real you could almost see yourself in it. It was called *The Arnolfini Portrait*.

'Look at the way he's holding her hand,' said Minnie. 'They're both in their best hats. It's a wedding photograph. Except it's not a photograph, of course. It must have taken ages to paint. Look, there's mud on her shoes.'

It's true. When you looked closely you could see it.

Anyway, we decided on that one.

There was trouble at bedtime. Marie was still barricaded in her room, and she wasn't letting Minnie in.

'I want to go to sleep.'

'Go and sleep in Mam's room.'

'I've got no duvet.'

Marie opened the door and poked a wodge of

duvet through. Minnie tugged it out and the door banged shut again.

We went to complain to Mam. She said, 'Don't worry about it. We all have our off days. Marie's having one today.'

The moment she said it we heard a drill start up. Marie had taken the padlock off Dad's big toolbox and was fixing it to her bedroom door. It took her about five minutes. She really is handy with power tools.

Mam said, 'Never mind. Come and look at this.' There was this big fancy book on the bed, which she'd been reading and Max had been chewing. 'It's my wedding photos,' she said. I'd seen the book before, but I'd never bothered looking at the pictures until now. There was Dad with loads of curly black hair and Mam with a skinny little waist. And practically everyone in Manod, all looking magically younger.

'Hang on,' said Minnie. 'Isn't that Mr Davis there, with Uncle Ivor?'

'Yes. He's a lot thinner there.'

'But he's sort of . . . well, you know . . . he's smiling.'

'It was a wedding.'

'But Mr Davis doesn't smile. Not ever.'

'He did then, though.'

'So what happened?'

'What d'you mean?' asked Mam.

'Once he used to smile and now he doesn't,' said Minnie. 'What happened in between?'

'Well, you know,' said Mam. 'Stuff. Life. Things that happen.'

'What sort of things?'

'I'll tell you,' said Mam. And she did. And it was something really bad. It turns out that Mr Davis used to have a little boy. The boy and his mam went to the swimming baths in Harlech. Mr Davis went to collect them. He was backing into his parking space when his wife let go of the little boy's hand. The boy got behind the car, where Mr Davis couldn't see him, and he was crushed between the car and the wall. Imagine that.

'I didn't even know Mr Davis was married.'

'It was very bad. They blamed each other. He was driving the car, so you could say it was his fault. She was in charge of little Ben – that was his name – so maybe it was her fault. It was all very bad. No one wants to remember it. When it first happened, Mr Davis was angry. He used to stand outside his shop and yell at people if they tried to cross the road. "*Don't you know it's dangerous? You could be killed at any time.*" All that. And outside the school he'd shout at the kids if they were running too fast in the playground, in case they got hurt. It was him who called the insurance about the boating lake. He said there weren't enough lifebelts. The insurance people came down and they agreed with him. The council said that lifebelts weren't a spending priority, and that's when they boarded up the lake. Just after that is when he saw Elvis. That made him a bit happier. Seeing someone everyone thought was dead. He thinks King Arthur's still alive too.'

'And liver,' said Minnie.

'Actually liver *is* alive.'

'It isn't,' I said. 'Is it?'

'No, of course it isn't.' She gave me a shove. Then she looked at the wedding photographs again. 'Go and get your book of paintings. Cheer me up.'

We flicked through *The National Gallery Companion* together. A massive horse rearing up. A woman with a huge bottom. Men with goats' legs. People playing cards. And, near the end, quite a splodgy one of some people in a rowing boat on a river on a sunny day.

'There,' said Mam. 'See that? That's what Manod used to look like. Just like that.'

It was called *Bathers at La Grenouillère*. No one getting beheaded. No one running round in the nuddy. Just some rowing boats tied to a wooden jetty and people standing around, talking to each other. Oh, and the sun shining, like on top of the mountain. I said, 'OK. We'll send them that one instead of the wedding one.'

'No, send the wedding one. That's the one you liked.'

'No. If we send this one to London, maybe Dad will see it and maybe it will cheer him up.'

Then Mam hugged me so tight, I thought she was going to behead me.

17 June

Cars today:
RED FORD KA — Ms Stannard (petrol and Snickers)
WHITE MONTEGO — Mr Evans (returning box of fudge)
RED TOYOTA PRIUS T4 AUTOMATIC —
Dr Ramanan and family (a social call — all had coffee)
TWO WHITE COMBI VANS — men from the quarry (box of Crispy Choc Constables and a Tintoretto Turnover)
VAUXHALL ASTRA ESTATE 1.9 CDTi —
Mr Davis (Petrol! Cigarettes! Eggs! Shoe polish! Video — 'Shrek')
PLUS VW BEETLE, AUDI QUATTRO, SUBARU FORESTER — all visitors

Weather — sunshine!!!

Note: THE FIRST BOY ON THE BOATING LAKE SINCE MR DAVIS SAW ELVIS

This is the utterly hectic day when I became the first boy on the boating lake since Mr Davis saw Elvis. And it was all down to good customer relations, namely mine.

I remembered that Lester liked to open the box with the painting in on a Thursday evening, so Friday morning I asked Mam if she'd like to come and see the painting she picked, the one with the rowing boats.

'I've got a lot on my mind,' she said. 'I don't think I'll bother.'

I think she was worried about our Marie. It was over a week now since the Sellwoods had dropped off the painting, and in all that time no one had really seen Marie. Every morning she left early for school, padlocking the bedroom door behind her. As soon as she came home in the evening, she locked herself in again. The only time anyone saw her was when Mam called through the door and asked her to hold Max while she had a shower. Then Marie would take Max into her room for ten minutes and we'd hear laughing noises and sometimes see this weird flash of light. But mostly she was too cross to talk to. On the Tuesday, for instance, I saw her on the landing – which was where we'd put the picture – and she said, 'Put that where I can't see it. Or I'll burn it.' We put it in the utility room.

Anyway, when me and Minnie were walking up after school that Friday, we passed the butcher's and I looked in the window and saw Mr Davis there, with his cleaver, and I thought about all the stress he must be having – a butcher who's scared of liver. So I went in. I said, 'Mr Davis . . .'

He said, 'Are you here to have a conversation or are

you here to buy meat? If it's meat, just point. If it's a conversation, I don't do them.'

'I think,' I said, 'I can get you in. Up there.' And I nodded my head towards the mountain.

He put down his cleaver. 'What? Up there?' And he nodded at the mountain too.

'They let me in. They think because I'm a kid I'm harmless. I won't care about, you know, King Arthur, the Grail, who really rules the world and . . .'

He shushed me. 'That's dangerous talk. Their agents are everywhere.' Then he came round to my side of the counter and closed the door.

'Can you really get me in up there?'

'No problem. We can go now if you like.'

'I've got to make up a big barbecue pack for the Nirvana Retirement Home in Llechwedd. After that, I'll come with you and we'll Strike a Blow for Truth, eh?'

Mr Davis came and got me in the Astra Estate 1.9 (top speed a surprising 129 mph). In case you don't know, it's a diesel, but don't let that fool you. It's got very cool headlamps, a tinted rear window and alloys. It's also got ESP, ABS and CDC. And IDS, HSA, UCL and DDS. HSA, by the way, is Hill Start Assist, which means you get extra time to find the accelerator after you take your foot off the brake, which is handy if you have to drive up Manod Mountain. DDS is even beastier. It's a Deflation Detection System, and it tells you if your tyres are going down. That meant we could drive up feeling relaxed about the car. Mr Davis wasn't relaxed though. He kept leaning forward, like a sheep that's got wind of a packet of Quavers.

When we got to the top, I could see that Lester wasn't happy. I thought it must be something to do with Mr Davis. He said, 'The painting's ready but I'm afraid I'm not convinced.'

He led us through to the room with the easel. Mr Davis whispered. 'Nervous. Knows I'm on to him, see.'

Lester opened the door and stood back to let us in.

'Going to show us a pretty picture then?' said Mr Davis. 'One of the ones you don't mind us seeing.'

Lester looked a bit bewildered. 'It's the one the boy requested. As I mentioned, I'm far from certain myself.'

'We're not going to see the ones you don't want us to see though, are we?' said Mr Davis. 'Just some pretty picture that anyone can see. Well, I'm on to you. Don't think I'm not. We all are. We're not easily fooled in Manod.'

He was right about the picture being pretty. It was also very bright. The ripples on the river looked like they were really moving.

Mr Davis said, 'Oh.' I thought for a minute he

must have found the answer to his secret code or whatever, he seemed that surprised.

'You see my problem,' said Lester. 'London has, as you know, suffered from a series of floods. I'm anxious that, in the circumstances, sending a picture of people messing about in boats might be considered insensitive. Or even insulting.'

'Where is that?' said Mr Davis. 'Where's it supposed to be of?' He sounded like he was on to something. Maybe the picture was a clue to where the Holy Grail was hidden. I remember Minnie saying something about a lake with a lady in it.

'It's a little island in the Seine in the summer of 1869. It's called the Camembert, because it's shaped like a cheese. Monet used to go there with Renoir. They were supposed to be working on sketches to make a large tableau painting for the Academy, but I think the summer and the wine distracted Monet somewhat, and he only completed these small, slightly hurried *pochades*. It's not without charm or interest.'

'Very nice,' said Mr Davis. 'Reminds me of Manod back in the day.' Which is exactly what Mam said, so it must be right.

'A painting like this would simply not have been possible before then. It was around this time that oil paint first became available in metal tubes, so the artist could paint easily in oils outdoors – almost impossible before then. The tubes made them portable and kept the paints soft and ready to use. In planning to do a great painting back at the studio later, Monet was thinking like a nineteenth-century artist. But his instincts and his hands were already those of a twentieth-century artist – not necessarily a good thing, of course. But looking at this does make you reflect. How wonderful it would be to have something so spontaneous and immediate by Michelangelo, of the marketplace in Florence, say, or a picnic in the Umbrian hills.'

Mr Davis said, 'The boats. Were they private property? Or were they for hire?'

'I'm afraid I've no idea.'

'They look like they're for hire. How much would they charge, d'you reckon?'

'Again, I couldn't say. Colour and brushwork are my field. That's more a matter for a municipal park keeper.'

'It was popular though?'

'The Camembert? Oh, enormously so. But you can see my problem. Water. Boats. Bad memories for Londoners, I'm afraid.'

'Maybe . . .' I said. 'Maybe it will make them see that floods can be fun. Like the man you were talking about, who realized that pots and pans were beautiful.'

Lester looked at me, looked at the painting and

the ground and Elvis in Home and Bargain sort of twisted round and split in two. 'There it is,' he said, pointing through the gap he'd made in the fence. It wasn't the Holy Grail or anything. It was just Manod boating lake, but it did look lovely – all velvety and silvery now that it was getting dark.

'Is it at the bottom of the lake then?' asked Minnie.

But Mr Davis wasn't listening. He'd already walked over to the old boathouse and cut the padlock off that too. He disappeared inside.

'He seems very focused,' said Minnie. 'Do you think he has found it?'

He came out again, dragging one of the old rowing boats behind him. 'Come on then! Give us a hand!' he shouted. It was pitch black in the boathouse with thick curtains of cobwebs hanging down everywhere. It was the kind of place you'd expect some secret treasure to be hidden. Maybe it was behind the boats. Mr Davis was pulling another one out. I helped him. Then we pulled out another and another. There were eight altogether. He started poking and kicking at them. 'Seem sound enough,' he said. 'Just need a lick of paint, that's all. What about this jetty?'

He walked out on to the jetty, bouncing up and down on his heels. 'Not bad, not bad,' he said. But he wasn't talking to us. He seemed to have forgotten we were there.

'I'm freezing,' said Minnie. So we went home.

*

The next morning, Mr Davis's shop didn't open for business. It turned out he was still in the park. He'd taken down the rest of the Elvis mural and he was painting the boats blue and red. Mr Elsie – chemist and parish councillor – went up to give him a talking to: it was all illegal, what he was doing, and they weren't properly insured.

'The interesting thing is,' said Mr Davis, 'I don't seem to care.'

Everyone said that Mr Davis had finally gone mad. But we went to look at him, and he seemed happy enough. He asked me to shove one of the boats into the water to see if it would float. It did. It was a bit wet in the bottom but it was floating.

The next time we went down to the park, Mr Morgan had brought his tractor (Massey Ferguson, seventies classic, top speed 47 mph) and he was using a hay thingy to drag all the weeds and mud out of the lake. Minnie asked him if he thought that Mr Davis had finally gone completely mad.

'Maybe he has and maybe he hasn't. If he has, it's best to humour him, don't you think?'

We asked Mr Elsie the same question the next day when we found him down by the lake in his overalls, creosoting oars. 'He's mad as a box of frogs,' said Mr Elsie. 'You couldn't hold this oar up, could you, so I can do the other side?'

*

The next day, one of the vans from up the mountain pulled up and about five men jumped out. 'We're bored witless up there. Mind if we join you? This looks like it'll pass the time,' they said. One of them mowed the lawns and one of them cut the hedges. Then another van came down and the men in that one took all the litter away. Mr Davis rewarded them with pork pies. For as long as I could remember no one had ever wanted to talk to Mr Davis. Suddenly people were queuing up to talk to him – and there he was, giving orders, cracking jokes and handing out pies.

And an amazing thing happened. Mr Evans – Terrible's dad – he turned up! He said he'd had enough of London and he'd heard that things were finally moving in Manod. Terrible asked for the morning off to help him cut the grass around the lake and Ms Stannard said, 'Let's make a school trip of it.' She took us all down to the park.

When we got there, Mrs Porty was putting up some hanging baskets on the boathouse. Mr Elsie was screwing some big iron rings into the end of the jetty, and Big was with Terrible. They were carefully painting numbers on the sterns of all the boats, which were lying, bottoms up, on the grass, like a row of little huts. It was Minnie – obviously – who noticed that they were painting the numbers upside down.

Everyone laughed and then we had a vote about

whether to leave them like that or clean them up and start again. We voted to leave them upside down.

I waited till he was on his own, then I asked Big if he'd seen Dad.

'Isn't he up in his workshop?'

'No. He went away on business. We think he went to London, like you. That's why I was asking.'

'Ah, well, London's a big place, you know.'

'Yeah, but he was working on the New Barrier, like you.'

'Well, it's a big barrier too,' said Big, which was true enough.

Then Jade Porty shouted, 'Look!' And we all did. It took us a minute to realize what we were looking at, though. Because she wasn't pointing at something that was there. She was pointing at something that wasn't there. It had stopped raining.

'It's stopped raining!'

The sky was completely blue, like in a Monet, and the lake was brown and still.

Big turned one of the boats over and pushed it into the water.

Mr Davis said, 'Wait, wait. Before we declare this boating lake well and truly open . . .'

'If uninsured,' said Mr Elsie.

'Before we do that, I would like to thank you all for helping and I'd like to thank especially Mr Lester from up the mountain and little Dylan Hughes. They gave me this idea. It's a pity the gallery fella's not here, but I think Dylan should have first go, don't you?'

And then I got this big, hectic round of applause. I thought it was going to go on forever but Mr Elsie shushed everyone and said, 'Just to remind you, we are not insured. You take these boats out at your own risk.'

I said, 'That's all right.'

Then everyone clapped again and Mr Davis pushed the boat out, and that's how I became the first boy on the boating lake since Mr Davis saw Elvis. It was beastie. You have to be careful because when you lift the oar the water runs down your arm and up your sleeve and you get soaked. But they say you get better with practice.

One of the men from up the mountain was really brilliant at rowing and his boat went up and down the lake in a straight line. It was amazing.

Later on, Tom came down and helped Big set up a barbecue while Mr Davis went to get a bag of sausages from his shop. And everyone in Manod had Davis's Own Make sausages (except Marie, who was still in her room).

And that's all anyone did for days. Every night after school, everyone went down to the lake and raced the boats. Mr Davis bought all the discount garden furniture from the Oasis and brought that down so that people would have somewhere to sit and wait. He sat outside the boathouse himself, and the more people talked to him, the more normal he sounded. Tom came down. Mam came down with another big tub of umbrellas.

I thought it might be nice to get Marie to come down, so I played with Max outside her door, quite noisily, to see if that would tempt her out. He was toddling past her door shouting, 'Hot! Hot!' for some reason, when it opened, Marie's hands shot out and pulled Max in. Then the door shut again.

'Hey!' I shouted. 'I'm trying to play with him.' I know better than to knock on that door, but I did some noisy walking up and down outside for a while and even sighed a couple of times. Suddenly there was a flash of really bright light from under the door, just one quick flash. I shouted, 'Are you OK?'

'Move away from the door.'

'What was that flash?'

'Move away from the door.'

I stepped back. The door opened a crack and Max came waddling out on his own. Then the door was closed behind him. I picked up the baby and took him downstairs again.

So Marie never did come down to the boating lake.

Lester did though, in the end. Mr Davis couldn't stop shaking his hand. 'This is all down to you,' he said.

'All this. If I hadn't seen that picture, none of this would have happened. You see, I lost a lot in my life. But seeing that picture, I realized I didn't have to lose it all.'

'Well, I'm glad you like it,' said Lester. 'It was quite popular in London, too.'

'You know I've got a phobia about liver?' said Mr Davis.

'No. No, I didn't.'

'A butcher with a phobia about liver.'

'But seeing the picture has cured you?'

'No, I'm still frightened of it. It's alive, you know.'

'No, I didn't know. I had no idea.'

'A lot of people don't. It keeps me awake at night. I've tried drugs, therapy, acupuncture. But being out here, digging this lake, mowing the grass, it knocks me out. I sleep like a stuffed pig.'

'Well, that's nice.'

'Nice? It's fantastic. There's powerful stuff in those pictures.'

'Yes,' said Lester, 'I've always thought so . . .' And he looked around the park like he was dreaming it all.

20 June

Cars today:
RACING RED MINI COOPER S - me!

Weather - too excited to notice

Note: THE LADY IN THE LAKE

The Mini is the one that was nicked, and this is the day that we got it back – and the way we got it back was immense. I really thought this was it, that our troubles were over.

We were just finishing school and Terrible Evans cornered me in the cloakroom and said, 'My dad's starting work on the old pavilion tonight. You'd better come and help us . . .'

'I can't,' I said. 'I've got to sort out the cake orders and make sure the Gaggia is cleaned and—'

'You'd better come and help us,' said Terrible, 'or I'll kill you.'

I said, 'What time?'

'Five o'clock. I'll give you till ten past, and then I'll come looking for you.'

At five o'clock Terrible was waiting for me by the lake without her dad. Apparently he was 'running late'. 'Get in a boat and row till he turns up.'

I didn't really fancy getting my sleeves wet again,

but I always find it hard to say no to Terrible because of my fear of being poked in the eye.

There was already one boat out on the lake. It had a man at one end and one of Mam's big umbrellas at the other. Terrible wanted me to row over and ram it. I didn't like the idea, but sometimes it seems easier to sink a boat than it does to think of a reason why not. It was only when we got right up close that I saw the man was Lester. Which was a bit random. But then I saw what was behind the umbrella and that was a lot random. It was Ms Stannard.

Ms Stannard and Lester out in a rowing boat together! What's going on?!

'Ram them!' snarled Terrible.

'No! Look who it is.'

Even Terrible had to gasp. Ms Stannard seemed to be shouting at Lester. She was going on about art again. He was so listening to her that he didn't even notice us.

'Quentin,' she was saying (she calls him Quentin!), 'the whole point of art is to rescue something of ourselves from the ravages of nature. By those criteria, of course, the whole of Manod is a work of art. It's very difficult to live up here. Just being alive is a work of art. The Sellwood sisters live halfway up the mountain and they keep their hair that preposterous shade of blue. Surely even a prig like you can see that they're a work of art?'

'They're something, but they're not art. I don't know why you would want them to be a work of art . . .' and more stuff like that. Ms Stannard was using her 'patiently explaining' voice, which is the voice she uses when she is finally running out of patience. I thought she might be about to drown him.

Terrible said, 'They're in love.'

'What!? Listen to her. She's shouting at him. She hates him.'

'That's how people talk when they're in love, you moron,' said Terrible.

Lester finally noticed we were there. He gave us a little wave and carried on rowing while Ms Stannard carried on patiently explaining.

Big Evans finally turned up. He backed his Montego up by the steps of the old pavilion and took shovels, mops, buckets and bolt cutters out of the boot. 'Oh,' he said to Terrible when he saw me, 'you've brought your little friend along to help.'

'He's not my friend,' she said. 'He's an idiot. He came because I told him to.'

'Fair enough,' said Big. 'Gonna help us clear this place out then, Dylan?'

'If you like.'

'We're going to see if it can be restored. And after that, we think this bit of grass in front here has potential as a putting green. What d'you think?'

'OK.'

The old pavilion had massive doors that folded back, like fire-station doors. In the winter you could open just the middle bit so that it stayed warm and dry inside. In the summer, if it wasn't raining, you could fold the whole thing right back and let the sun shine in. Now, though, the doors had great planks of wood nailed across them, top and bottom, to keep them shut. The windows were boarded up and the steps were all covered in bird muck.

'We'll start with the doors,' said Big. And he gave me and Terrible each a claw hammer so we could get the nails out of the planks. It was easier than you'd think. The wood was soft and the nails slid right out. They were still quite bright and shiny. You wouldn't think they'd been out in the rain all that time. We got the bottom planks off and stacked them up on the potential putting green. Big had to help us with the top ones. As soon as he'd pulled out the first few nails, though, the whole thing started to look a bit wobbly, and then suddenly the whole front started to fall off. Big stuck his hands in the air quickly and yelled, 'Go on, get back!' and we ran off the porch on to the grass. Then he walked his hands backwards up the door towards us, so that it came down slowly. We rushed forward and grabbed the edges and helped him lower it. And there it was, the old pavilion, with its front completely off like a doll's house. Inside, we could see the famous snooker table, shoved up against the wall with a dead pigeon lying on top of it. And cobwebs that were so thick they looked like washing hanging out to dry. But we didn't notice these things at first. Because there, tucked neatly into the far corner was something else – a Mini Cooper S (racing red). *Our* Mini Cooper S.

I yelled, 'That's ours! The one that got nicked! I've found it!'

'All right,' said Terrible. 'It's just a car.'

But I thought I was going to explode. Ever since it had been nicked, I'd been wanting to find a clue to who nicked it. And now I'd found the whole car. I said, 'Wait till Dad hears about this!'

As Big Evans said, it was unusual to find a stolen car at all, and even more unusual to find one in such perfect condition, and most unusual of all, the keys to the ignition were tucked under the sun visor, on the driver's side. 'It's all a bit mysterious,' he said. 'And the real mystery is how the hell they got it in here. Up the steps and through the door and round the back of the snooker table.'

I said, 'Pure manoeuvrability, Mr Evans. Anyone who's seen the film *The Italian Job* . . .'

'Oh, yeah. I love that film.'

'. . . will know that the Mini can easily cope with flights of steps and can turn on its own axis to slot into the narrowest space.'

'Excuse me,' said Terrible. 'Who cares?!'

Mr Evans started the engine and bumped the Mini down the steps and out on to the grass. It was a bit dusty but that was all.

By this time Lester and Ms Stannard were getting out of their boat. Lester had managed to row all over the lake without getting a drop of water on his shirt, or even on his shoes.

Ms Stannard said, 'What's this then, Dylan?'

I told her what had happened and I showed her the Mini.

'Now that,' said Lester, 'is a work of art.'

'No,' said Ms Stannard, 'that is a work of engineering.'

'Let's not go down that road again.'

'No, let's not.'

'Though I would point out that it is a very striking colour.'

'I wonder why they put it in the pavilion.' Then she said, 'Tell him your idea, Quentin.'

'Well, it was your idea,' said Lester.

'He's not interested in whose it is, he's interested in what it is . . .'

'I'm simply saying that . . .'

I could see that this was going to go on for a while. I was too excited about the car to wait, so I said, 'Got to go. Tell me later.'

Big drove us up through town in the Mini. Someone had taken one of the panels from the Elvis mural and propped it up outside Curl Up N Dye. It was the one of Elvis having his hair cut before he joined the army.

As soon as we hit the forecourt, Mam came running out – and that wasn't good, because she looked so excited I knew she must have thought that it was Dad's car and so Dad must be inside. She was disappointed that it was just me and Terrible.

'Oh,' she said. 'Where did you find it?'

'In the pavilion in the park. Someone must've hidden it. But I found it! Well, we found it.'

'That's good.'

Then Marie came running out as well and she looked all excited too.

'Where is he?' she said.

'It's not him, pet,' said Mam. 'It's just the car. Dylan found it.'

Marie glared at me and went straight back inside. Mam went after her, but it was pointless. We heard the door slam and she was locked in her room again.

The only person who was pleased to see us was Minnie. 'This is very unusual,' she said. 'Normally, if a car is used in a bank robbery or a drive-by shooting, they burn it out.'

'Maybe it wasn't used in a bank robbery.'

'Why would anyone steal a car and then put it in the pavilion? This is truly fascinating.'

'The point is, I've found it. This makes up for losing it in the first place, doesn't it?'

Mam said, 'It's very good, Dylan. Very good.'

'So you'll tell Dad, won't you? Phone him and tell him that we've got the car back? And that I found it?'

'Yes, of course I will.'

'And about the oil change, as well.'

'Yes.'

'Isn't this the best thing ever?'

'It's very good.'

And later on, something else brilliant happened. Ms Stannard and Lester came in and she said, 'Tell them, Quentin.'

He coughed like he was about to make a speech. 'Well, I am – as you know – impressed and touched by the way the village has responded to the paintings . . .'

I said, 'What village?'

'This village.'

'This is a town! Do you think this is a village?'

'Let's not get involved in geography. The point is, I am impressed and I would like to pay tribute.'

At last! Hidden Beauty! Finally he was admitting that Manod was legend.

'What kind of tribute?' said Minnie.

An immense kind, that's what. Lester's idea (it was Ms Stannard's idea really) was that on Sunday, before the picture set out on its journey to London, it would stop here, on the forecourt of our garage, and Lester and his men would bring the picture into the shop and people – invited people – people invited by us – would be allowed to look at the painting. 'A private viewing', he called it. 'It's a kind of thank-you present. To Manod. And especially to you, Dylan. Verbal invitations only, of course. There must be no mention of it in the press.'

I said, 'You don't need to worry about that, Mr Lester. The press doesn't come out for another three weeks.'

'Please call me Quentin.'

I said I would, but I couldn't.

How legend is that? We wanted the Oasis to be more than a garage and now it was a copier centre, coffee shop, and the National Gallery!!! Beat that, Little Chef!

I said to Mam afterwards, 'Tell Dad about this and the car, and he'll be back before you put the phone down.'

'We'll see,' said Mam. Mams are always a bit cautious.

That night while she was putting the baby to bed, I remembered about Barry and Tone – the men from the insurance company – who'd asked me to ring them if ever I found a clue about the missing car. I still had the pen they'd given me with the phone number on it, so I called them. They were really interested that we'd found the car. They said they'd come over as soon as possible. I thought Mam would be really pleased with me for that.

It turned out to be my biggest mistake yet.

22 June

Cars today: too many to keep track of

Weather — too busy to notice

Note: A DIFFERENT ANGLE

This is the day that the Snowdonia Oasis Auto Marvel and Coffee Shop and Copier Centre finally became Manod's premier Indoor Attraction.

On Sunday, I made sure that Mam got lots of milk and coffee for the Gaggia and even polystyrene cups, just in case. I got Tom's mam to make a massive load of Crispy Choc Constables. Then we sat in the shop, waiting. And waited. And waited.

'Is there maybe a big football match on?' asked Mam.

But there wasn't.

No one came all afternoon. Mam decided to cut Max's hair because his fringe kept flopping into his eyes. He wouldn't stop wriggling, so I had to hold him on my knee. When she'd fininished, Mam said, 'There. That's better. Oh!'

'What?'

'I've cut too much off. He doesn't look like a baby any more. He looks like a little boy.'

'No. He looks like a baby with short hair.'

She picked him up and took him off to her room.

Minnie had been flicking through the *Revised and Expanded*. 'Hey,' she said, 'look at this.'

It was a piece of paper, folded in four, with lots of typing on it and 'CONFIDENTIAL' stamped across the top.

'What is it?'

'Suffering sherbet!' said Minnie.

'What is it?'

'It's a list of all the paintings he's got up there. And it tells you how much they're insured for. Hang on.' She searched through the book and held it open at one of the pictures – a woman looking up to heaven with her hand on her hip – and said, 'How much do you think that's worth, then?'

I said, 'A thousand?'

Tom said, 'Is it for sale?'

'No.'

'Ten thousand?'

'Twelve million,' said Minnie. 'Which is more than this whole town is worth.'

'So if anyone did rob one of the paintings, they'd be a very rich robber,' said Tom.

'Tom,' said Minnie, 'you're tempted!'

'No, I'm not.'

I said, 'If it says "Confidential" on it, we should give it back.'

'I suppose so,' said Minnie. 'Except . . .'

'Except what?'

'Well it's like Fate, isn't it? All we've got to do is look down this list and we'll know which is the most valuable painting in the gallery. He's almost asking us to do a robbery really, leaving it in his book like that.'

'He is not asking us to do a robbery.'

'He left the paper in our copy of the book. He's trying to tell us something.'

I said, 'Minnie, that painting is worth twenty-five million, right?'

'Right.'

'Can I just ask you something – who do you know with twenty-five million pounds?'

'No one.'

'Then who is going to give you twenty-five million for that painting?'

'That,' said Minnie, 'is a very good point. Tom, stop talking about robbing paintings.'

'I'm not talking about robbing paintings,' said Tom.

Then Minnie invented this great game called Masterpiece. In the back of the *Revised and Expanded* there was a set of postcards of the most famous pictures. She wrote down the insurance value of each painting on the back of the postcard and then dealt them out like cards. And we played this game where we had to see whether Tom, say, would swap my picture of a knight for his one of a woman in a big hat.

Then, when we'd decided, we'd look at how much they were worth.

If it hadn't been for the game, we'd've gone mad waiting. Nothing happened till it was starting to get dark. Then suddenly headlights lit up the inside of the shop. Then more headlights, and more and more. And we went outside and cars were parked all the way down the road. And people were walking up the street towards the garage. It seemed like there were hundreds of them, all walking, talking, laughing, all coming to our garage. You couldn't make out their faces, but I was pretty sure Dad would be one of them.

Mam said, 'I thought he said invited guests only.'

Minnie said, 'We didn't want to miss anyone out.'

'But there's people here we've never seen before.'

'I think everyone thought they should invite some-one else. Great, isn't it?'

'Yes, it is.'

The reason that no one had turned up until now was that they were waiting to see the truck come down the mountain road. If you looked up, you could see the headlights jerking backwards and forwards as the combi negotiated the tight turns.

Someone tapped me on the shoulder. I looked behind me and there was Mohan, his face lit up by the halogen security lights.

I said, 'Mohan! Fantastic!'

He said, 'Fancy a kick-around?'

He dropped the ball and I dribbled it over to the grass, shouting, 'The butane rack is goal!'

We'd barely kicked it once when suddenly the Ellis brothers were running round, shouting, 'Over here! Over here!' And then someone else joined in, and someone else, and we were playing this massive game of football. People were standing on the invisible touchline with cakes and coffee, shouting things like, 'Go on, Jimmy!' Names I didn't even know.

The ball landed at Tom's feet and he took it forward. I drifted over to the left and shouted to him, but he just kept going forward till it looked like he'd go past the goal. Then he kicked the ball and it swung round and slid in from an incredible angle. Everyone cheered. I'd never seen him look so happy.

'Amazing geometry, Tom,' said Mohan.

Tom said, 'It's a Ninja thing,' and grinned again.

Doctor Ramanan came over and ruffled Mohan's hair. He said, 'Busy like this every night, is it then, Dylan?'

I said, 'Not yet, but it will be one day.'

'I think everyone I've ever met in Manod is here.'

'Except my dad. But I think he's coming. You haven't seen him, have you?'

He hadn't.

*

And then the gates opened and the van came in. Everyone watched while the men got in the back and passed out a box the size of a dining table. They carried it into the shop.

Then Lester stood on the back of the van, 'I was only expecting a few dozen people. It seems the Hughes family are more popular than I'd imagined,' he said. 'Deservedly so. Perhaps the wisest thing would be if you formed a queue to see the picture and Mrs Hughes and her children will entertain you with their excellent coffee and cakes.'

So that's what everyone did and, for the record, we took nearly £600 that night. We ran out of polystyrene cups and Tom had to wash a load of them so they could be reused.

Whenever the shop was full, Lester gave a little talk about the painting, which was two big blokes with beards and cloaks standing in a room with loads of stuff all about the place, like it was a junk shop maybe. It was called *The Ambassadors* by Hans Holbein. It's insured for £15 million.

'Note the detail of the collar,' Lester was saying. 'Because court officials wore so much fur, of course, a court painter had to be particularly adept at painting fur. The fur here – it almost looks fluffy.'

It did look fluffy – but £15 million! Come on! And it had a kind of big white smudge across the bottom by the men's feet.

'Ah. Now that,' said Lester, 'is very interesting . . .'

Terrible whispered to me, 'Pity your dad couldn't come tonight.'

I said, 'He might come yet.'

She looked surprised. Then she said, 'He didn't mention it earlier. We saw him. In Harlech.'

Lester was saying, 'If I can invite the children to come right over to one side of the picture – to a very tight angle. Almost parallel. That's it . . .'

Terrible moved over. I pulled her sleeve. 'What d'you mean, in Harlech?'

She shushed me. Lester was saying, 'Now, if you crouch down and look at the painting from over here, what can you see? The smudge has become . . .'

'A skull!' shouted Terrible, right into my ear.

'Very good.'

Then she whispered to me, 'He drives the monster truck at Diggermania. You must know.'

Lester was saying that the skull was hidden because it was drawn in a special way called fore-shortening. 'Most pictures – because of the nature of perspective – compel us to stand right in front of them, like television sets. But this one invites us to move aside and look at things from a different angle. And when we do, what do we see?'

Another angle. You just look at things from another angle. And what do you see then?

I tried to look at it from a different angle – Dad

driving off suddenly, Mam doing nothing but look out of the window for days, Marie locked in her room . . . I don't want to talk about it.

Lester and his men packed up the picture and took it back out to the van. Everyone stood around, watching it go. They were still drinking coffee and eating cakes and talking. Some of them were even laughing. I wanted to shout at them. And I realized that that's how I must've looked to Mam all this time. Like one of these people who were happy when things were actually sad. Someone looking from the wrong angle.

23 June

Cars today:
JAGUAR XJ 4.2 V8 SOVEREIGN – Barry and
Tone from the Insurance

Weather – don't care

Note: THE CASE OF THE MINI IN THE
PAVILION

So this is finally it. This is the day that the Snowdonia
Oasis Auto Marvel officially ceased trading as a
garage.

At first I didn't believe what Terrible said about
Dad. I couldn't ask Minnie about it, because she's
younger than me and she shouldn't have to know sad
things. I wanted to ask Mam, but she was always busy
with Max, so I went and knocked on Marie's door.

She didn't answer, so I knocked again. Still no
answer. Knocked again. This time she came out.
'What,' she said, 'do you want?'

'Do you know where Dad is?'

'Dylan. This door is locked. It's been locked for
weeks. Can you figure out why?'

'I think I know where he is.'

'It's locked because I don't care. I don't care about
him. You. The garage. Mam. Anything. Go away.' She
slammed the door.

I knocked again. She started screaming.

Mam came running up the stairs with Max on her arm. 'Dylan, what are you doing?'

'Trying to talk to Marie.'

'Well, she doesn't want to talk to you. Let's go.'

Marie must have heard, because she stopped screaming. The bedroom door opened a crack and her arms shot out like two white tentacles and plucked Max away from Mam. Then the door shut again. Mam didn't even blink. Like this happened all the time.

'Dylan,' said Mam, 'Marie is a teenager. Lots of teenage girls get grumpy and we just have to live with that. It's a phase. All girls go through it.'

'All girls lock themselves away for weeks on end? Really?'

'Leave it, Dylan.'

There was that flash of light from under the door again. Then the door opened and the two arms passed Max back to Mam. She cuddled him. She was going to walk away.

I said, 'Mam, can we go to Diggermania?'

'Where?'

'Diggermania. You know, it's . . .'

'I know where it is.'

'It's got . . .'

'And I know what it is.'

'Well, can we go then?'

'No.'

'Why not? It looks immense and . . .'

'Just no.' She was snapping now and there was a big fat tear lying on her bottom eyelid.

'If I'm really good, can we go?'

'That's enough, Dylan. All right? That's enough.'

And it was enough. Enough to tell me that she knew. Enough to tell me it was true.

When I saw Barry and Tone's Jaguar turning on to the forecourt I felt a bit more cheerful. At least they'd be happy that I'd found the car. And even though it's weird that Dad's only in Harlech, it's also good because it means that, once I've sorted this car business out, we can go and tell him.

I ran out on to the forecourt. Tone handed me the car keys and asked me to fill her up. I know I was only opening the petrol cap, but there's something about holding the keys to a classic-marque car that makes you feel good. I said, 'The Mini's in the workshop now, by the way. It was just sitting there in the pavilion.'

'We heard.'

'How lucky was that, though, that I found it just like that?'

'I'm not sure,' said Barry.

'How lucky was it?'

They went into the shop to pay and started asking Mam all kinds of random questions.

'We noticed from the paperwork,' said Barry, 'that you had difficulties meeting the financial requirements of your petrol supplier.'

That was when we sold the Lego.

'Would it be true to say,' said Tone, 'that Mr Hughes was having financial problems before he disappeared?'

I said, 'He has not disappeared.'

They all looked at me. Mam was glaring.

I said, 'My dad has not disappeared. He's just gone to Harlech.'

'Dylan . . .' said Mam.

'He works in Diggermania,' I said, and went upstairs.

I could hear Mam arguing with them for ages. I tried to listen to what they were saying. Minnie came bothering me with her *Crime and Criminals* book.

'Look at this one,' she said.

I wasn't interested.

'Just look. This guy is Lord Brocket. He had loads of debts, but he also had loads of Ferraris.'

'No one has loads of Ferraris.'

'He did. Have a look.'

I was still trying to listen to what Mam was saying but, I have to admit, the Ferraris were distracting.

This man had had the first-ever road Ferrari, Niki Lauda's F1, a 340 America, and a Maserati Birdcage.

'And he couldn't sell them because no one could afford them. But he needed the money. So what did he do?'

'I don't know.'

'He pretended they'd been stolen and then claimed on the insurance.'

'How do you pretend a car has been stolen?'

'Well, you could drop it in a crusher . . .'

'He didn't! Ferraris? No. That'd be the worst thing ever. No. No one could crush a Ferrari.'

'No. He didn't. If you're doing an insurance job, never do anything irreversible. Just in case they don't pay out.'

'So?'

'So he buried them.'

'Buried them?'

'Yeah. Buried them in the ground. Genius, eh?'

I had to admit, it was quite good.

'Just like Dad,' said Minnie, 'in the Case of the Mini in the Pavilion.'

'What?'

'Well, it's obvious, isn't it? He got into a bit of financial trouble – like Lord Brocket – and – like Lord Brocket – he decided to do an insurance job. Our Dad's a bandit.'

'No, he isn't.'

'Yes, he is. And Barry and Tone got suspicious so he went on the run. Our dad's a bandit—'

'Be quiet.'

'You see this pull-out chart of Master Criminals? It's wrong. All this lot – Ronnie Biggs, Jonathan Wild – they all got caught. That's how we know they're criminals. The real Master Criminals, they don't get caught. No one even knows they're criminals. Like Dad.'

'I said, be quiet.'

'I bet Manod doesn't have the lowest crime rate. I bet we're just better at it. We don't get caught. I'm telling you, Dad is a bandit and now he's in hiding.'

I yelled at her again to be quiet. 'You're talking rubbish.' But I was thinking, What if she's right? And I've just told Barry and Tone where Dad is.

It got worse. After Barry and Tone had gone, Mam came upstairs and explained that they worked for our insurance company. They were pleased that the car had been found so they didn't have to pay out, but they now had a number of other concerns. For instance, why the car had gone in the first place. Plus they had found out that Nice Tom had once tried to rob the garage he now worked in, which they thought was a security risk.

'You're not going to sack Tom?' said Minnie.

'Not directly,' said Mam. 'They said they were also

aware that valuable paintings from the National Gallery were crossing the forecourt on a regular basis and they regarded this as an unacceptable insurance risk. They said they weren't able to insure us any more unless we paid them thousands of pounds, which we can't. Plus they bought our last drop of petrol. So we're closing down.'

'Closing down!' We both said that together.

'But . . .'

'Please don't argue.'

But I had to argue. 'Couldn't you just stay open not insured, like the boating lake?'

'No.'

'Why?'

'Because I've had enough,' said Mam. And she took the baby and went to bed.

24 June

Cars today:
SILVER FORD MONDEO TDCi ESTATE –
Richardson's

Weather – persistent, incessant, heavy rain

Note: CRIMINAL TYPES

Even though we were closed now, I still kept writing the petrol log. Obviously there wasn't so much to write in it because we had no petrol. But some things just seemed so important, you had to write them down. Like when this Mondeo (top speed 127 mph) came. It was the TDCi, the one with the push-button shifters on the steering wheel. I went out to see what he wanted. I'd forgotten we weren't the Snowdonia Oasis Auto Marvel any more. He waved at me, opened the boot and took out a 'FOR SALE' sign. He nailed it to the telegraph pole where we used to put up the special offers.

So that was that. The end of the Snowdonia Oasis.

Tom turned up for work, even though Mam had told him not to and even though there was no work to do. He said, 'Maybe I could feed the chickens or take Max for a walk or—'

'Tom,' said Mam, 'one of the reasons they withdrew

247

our insurance is that we had a criminal type working here. Namely you.'

'But I'm not a criminal type, Mrs Hughes. Mr Hughes said—'

'Mr Hughes – in case you hadn't noticed – is not here. And has not been here for some time.'

'So it was all my fault.'

She looked at him for a minute. Then she said, 'Yes.'

I said, 'No, it wasn't.'

She said, 'You be quiet.'

Tom had gone by then.

'What did you say that for?' said Minnie.

'It made me feel better,' said Mam.

Sometimes someone would drive up, but when they saw the 'CLOSED' sign, they'd back up and turn around again. Even the hens seemed to be sulking. They sat in their hutch all day and Donatello stopped laying (Michelangelo never started).

A couple of times Tom went by on his bike. At first we thought he was just confused, then we thought it was nostalgia. Finally we got the idea that he wanted to talk to us.

After school he was waiting for us on the porch of the pavilion in the park, wearing his Turtles crash helmet. He said, 'I think I've got a Master Plan.'

'Go on then.'

He looked around to make sure no one was listening. There was just a duck on the putting green. He whispered, 'Nick a painting.'

'I knew you were going to say that!' said Minnie. 'You've been planning that right from the start, haven't you?'

'No, I haven't,' said Tom. 'I'm reformed. Or I was reformed. It's just I can't think of anything else we can do now.'

'So what's the plan?' said Minnie.

'Just that really. Nick a painting.'

Minnie said, 'The boxes are in a quarry underground, Tom. It's only got one entrance. The reason the government has put them there is so they can't be nicked. And that's exactly what they can't be – nicked.'

'Oh,' said Tom.

I said, 'You've got to stop trying to solve problems by robberies. Look what happened when you tried to rob our garage.'

'Nice things happened when I tried to rob your garage. Your dad gave me a job.'

I said, 'I'm not sure the National Gallery will take the same approach. My dad is special.'

'Yes, he is,' said Tom. 'All the same, it's got to be worth a go.'

'I'm not sure you're right about that.'

"The only time the paintings are vulnerable is when they're crossing our forecourt,' said Minnie. 'We'd have to gain access to the van, maybe when it was getting petrol. And we haven't got any petrol. And anyway, the painting in the van is going to be on the gallery wall in London first thing the next morning, so everyone would be looking for it almost right away. If you were going to get away with it, you'd have to replace the one in the van with a plausible copy.'

Tom and I stared at her.

I said, 'You've really thought about this, haven't you?'

'From time to time,' said Minnie.

Next morning, Tom came riding past the garage again. He saw me looking and tried to make some kind of signal with his hands, and fell off his bike. I went out to help him. 'Meet you after school,' he said. 'Same place.'

When I went back in, Mam said, 'What did he want?'

'Nothing. He just fell off his bike.'

Tom was sitting in the pavilion in the park with what looked like a pile of Monopoly boxes on his knee. Only they weren't Monopoly boxes.

'I was thinking about what you said, Minnie, about how if you stole a painting you'd have to swap it for a copy.'

'And?'

He tipped the boxes up so we could see the covers. 'Painting by numbers,' he said.

'Oh,' said Minnie, 'painting by numbers. Right.'

'Your mam is short of money. The paintings up there are worth millions. We could nick one and swap it for one of these.' He had three pictures to choose from. One was of a collie dog. One was of an alpine scene. One was of a vase of flowers.

I suddenly remembered that Nice Tom used to be called Daft Tom.

'Painting by numbers,' said Minnie.

'All we have to do is find a painting up there that looks like one of these, and swap it.'

Minnie pulled out the one of the vase of flowers and looked at it.

'Tom,' I said, 'remember what Minnie said? Even if you did nick a painting – which you couldn't – how would you get rid of it? Who do you know with twenty-five million pounds?'

Tom looked thoughtful – like he was going through his mental address book, looking for forgotten millionaires.

I said, 'You know, Tom, maybe the insurance people were right. Maybe you are a criminal type.'

'I'm not! I even paid for these . . .' He pointed to the painting-by-numbers sets.

'Tom,' said Minnie, 'this is not a good idea.'

Tom stared at her. 'But you were always telling me to go and steal a painting.'

'I was only joking. This isn't going to work.'

Tom could argue with me. No one can argue with Minnie. He didn't say anything. He just seemed to shrink. 'I know. I know it's not. I just wanted to do something. There must be something I can do! It's all my fault.'

Then Minnie said something which was meant to be kind but maybe was a fateful mistake. She said, 'We might as well make the picture anyway, just in case.'

Tom did his famous big smile and offered her the boxes. 'Which one?' he said.

She chose the vase of flowers.

When we got back home, we looked in the *Revised and Expanded*. The vase of flowers was in there. It was based on a real painting in the National Gallery. It was called *Sunflowers*, by Vincent Van Gogh. It was the most valuable painting in the whole gallery.

'Jesus Jellybeans,' said Minnie. 'Bang on the money. If we had a plan, this would be going according to plan.'

'Except we don't have a plan.'

'No. We don't. That's right.'

We decided to make the picture in the workshop. We told Tom it was because it was all top secret and no one was supposed to know. Really, it was so that Mam wouldn't see him and lose her temper with him again.

The paint comes in little numbered pots. The picture is split up into little numbered shapes. All you have to do is match the colour to the space. We decided to have a colour each so that we'd get it done quicker. So I was yellow ochre (9). Minnie was burnt umber (4) and Tom was crimson lake (13). At first it was just spots of bright paint on a big board.

'It looks like different flavours of chicken pooh,' said Minnie, and we all laughed. 'Like the hens have pigged out on icing and then come in here and just let go. Like they had a big pooh party.'

Mostly we were quiet and concentrating. It felt like we were doing something about the garage, and even though we weren't really, that was still a good feeling. We thought we didn't get much done the first day, but when we came back the next morning we realized we were nearly halfway there. You could already tell what it was supposed to be. That got us moving faster, like when you've nearly finished a jigsaw and you're racing for the last piece.

It was unanimously decided that Tom should paint the last number. It was a dab of vermilion (15) on one of the leaves. The effect was immense. It made the whole picture look like a painting. A painting that we'd painted. We were so proud, we stood there staring at it for about five minutes. Minnie went and got the *Revised and Expanded* so that we could look at it next to a photo of the original.

'That's amazing,' said Tom. 'No one could tell that wasn't the proper one.'

'Except,' said Minnie, 'ours is wet.'

'Oh, yeah.'

And then she said – but I wish she hadn't, 'Then again, it will dry.'

And it did dry. Each morning we'd look into the workshop. By Sunday it was dry. It looked even more like a painting. It looked a lot like *the* painting.

Mam sent Minnie and me down to Mrs Porty's for a pint of milk. I noticed that they had a new window display in Curl Up N Dye. It was mostly big bottles of shampoo with wigs on top. It looked like an invasion of tiny, hairy aliens. But with nice hairdos. Like tiny aliens going to a wedding or something. Minnie said, 'If we did have a plan, the next thing would be for you to ask Lester to send *Sunflowers* to London and ask him if he could show it in our garage just like before, so that we'd have an opportunity.'

'But we haven't got a plan.'

'No, we haven't.'

We walked on. I said, 'I'll tell you what else we haven't got.'

'What?'

'A frame. Our *Sunflowers* is on a piece of cardboard

with "Painting by Numbers" written on the back. D'you think when they got it to the gallery they'd say, "Oh, no frame. That makes a nice change. We can Blu Tack this to the wall."?'

Minnie said, 'All right, all right.'

That night I woke up to find someone sitting on the end of my bed. I said, 'Dad!'

'No,' said Minnie, 'it's me. Minnie.'

'What?'

'You were worrying about us not having a frame for *Sunflowers*.'

'No, I wasn't.'

'Yes, you said that we'd be rumbled if they saw it with no frame on.'

'Yes, but I wasn't worried about it. Because we're not going to nick a painting and therefore we don't have to swap one.'

'The Misses Sellwood's dad's picture. The one of Elsa when she was a little girl.'

'What about it?'

'Got a proper frame on it.'

Which it did. A big, heavy, gold frame with leaves carved into it. The kind of frame you see in an art gallery. While everyone else was still asleep, we got the painting by numbers from the workshop, unclipped the back of Mr Sellwood's picture and dropped our picture in. It looked amazing.

'It looks like a masterpiece,' I said. 'No one would know that wasn't a masterpiece.'

'It would be a crime NOT to send it to the National Gallery,' said Minnie.

30 June

Cars today:
BLUE AUDI A8 V12 – valuer from Richardson's

Weather – rain

Note: SOME SORT OF GENIUS

Even though we were definitely still not really planning to steal a painting, we were already scared we might get caught. Like when we got home and saw this random Audi Quattro A8 V12 (top speed a remarkable 155 mph) on the forecourt, we both thought it was the police come to get us.

I said, 'How can it be the police? We haven't done anything yet.'

Minnie said, 'Conspiracy.'

A man in a stripy suit got out and said, 'I'm from Richardson's – the estate agents?'

We both said, 'Oh.'

'You've already been,' said Minnie.

'That was just the bloke with the sign. I'm the valuer.' He held up a camera and a clipboard. 'Where's your mam then?'

The Audi, by the way, has a V12 engine (like in a Bentley) and the distinctive Audi electro-hydraulic multi-plate clutch, which distributes power equally between the front and the back. So what?! It's not interesting if you aren't actually filling it up.

As soon as Mam took the man inside, Minnie grabbed my arm and hissed, 'Workshop. Quick.'

I said, 'What's going on?'

'If he's going to look around, he's going to see this.' She pointed to our masterpiece, which was propped up in the corner on top of the tyre gauge. 'If this is going to be a perfect crime, we've got to make sure no one can find any connection between us and the picture. This is a big, big clue.'

We sneaked it in through the back door. We could hear Mam showing the stripy-suit man round the kitchen.

'Where are we going to put it? They're going to go everywhere.'

Downstairs, Mam was saying, 'So that's the kitchen. This is the living room . . .' They'd be coming upstairs any minute.

'My bedroom?'

'They'll look in the bedrooms. Anyway . . .'

Before she could finish, Marie opened the door to her room and walked out. She was going to the toilet. She breezed straight past without looking at us, like a ghost. Her door was still half open.

Minnie grinned. 'Well,' she said, 'no one's going to look in there and survive.' She grabbed the picture and added, 'You stay here. Keep her busy if you need to.'

She dived into Marie's room. I could hear her moving stuff around. Downstairs, the stripy-suit man was talking about the view from the living-room window.

'Come on, Minnie . . .' I hissed. She should be out by now. I couldn't hear anything moving round.

The toilet flushed. 'Minnie . . . come on . . . she's coming.' It was surprising how frightened I was.

The taps were running. The sink was filling up. The man downstairs was looking at the coal-effect gas fire. 'Minnie . . . what're you doing?'

Suddenly the bolt on the bathroom door shot back and Marie was standing behind me. Almost at the same moment, Minnie appeared in the bedroom door-way. Oh, brilliant. Now there was going to be a big scrap and everyone would know what we were up to. And we'd go to jail and be in the paper and . . .

Marie glided back into her room. She didn't even look at Minnie as she passed her in the doorway. She went back in and shut the door.

I said, 'She is weird. Luckily. I thought she'd go mad when she saw you'd been in there.'

'She didn't, though,' said Minnie, 'so we're all right, aren't we? It's under her bed. We're all right.'

As she said this I noticed something strange:

Minnie was crying. I said, 'What's up? Don't do that. What're you crying for?'

She said, 'I'm not crying.'

I said, 'That's a relief.' But she was crying. She must've seen something in Marie's room. Anyway, just then the stripy-suit man came up the stairs with Mam so luckily I didn't have to talk about it. The man reached for Marie's bedroom door and turned the handle.

Mam said, 'I'm not sure . . .'

Marie's voice came out of the room like a flying dagger. 'Get out!' she shrieked. And he did. So our security was good.

When the stripy-suit man had gone, Mam said, 'He says we'll get quite a good price because of the exceptional view and because the garage provides room for development. He thinks someone might want to open a bed and breakfast here or a garden centre or something. Quite exciting.'

I know it's mad, but I'd not really thought about us moving out before. I looked out of the window at the exceptional view.

Minnie said, 'How long have we got? I mean . . . how long will it take?'

'That depends,' said Mam, 'on whether anyone wants to buy it. And if we can get Marie out of her room. No one's going to want to buy it with her in there.'

We told Marie about the house being for sale by slipping a note under her door.

Minnie came and slept in my room. She said, 'If we can get that painting, we could have that "For Sale" sign down quicker than it went up. We could build our own garden centre.'

'But we can't get the painting because we are not going to steal a painting.'

'I know,' said Minnie. 'I just don't remember why not.'

'Because, as you said, we don't know anyone with twenty-five million pounds, so what is the point?'

'You're right,' said Minnie.

I turned over and tried to get to sleep.

'Except . . .'

'What?'

'Well, we don't want twenty-five million pounds. Twenty-five million pounds is what the gallery would get if they lost the painting. If we offered it back to them for a lot less than that, they might be quite pleased. It wouldn't even be stealing. It would just be making a point.'

'It would be kidnapping.'

'Exactly. Well, kidnapping's not so bad, is it?'

'How much less?'

'Well, I was thinking about this. When you think

about it, it's all the gallery's fault. Before they moved in, we were ticking over nicely. Dad was happy. Tom was happy. Marie was happy. The gallery is the reason that Mam has to pay the extra insurance. They should pay it. They should pay our insurance. And some wages for Tom. That's all we want: everything back the way it was.'

Everything back the way it was was very tempting.

'Maybe a bit of cash to go on holiday or something.'

I said, 'No,' rolled over and pretended to be asleep.

'No completely?'

'No completely.'

'Not even to get Tom his job back?'

'No.'

'Fine. You'll have to tell Tom, though. You'll have to tell him soon, before he builds his hopes up.'

'All right then, I will.'

'Great. Goodnight.'

After a bit I said, 'Min . . . why were you crying when you came out of Marie's room?' But she must have fallen asleep because she didn't reply.

Tom was outside school next morning. When he saw me coming, he ran over and shook my hand, and carried on shaking it until I thought my teeth were going to drop out. He kept saying, 'I'm so happy. I'm so happy.'

'Good,' I said. 'Why?'

'Minnie says you have a great plan. She says you're going to put everything back the way it was. I get my job back, even!'

'When did she say that?'

'Just now. Thank you. Thank you. Thank you.'

'Well, the thing is, she shouldn't have said that . . .'

'Why? Did you want it to be a surprise?'

'No, but . . .'

'Dylan. Everywhere I go in this town I see the things that you have done. The nice shop windows. The boating lake. The pavilion. The sign. You did all of this to the town. You made the town better. And now you are going to make me better.'

'Well, the thing is . . .'

'Dylan, you are just like your father. You fix everything.'

That was on Tuesday. So I still had a day before Lester had to decide which picture to send to London.

When I got home, I put my big coat on, climbed over the gate and started off up Manod Mountain. I knew I had to try.

I followed the white stones through the cloud again. I passed the big boulder with the staring faces drawn on it. I came through the cloud and into the sun and took my coat off. I'd hardly got to the fence when Lester came out to meet me.

'Nice to see you,' he said. 'I thoroughly enjoyed our soirée last week. I hope you did too.'

'Yes, it was good.'

'And your mother?'

'Yes, she liked it. Everyone liked it.'

He was so pleased to see me, and I'd only come to rob a painting from him. I felt like telling him the truth there and then, but then he said, 'I hear you're moving on?'

'Yeah.'

'Where to?'

I looked at the exceptional view – at the shiny black peak of Blaenau Mountain, at the green slopes of Manod Mountain, at the big duvet of cloud that covered my town. Were we really going to go away and leave it all? I took a deep breath and said, 'Did you ever hear of a painting called *Sunflowers*?'

'Of course.'

'It's by—'

'I know who *Sunflowers* is by.'

'You haven't got it here, have you?'

'Yes, we have. Of course, he painted a whole series of sunflowers, but one of the best is here in our collection. I'm surprised it interests you. I was thinking that perhaps you'd like to see some Velázquez. Really *Sunflowers* is horribly overrated and . . .'

It would have been easy to let him talk me out of it. But I said, 'I'd really like to see *Sunflowers*.'

'Well, I have to admit I was thinking I'd have to send it up to London at some point. It is such a crowd-pleaser. Why not this week? Come in. I've got something to show you.'

Lester led me inside the mountain and down into the big cavern where the paintings were kept. The lights were off. It was pitch black.

He said, 'Dylan, when I came here, I was looking forward to having these pictures to myself. I had come to hate seeing them in the gallery, with crowds of trippers gawping at them. I was going to hoard them here in my cave like an old dragon with his treasure.'

'Shall I put the lights on?'

'In a moment. When I came here, I discovered that I didn't appreciate these pictures any more than those day trippers did. To me they were just . . . dead, like dead butterflies in a museum case. Then someone came along and opened the case, and they weren't dead any more. They flew away. And I finally understood them at last.'

'That's nice.'

'That person – the person who let them fly – that was you, Dylan Hughes. I just wanted to say thank you. And now I'll turn the lights on.'

And he did. Then he said, 'What d'you think?'

It was immense. Where all the rows of boxes had

been, now there were rows of pictures. Big pictures, tiny pictures, huge pictures, pictures of women in mad hats, pictures of men out hunting, cities, seas, ships, lions, tigers, everything.

'Quite an eyeful, eh? I thought the men working here, why should they be looking at boxes all day when they could be looking at the highest achievements of civilization, to quote your teacher? And this was your doing! This is all your doing. You are some sort of genius. Now let's find your *Sunflowers*. Impressionism this way . . .'

He set off down the rows of paintings. I looked at them all and all I could think was, Your fault. If it wasn't for those paintings we'd still be happy. We'd still have the garage. Dad might come home even. It was all down to the paintings.

I said, 'Lester . . . Mr Lester, I . . .'

'Yes?'

'I'm not a genius.'

'Well, genius is a much misused word.'

'I'm not even clever.'

'Clever people always think they're not clever.'

'I don't know anything about painting.'

'To know we know nothing is the beginning of wisdom. As it says in *Bill and Ted's Excellent Adventure*. Ha ha.'

'My chickens . . .'

'Your chickens? Ah yes. Donatello and Michelangelo . . .'

'They're not named after the painters. They're named after the Turtles.'

He looked a bit baffled.

'The Ninja Turtles. The Teenage Mutant Ninja Turtles. They're called Raphael, Michelangelo, Leonardo and Donatello. And Splinter. But he's not actually a Turtle. He's a mutant rat.'

Lester just stared at me for a while.

'That's who my hens were named after. Not the painters.'

'But . . . you . . .'

'I'd never even heard of the painters.'

He didn't say anything. After a while, I said, 'Sorry.'

He still didn't say anything.

I thought I'd better go. I said, 'D'you want me to turn the lights out?'

But he still didn't answer.

2 July

Cars today:
ROVER 3500 V8 — the Misses Sellwood

Weather — very wet

Note: PLAN B

So first of all we didn't get to pump petrol any more or help in the shop. And now I'd stopped being a genius. For the first time in Manod there was nothing to do. No wonder we were thinking of turning to crime. Every day was like Wednesday. In fact, Wednesday was more interesting, because at least the Misses Sellwood came. Miss Edna pipped the horn and when I came out she asked for her copy of the *People's Friend*.

I explained to her that we'd closed down.

Miss Edna said, 'Elsa, he says they've closed down.'

'Oh dear,' said Miss Elsa, 'Have they got your *People's Friend*?'

'No, they haven't. We'll have to go to Mrs Porty.'

'Closed down,' said Elsa. 'And only open the twinkling of an eye.'

'I've only just got used to them being here,' said Edna.

And they drove off.

I'd lived nearly all my life in the Snowdonia Oasis. But the Sellwoods had lived all their much longer life on the mountain. To them, we seemed like a novelty. Somehow that made me feel a bit better. That's why, when Minnie came out, I felt quite comfortable saying to her, 'The robbery's off. Lester knows I don't know anything about art. He's not going to let the van stop and show us the painting. He's not even talking to me. I'm not even sure it's going to be *Sunflowers*.'

Minnie said, 'Doesn't matter. We've always got Plan B.'

'Plan B? I didn't even know we had a plan A!'

'See you in the workshop after school.'

When we got to the workshop, Minnie had it all set out. Two shop-damaged discount chairs – one for me and one for Tom. A tray of drinks. Notepads and pencils. And, on the workbench, some toy cars and a monkey wrench to help her explain her plan. She'd put a lot of work into this. It made you worry about her. This was Plan B:

1. Put our painting in a wooden box like the ones from the gallery

Minnie said, 'You may be wondering where the shell we are going to get one of those,' and then she smiled and pulled one out from under the tow truck. It had 'National Gallery Collection' written across the front.

It was the one Lester had left behind, the time he forgot *The Wilton Diptych*.

So that was Step One sorted.

We left it to Minnie to sneak into Marie's room, get our picture and put it in the box, which she did. She also borrowed Marie's phone.

2. Take the box up the mountain, ready to swap boxes

We had to wait until Sunday night because that was when Lester put the picture back in its box so that it could be loaded on to the van and driven to London on the Monday.

On the night, Tom hid in the workshop, waiting for us to come out, which we couldn't do until Mam had gone to sleep. Mam stayed up really late, though. She was sorting things into boxes – some to take with us and some to take to a car-boot sale (Dynamo Blaenau Floodlit Car Boot Super Sale was coming up). I fell asleep but Minnie woke me up.

We were quite worried about being seen by the guards. Then I remembered the shoe polish Dad had got from the Cash and Carry. We rubbed it on our faces so we wouldn't show up so much in the dark. We almost forgot to get Tom out of the workshop. When we opened the door, he said, 'Look! I brought these!' He had three Turtles masks. I'm not sure they were that good as a disguise, but he'd always wanted to wear them so we did.

The box wasn't so heavy and it was easy to follow the white stones. Every now and then a sheep coughed, which was a bit scary. But we got up to the top.

3. Swap our picture for their picture

I said, 'Hang on. How do we do that? There's an alarm and—'

'I can get round the alarm.'

'Nothing to do with wasps, is it?' said Tom.

'No wasps.'

'Good then,' said Tom. 'I hate wasps.'

I said, 'No, Tom, not good because not true.' I turned to Minnie. 'How can you get round the alarm? What are you? The Fugitoid?'

The Fugitoid is this robot who was the Turtles' main ally in their fight against General Blanque on Planet D'Hoonnib in the Sidayom System. He can drill through stone.

Minnie said, 'We won't need any of that. I can do it with a packet of Quavers.' And she produced a packet of Quavers she'd already acquired.

On the night, I worried about the alarm all the way up the mountain. When we got to the top, Minnie pulled the bag of Quavers out of her coat. Within a couple of seconds, you could hear sheep crowding in from all over the place. They followed her right up to the barbed-wire fence.

She hissed, 'Lift it up. Lift the wire up and let a couple in.' We did. Then she said, 'Wait here. I'm going to set the alarm off.'

'What?'

But she was gone. We hid behind a great big boulder, the one with the doodles on. We could just see her heading towards the Technodrome, where Lester kept the paintings.

Tom said, 'She forgot the painting!' We still had the gallery's wooden box with us. 'I'll go after her.'

I said, 'No, no, no, no, no, no, no. Wait and see what she's up to.'

Suddenly the alarm went off. It echoed round the caves and cliffs like the whole mountain was a massive bell. Blue lights were flashing. Men were running. Sheep were going crazy for miles.

I was worried. Tom was terrified. But all of a sudden Minnie was sitting next to us, looking at her watch.

Four quad bikes came roaring out of the dark, their headlights blazing. 'Two minutes,' said Minnie. 'Pretty good.'

The quads rumbled up and down the fence looking for intruders. We crouched behind the rock. After a while they trundled back towards the Technodrome and the alarm stopped.

'Did you get the painting?'

'Not yet,' said Minnie. 'Wait about half an hour.'

'Why?'

'You'll see.'

So we waited and watched. Men were running round with torches. Eventually they found the sheep that we'd brought with us. We could hear them shouting to each other, 'It's only sheep.'

A few of them tried to chase one of the sheep towards the fence, but it wasn't interested. Luckily they didn't have any Quavers.

We sat there, looking up at the stars. They were really, really bright up here, not like in town.

Tom said, 'Why was General Blanque so obsessed with the Fugitoid?'

'Because he wanted to use its teleportal device to help him achieve galactic domination.'

'Ah,' said Tom.

Then Minnie got up. 'I'm going to set the alarm off again,' she said. 'The trick is to make them think there's something wrong with it, so they end up ignoring it.'

So off she went.

A few seconds later the alarm went off again. There was the same palaver with the men and the sheep.

When Minnie came back, she said, 'Four minutes to scramble the quad bikes this time. They're getting slower already.'

She set the alarm off three more times. Each time it took the guards a little bit longer to come out of their hut. Each time we stayed huddled together behind the boulder and talked about, well, stuff. It turned out that Tom knew the names of some of the stars.

'That one's Vega,' he'd say. 'I wish we'd brought a flask of hot chocolate. And that's Cassiopeia. I'm freezing.' And on like that.

The moonlight made the big boulder shine like silver and it made the lines of the drawing on its side really black, like ink. All the faces in the drawing were looking in the same direction. Up towards the corner where the big mop of moss was. What were they looking at? I don't know what gave me the idea, but I lifted up the big mop of moss – and tried to see what was underneath. Suddenly there was a noise like a tiny machine gun right next to me. I dropped the moss and crouched down quick. 'Only me,' said Tom. He was holding up a torch. 'My wind-up torch.' He lifted the moss and shone the beam on the corner of the boulder. There was a drawing where the moss had been. This one was two women with their hair hanging down. The men were all looking at the women.

Some of the quarrymen must have scratched it on, years back.

The sixth time Minnie went, the alarm didn't go off at all. She came back grinning. 'They've turned it off,' she said. 'The place is wide open. Maybe we should take a few extra paintings?'

'No.'

We all got up and carried our painting by numbers over to the Technodrome. The moment we opened the door, a different alarm went off. It was like being punched in the ears. I had to bite my lip so I wouldn't scream. We just stood, frozen to the spot. The moon cast our shadows on the grass. They were as still as fossils. Even the steam from our nostrils seemed too scared to move.

But nothing happened.

There was the painting, all boxed up. We put our painting down. We picked up the other one. Then the alarm stopped. The quiet was almost worse than the noise. We stood there, holding our breath. Then Minnie walked out and me and Tom followed.

It was only when we got to the barbed-wire fence that I thought, 'Twenty-five million pounds.'

4. Put the Misses Sellwood's painting in the *Sunflowers* frame

This was Minnie's idea, and you have to admit it was impressive.

The plan was to take *Sunflowers* out of its frame, put the picture of the young Miss Sellwood into the front of the frame and then put *Sunflowers* in behind it, and put it all back together again. Now if anyone searched the house, they could be looking straight at the Van Gogh and never know it. Because it was hidden behind old Mr Sellwood's picture of his daughter.

Genius.

As soon as we got back down off the mountain, we went into the workshop. I got the jemmy, found the special groove under the 'T' of National and then slipped the box open. There was some bubble wrap on top. We moved that, and there was *Sunflowers*.

It didn't look anything like our painting by numbers.

We thought that was a masterpiece – but this . . . the yellow was so yellow it nearly lit up the garage. And even though it was only flowers, it seemed really sad and happy at the same time. How can flowers be sad? Or happy, for that matter? But these were. We just sat there, staring at it for ages. The weirdest thing was, we were freezing when we came off the mountain, but looking at *Sunflowers* was like warming yourself at a fire. It had so much sunshine in it, it was like being back on top of the mountain that first day when I hadn't known it was going to be sunny.

Then the birds started singing outside. It was nearly morning.

Minnie said, 'We need a photo.'

'What?'

'To prove we've got the painting. During negotiations. I sneaked Marie's Polaroid camera out of her room. You have to take it, Tom.'

'But I want to be in the picture,' said Tom.

'You can't. Then there'd be evidence linking you to the crime.'

'There'll be evidence linking you to the crime.'

'We're under age. We can't go to jail.'

'I could wear my Turtles mask.'

So that's what we did. We put the camera on automatic and we all stood there, holding up *Sunflowers*, disguised as Turtles. It was a rubbish disguise. There's only one person in Snowdonia with that many Turtles masks, and everyone knows who that is.

We unscrewed the back of the frame. I lifted the painting out. The paint was really thick and I was scared it was going to start flaking off. Minnie dropped Mr Sellwood's painting into the frame. I was supposed to drop *Sunflowers* in just on top of that, but I was scared the paint would rub off on the back of it.

'Put some tissue in or something.'

Dad had a big roll of tissue with the Swarfega on the shelves. We padded the back of the other painting with it and then we put *Sunflowers* in. Then we sealed it up. And, 'There you go,' said Minnie. 'Perfect crime.'

'What do we do next, then?' said Tom.

'Just hold tight,' said Minnie.

7 July

Cars today:
WHITE COMBI VAN — just passing through
CARBON BLACK BMW M5 — Mr Q. Lester
(criminal investigation)

Weather — didn't notice

Note: INSURANCE COMPANIES TEND TO
SPECIALIZE

This was the Monday. The white van crossed the fore-court. Lester came right after it in his own car. He waved to us and we thought, There it goes.

Minnie said, 'There you go. Job done.'

'Painting by numbers heading for London.'

Suddenly there was a terrible scream from upstairs.

'What's that?!' For some mad reason I thought it was something to do with the robbery – like the police had come in through the window or something. Then the scream turned into shouting and throwing things. It was Marie. Something had upset her.

'What's going on?'

'Nothing,' said Minnie. 'Come on, let's get to school.'

And she more or less dragged me out of there and we ran to school.

*

Normally, when we get to school, me and Minnie go our separate ways. This day we stuck next to each other all day. Like we were both worried that one of us would give the game away. Minnie spent the whole day grinning. She was so chuffed that she'd finally become a Master Criminal. She was so happy, she hummed when she was doing her maths. Ms Stannard told her off and she just smiled this *Mona Lisa* smile, like she was thinking, And they told the Master Criminal not to hum . . .

When we got home, Lester's car was parked on the grass, just the far side of the mountain gate. He'd just got back from London. He looked as though he'd driven non-stop. Even though the BMW has ergonomic seats and excellent cruise control for longer journeys, he still looked tired.

'Stay calm,' I said to Minnie. 'He must know by now that it's gone, but he can't possibly suspect us.'

Lester said, 'Right then. Where is it?'

I said, 'Where is what?'

'I've said nothing to your mother because I have no wish to add to her troubles. Just return the painting immediately, and we'll say no more about it.'

He was looking straight at me. But I couldn't look at him.

Minnie said, 'We were hoping for a reward.'

'Reward?' said Lester. 'The reward will be that you won't go to jail.'

'We're too young to go to jail.'

'In that case, your mother and your friend Tom, they can go to jail.'

I gasped. 'No, listen,' I said. 'It's all right. We—'

Minnie interrupted, 'Do the police know?'

'I was there when they opened the box. I almost fainted. Luckily for you, I had the presence of mind to invent a story about a community arts project. So far, only I know. Give it back immediately and you may yet avoid a custodial sentence.'

I said, 'OK. Thank you,' and I was just going to go and get it, only Minnie stopped me.

'It's hidden,' she said. 'It's completely safe. But we'll need a bit of time.'

'A bit of time you can have. Just a bit. Understand?'

'Sure,' said Minnie. 'So what are they doing with the other picture?'

'They're going to hang it. For the week.'

'Rocking Rollos,' said Minnie. 'Cowabunga!'

'Not cowabunga at all,' said Lester. 'Just give back the painting. Do you have any idea how fragile it is?'

'You've made your offer,' said Minnie. 'We'll sleep on it.'

I'd read about people's eyes narrowing before, but

I'd never actually seen it till now. Lester's were like little razor blades of fury.

He got back into his car. Then he wound the window down and looked at me.

'Dylan, I want to apologize,' he said, which was a bit weird, 'for overestimating you. I thought very highly of you. I was mistaken. I should never have shown you those paintings. I should never have shown anybody any paintings.'

Then he drove off.

I said, 'How did he know it was us?'

'All part of the plan,' said Minnie. 'I suddenly thought, it's no good nicking the painting if no one knows it's nicked. So instead of putting *Sunflowers* in, I put our Marie's collage in. That's why she was screaming this morning – because I'd taken her collage.'

'What collage?'

'She'd made this collage. You know, like she did with "Be Lovely", only different.'

'And you swapped her collage for our *Sunflowers*?'

'Yeah, and now it's in the National Gallery. That'll cheer her up when she hears about it.'

'Yeah. That'll really make up for us going to jail.'

She said, 'Can I borrow your pen?'

I passed her my pen, the one with Barry's phone number on it. She took out Marie's phone and started dialling.

Upstairs, Marie was still wailing.

I followed Minnie in and said, 'What are you doing?'

'If your friend Lester won't play ball, I know someone who will. After all, it's the insurance company, not the gallery, that will have to pay out if the painting's not found. It's the insurance company who've got the motivation to cough up. Hello?'

She'd got through.

'It's Minnie from the garage. We'd like to meet up and talk.'

We met them in the pavilion. They drove their XJ 4.2 straight on to the potential putting green and climbed out.

'Is this about the Mini?' said Barry.

'Because we don't want to be messed around any more,' said Tone.

'This one,' said Barry, pointing at me, 'told me his dad worked at Diggermania. He left there days ago. No one's seen him since.'

'So don't waste any more of our time.'

I was so surprised about the Dad news that I forgot to be scared of them. Anyway, it was Minnie who was the really scary one. She said, 'We don't care about the Mini. We're here about this . . .'

And she showed him the Polaroid of us in disguise holding up *Sunflowers*.

Barry looked at it closely. He seemed confused. Tone looked at it closely. He looked even more confused.

Tone looked at Barry. Barry looked at Tone. They both looked at me. I looked at Minnie.

'That's *Sunflowers* by Vincent Van Gogh,' said Minnie. 'Stolen from the gallery this weekend. We know where it is. We'll reveal its whereabouts in exchange for a Handsome Reward.'

Barry and Tone looked at each other again. 'That's interesting,' said Tone.

'But what's it got to do with us?' said Barry.

'Well, if we don't hand it back, the insurance company will have to pay out twenty-five million pounds. We'll be saving your company tens of millions. Do you want to make a deal?'

'Not really,' said Barry, 'because it's not our insurance company. It's a different insurance company. Insurance companies tend to specialize these days. We specialize in late-night and rural garages, service stations, that kind of thing. Not national art collections. This is way out of our league.'

Minnie said, 'Oh.'

And that's when I remembered that, as well as being a Master Criminal, she was just a little girl.

'So . . .'

Barry and Tone were laughing. 'So you were going to try a little insurance scam of your own, were you?

Just like your dad. Criminality is in your blood, isn't it?'

That was it for me. I turned and walked away. Minnie came with me. She was going to cry. Then Barry called her back.

I said, 'Ignore him.'

But he said, 'Listen, I could do something for you – freelance type of thing.'

'Yeah, we could do it freelance.'

'There'll be a reward when this gets out. We could take it off your hands, turn it in, split the money with you. What d'you reckon?'

Minnie looked like he'd asked her if she'd like an extra birthday.

'Is that a "Yes" then? What shall we say? Seventy–thirty. They'll probably go to a mid six-figure sum as long as it's kept out of the papers. It affects their shares, you see, if people hear they have to make a big payout. If you can keep this secret, I can get you . . . oooh, twenty grand.'

'Twenty-five,' said Minnie.

'Done.'

She handed him the Polaroid and said, 'That's on account. You can have the real one when we get the money.'

When we were clearing up that night I said, 'What if we get caught?'

'Master Art Criminals don't get caught. Look at Vincenzo. They had to invent the whole science of fingerprinting to catch him.'

'Say that again.'

'They only caught him by inventing fingerprinting.'

'They caught him?'

'Well, yeah. Eventually.'

'You never told me they caught him.'

'No. I sort of skipped over that bit mentally.'

'Oh.'

'Oh.'

9 July

Cars today:
ROVER 3500 V8 — the Misses Sellwood
CARBON BLACK BMW M5 — Lester, me,
Minnie, Max, half the National Gallery — and
Ms Stannard

Weather — rain

Note: COLLECTABLE SPLINTER ACTION
FIGURE WITH SIXTY-SEVEN POINTS OF
ARTICULATION

This is the arrangement Minnie made with Barry and Tone:

Mam was going to take all our stuff to the Dynamo Blaenau Floodlit Car Boot Super Sale on Wednesday evening at the rugby ground. We were going to stay in and babysit Max. Barry and Tone were going to call round with the money and we were going to give them the painting.

This is what actually happened:

We helped Mam load all the boxes in the car. Just as she was about to leave, a car horn beeped over by the gate. It was the Misses Sellwood. I ran over to open the gate.

'You haven't gone yet, then, Dylan?'

'Not yet.'

They got out of the car. Mam said, 'We're closed, I'm afraid, ladies. Got no petrol at all, if that's what you're after.'

'Oh, no, no, no,' said Edna. 'We saw you putting everything in boxes and we were inspired, look.'

They had a box on the back seat with old records and a lamp in it. 'We're going to the car-boot sale in Blaenau. Going to sell some of this rubbish.'

'I see.'

'In regard to which, we wondered if we could have our picture back?'

'Your picture?'

'The one Father painted. The one of Elsa.'

Me and Minnie looked at each other. We were both thinking the same thing. Namely, 'Oh, shell!'

Mam said, 'Oh yes. Surely. I'll get it right away . . .'

Minnie and me both said, 'I'll get it!' Thinking, maybe we'd have time to get *Sunflowers* out of the frame.

'You stay with the baby,' said Mam, 'and I'll get it. Don't get me wrong, it's a beautiful painting, but it's had a very bad effect on Marie. I'll be glad to see the back of it.'

And off she went.

Minnie said, 'But you're not going to sell it, surely?'

Edna said, 'It's no good to us, after all. Elsa can't

see it and I'm tired of looking at it. What would I want a portrait of Elsa for when I'm looking at the real thing all day long, whether I like it or not, so to speak?' She had a point. 'It's always caused bad blood between the two of us. Why he painted a picture of her and not of me, I'll never know. Anyway, that's it now. It's going.'

Mam came out and gave them the painting.

And they drove off to the Dynamo Blaenau Floodlit Car Boot Super Sale with our priceless Van Gogh in the back of their Rover.

About ten minutes later, Mam went too.

I was just recovering my powers of speech. I said, 'What are we going to do?'

'Well, we can't stay round here, that's for sure.'

'Why not?' My plan was to get into bed and pull the duvet up over my head.

'Because when Barry and Tone get here, they'll kill us.'

Oh.

'It's all right,' she said. 'Every good plan has a wide margin of error. We've just got to make use of it. This is what we'll do. We'll go to the car-boot sale. We'll buy the picture. We'll bring it back here and everything will be fine.'

'What if it's already been sold?'

'Let's minimize that possibility.'

'How?'

'By getting a bloody move on.'

Jade Porty was on the bus. She gave Max a big smile and tickled him under the chin – which he didn't like. Then, in this baby voice, like she was still talking to Max, she went, 'Where oooo going den? Blaenau Car Boot Super Sale?'

'That's right.'

'Looking for bargains, are you?' she smarmed. She was hinting that we were going there because we were poor. I wanted to say to her, 'No, actually we're going to collect our twenty-five-million-pound Van Gogh,' but I didn't.

Obviously we had to avoid Mam when we got to the rugby pitch. That part was easy because the flood-lights made big wedges of deep shadow all over the place.

We found the Misses Sellwood's car and saw that the painting was still there. The whole plan was back on track. So it was a pity that the Misses Sellwood wanted twenty quid for their painting and we only had a fiver.

'It has enormous sentimental value to us, see,' said Edna. 'So we couldn't sell it for less. Besides, I've got my eye on a Wedgwood cake stand over there. So I need the money.'

Minnie pleaded with them. 'We could give you five pounds as a deposit, and pay you the rest as and when.'

'I'd like to, Minnie.'

'Great.'

'But we can't always do what we like, can we? If I did that, I wouldn't have enough money for the cake stand, and then how would the world go round?'

Then Minnie had the idea of phoning Tom and telling him to bring some money. 'Get your mam to drive you here,' she said. 'We need it right now.' Tom said he was on his way.

We hung around the cars, trying to keep out of Mam's line of vision. They were mostly estate cars and 4x4s, but there was one interesting old character car called a Morris Traveller, which seemed to be made of wood. People were selling lamps and crockery and car batteries. One woman was selling reproduction Victorian toilets.

Then we saw Tom.

'Thank gumdrops!' said Minnie. Tom was striding across the field towards us, waving happily. Only he wasn't just waving his hand. He was waving some sort of doll. He held it out for us to look at. It was a model of Splinter – the Turtles' guru. 'Sixty-seven points of articulation.' He beamed. 'I was beginning to think it didn't exist. I've been looking for this all my life.'

It was pretty good, to be honest. It really had that Splinter, faraway look.

'Where did you get it?' said Minnie.

'Over there. Man in a Škoda.'

'That's what I was afraid of. How much was it?'

'Seventeen pounds and ninety-nine pence.'

'So how much have you got left?'

'Two pounds and one pence.'

We didn't feel like explaining it to him. He was so happy with his Splinter model, it didn't seem right to spoil his moment.

That's when the Jaguar trundled on to the field. Barry and Tone got out and looked all around.

'One last try,' said Minnie.

We sneaked round the front ends of the cars and came up just short of the Misses Sellwood's stall so we could keep an eye on the painting. Barry and Tone were about to walk past us, but Minnie stepped in front of them and said, 'Where's the money?'

'What?'

'No money. No painting.'

'I'm not going to hand over twenty-five grand under a set of floodlights in a crowded place,' said Barry. 'What are you doing here, anyway? You said up at the house.'

'Sorry about that. Babysitting.' She showed them Max.

'Your sister nearly gave us a heart attack. She knows how to wail, doesn't she?'

'She's had lots of practice. We need the money.'

'No.'

'Not all of it. An advance. In good faith. Or no picture.'

'How much?'

She glanced at the stall. The picture was still there. 'Twenty quid,' she said.

'Twenty quid!' said Barry.

'Twenty quid!' said Tone.

'What are you laughing at?' said Tom. 'We mean it, you know.'

'Go on, go on,' said Tone. 'Anything else? Bag of peanuts? Packet of crisps?'

'Just give me the money.'

Barry took a big wad of cash from his pocket and peeled off a twenty. Minnie grabbed it and said, 'Wait there.' Then we dashed over to the Misses Sellwood's stall. We were just in time to see that Lester was there, that he was picking up the painting and walking away with it.

We both froze. We knew that Barry and Tone were watching us. Without even thinking about it, I shouted, 'Hey!' at Lester.

He looked round, saw us and then looked away again. He blanked us completely. I thought of all the times he'd been pleased to see me and wished this was one of them.

I looked at the Misses Sellwood's stall. Maybe it was a mistake. Maybe it was a different painting. No, it had definitely gone. Where the picture had been, you could now see Miss Elsa sitting on the bumper of the Rover, looking very tired.

'I want my mam,' said Minnie. As I said, you forget, because she's a genius, that she is just a little girl. 'Where is she? Where's Mam?'

She was looking round for Mam's stall. I grabbed her by the elbow. 'Things are difficult enough for Mam,' I said. 'Come on.'

And we set off after Lester. I knew it was going to be embarrassing. I knew it might not work. But I also knew it was my job to sort this out and not bother Mam with it. We hurried through the crowd. Lester was moving quite slowly. The painting was slowing him down.

Nothing was slowing Barry and Tone down. They were right behind us all the time, keeping an eye on us. Not getting too close. Not sure whether to trust us or not. There wouldn't have been any point trying to shake them off. Max kept waving to them and shouting. 'Men! Hello!'

We got alongside Lester as he reached his car and I said, 'Hi.' He didn't look round. So then I did the hardest thing ever and said, 'Quentin.' He looked round. I smiled and glanced over my shoulder. They were still there. 'Are you going back up? Could you give us a lift?'

He looked a bit taken aback.

Minnie said, 'Please.'

I said, 'We'll give you back *Sunflowers*.'

He still didn't say anything. He just put the picture in the boot, opened the back offside passenger door and waved us in. He closed it with that satisfying *thunk* but still didn't say anything. I suppose if you steal a twenty-five-million-pound picture from someone, they are going to be a bit cool with you. All the same, the leather seats were completely beastie and we were safe. For the moment anyway. We could see Barry and Tone staring at us as the engine started up. Minnie gave them a little wave. I wish she hadn't because they snarled at us, and two minutes later we got a text. It said 'w8 & c'.

We were so happy to be in the car, we didn't notice that Ms Stannard was in the front passenger seat, with her shoes off.

'Evening, children,' she said. She was eating a Twix. She didn't offer us any. 'We were going to take a spin up to Bala, but Quentin suddenly became obsessed with sourcing TMNT merchandise.' She held up the book that Lester had bought. It was an old Turtles annual. Why had he bought a Turtles annual? He took it off her and put it in the ergonomic map-holder between the front seats. Still not talking. Even though Max was now singing, 'Fast car! Fast car! Fast car!' over and over. I normally join in, but I was too embarrassed, and he stopped in the end.

Minnie was feeling cheery and cheeky because she thought she'd cheated death. She said, 'You like Miss Elsa's picture then?'

'Not particularly.'

Ms Stannard said, 'Is that lovely young creature really Miss Elsa?'

Minnie said, 'Her dad painted it when she was little.'

'No he didn't,' said Lester, without taking his eyes off the road (A496). 'That picture is called *A Greek Captive*. It was painted in 1863 by Henriette Browne. It was one of the most popular paintings in the gallery. During the Second World War, the last time these paintings were evacuated to this quarry, the painting went missing. I deduce that some previous Sellwood stole it, for whatever reason.'

'Why do you deduce that?' said Ms Stannard. 'Why not deduce that the picture was left behind by useless people from the gallery and was saved for the nation by Mr Sellwood.'

'Because he didn't save it for the nation; he kept it in his kitchen.'

'Cowabunga!' yelled Minnie. 'Grandpa Sellwood wa a bandit. He did the perfect crime. That's why

Manod's got low crime figures. Because we're so good at it, we never get caught.'

'It's certainly no surprise to me that theft and lying are part of the culture,' said Lester.

'Thanks for that, Minnie,' said Ms Stannard. 'Thank you very much.'

Minnie looked up at the mountain and smiled. 'That's what we should have put on that sign: Manod – Welcome to Bandit Country.'

That wasn't the point. All I could think was, That is not Miss Sellwood and her dad did not paint it.

When we got back to the garage, Lester pulled over and said, 'Right. I believe the arrangement is that you now return the painting.'

Minnie said, 'OK. Are you ready . . . ?' But I shushed her.

'What'll you do with it then?' I said.

'I shall lock it up in my cave with all the others, and I shall never ever again make the mistake of letting people come to look at them. You show people art, and all they see is money. Where is the painting?'

'We want you to do something first,' I said.

'I'm not really in the mood to bargain.'

I made Lester bring the picture into the house. It was a bit depressing. All the books and most of our clothes were in big piles of boxes in the front room.

I said, 'Upstairs.' We used to have these photos of us all on holiday in little frames all the way up the stairs. Mam had taken them down and now there were these little white spaces on the wall where the pictures used to be.

We were outside Marie's room. I knocked on the door. She shouted, 'Drop dead!'

I said, 'Marie, it's Lester. He wants to tell you something.' Then I asked him to tell her about the picture.

'Your picture? Your collage with the photographs of the baby on? Yes, the National Gallery believe it to be a local project and they've hung it. It's attracting more visitors than the Meléndez, as a matter of fact. Ridiculous, really, but there you are. It's very success-ful and popular, even though it just seems to be pictures of your baby. That's how I knew what—'

'I don't care!' yelled Marie.

I said, 'No, not *her* picture. This one.'

Lester looked puzzled.

I shouted through the door, 'He's got something else to tell you. Something about the Misses Sellwood's painting. It's not a painting of Miss Elsa.'

There was a long silence from the room.

Then the door opened and Marie peeped out. She looked as though she'd been crying for a month. Her eyes were all red and her skin was all dry. She saw the painting and growled. I thought she was going to kick it. I said, 'Wait, wait. It's not her. This isn't Miss Elsa. It's nothing to do with her.'

'Who is it then?'

I looked at Lester. He can't help himself. Even when he's cross, he loves to lecture. He cleared his throat and said, 'Interesting question. The model's name was Maria Pasqua. She was quite famous for a while. As you can see, she was extraordinarily beautiful.'

'She's not even related to the Misses Sellwood?'

'Not at all. She was from the Abruzzi region of Italy, from a peasant family. Her family were extremely poor and, when this exquisite creature was born to them, they saw it as an opportunity to improve their lot. Her father took her to Rome. At the time it was the custom for people with interesting faces to wait on the Spanish Steps in the hope that artists would hire them as models. There was an old man with a big beard who was often hired to model God, a lot of young women who got to be the Virgin Mary, and so on. When this girl turned up, everyone wanted to paint her.'

'What as?'

'Well, nothing, really. She was just so beautiful, as you can see. She was painted by almost everyone that season. And when the time came for the various studios to exhibit, all the paintings of the little peasant girl were snapped up.'

'So did she get really famous?'

'More complicated than that, I'm afraid. An English countess fell in love with her face and tried to buy one of the paintings, but was too late. So she bought the girl instead.'

We all said, 'What?!'

'She summoned the girl's father and offered the child a good life and a good education if he agreed never to see her again. The family was poor. I'm not sure the father understood all that the countess was saying, but he agreed.'

'And what happened to her?' said Marie.

'She went with the countess, thinking that she was going to model for her for the afternoon, and she never saw her family or her country again.'

We all stared at the picture, thinking that when it was painted the girl didn't know this was going to happen to her. Even Max was quiet.

'But what happened then?' said Marie.

Lester said, 'I believe her father wrote to her quite often, but she never got the letters. She lived to be quite old.'

Marie said, 'I mean, what happened to her face?'

'Oh,' said Lester, 'she was always beautiful. And she married and had children and they were beautiful too.'

Marie looked at him and said, 'Of course! She had children! Why didn't anyone say that?!' And she threw her arms round Lester and kissed him. Then she kissed Max and she kissed Minnie. She'd've kissed me if I'd let her. And she went downstairs, talking nineteen to the dozen just like she used to, and said to Lester, 'D'you know, I've been locked in that room for weeks because of that picture, and now the same picture, well, it's set me free. Thanks, Lester.'

'Quentin.'

'Thanks, Quentin.'

I could see that he was sort of starting to be happy again. She asked him if he wanted to stay for tea, but he said he had some business to attend to, and he looked at me and Minnie.

Minnie said, 'You've had the picture back for ages. We hid it behind the other one. It's in that frame. Check if you don't believe us.'

He did check. He took *Sunflowers* out just as Mam was coming through the door. And we all sat in front of the picture for a while, as though it was a fire and we were warming ourselves. Mam stayed there longest of all. 'They make you feel like nothing else matters,' she said.

I went with Lester to the car. He said, 'Why did you do it? Was it all planned from the very beginning?'

'No. I really did enjoy the paintings, even though I didn't know about them. Everyone liked them.' Then I told him all about the insurance men and how they put the premium up because of the gallery being there and he said, 'Oh, is that all? You should have come to me with that. I've a small fund for community relations. I'm sure I could cover that for you. I'll let you know.'

And off he went and I thought, 'Well, why didn't we think of that in the first place?'

Just after that, the Misses Sellwood came through and I opened the gate for them. Miss Edna seemed quite cheery. 'We made a hundred pounds!' she said. 'Imagine!' But Miss Elsa was sitting there like a broken teddy. 'She's upset because she thought that Da made that painting of her. I told her not to be so silly – what difference does it make if you can't see it? I'm just telling Dylan about how silly you are, Elsa.'

That night in bed, a text message beeped in on Marie's phone. It said, 'RT and AB r an item. Official.' It took me ten minutes to figure out that it wasn't some strange coded threat from Barry and Tone. It was just someone from Marie's class, passing on some gossip. By then I was too awake to go to sleep. I just lay there thinking, and the more I thought the more obvious it was that everything was my fault. All the way back to Ms Stannard's Fiesta, everything was my fault. I told Barry and Tone about the Mini. I told them where Dad was. Even the robbery. It was

Minnie's plan. But she's my little sister. I'm her big brother. Big brothers are supposed to stop little sisters becoming involved in major robberies, aren't they? Big brothers are supposed to look after little sisters. And who is supposed to look after big brothers? Dads. And where was mine?

10 July

Cars today:
TAXI
JAGUAR XJ 4.2 V8 SOVEREIGN — Barry and
Tone

Weather — sunshine

Note: ZEBRAS ARE IMPROBABLE, NOT
IMPOSSIBLE

One reason I don't believe that anyone can do a perfect crime is that plans just never work. Because things just keep happening. Even Vincenzo Perugia got caught in the end. Look at Minnie. She had Plan A. Then she had to go to Plan B and that didn't work either. And look at me. I sat up all night planning what to do when Barry and Tone came. Then I heard a car roll on to the forecourt, first thing. I knew it would be them. I felt sick. But I got out of bed and went down to the front door. I didn't know what I was going to do. I just knew it had to be me and not Mam that did it.

I opened the door.

And it wasn't them. It wasn't a Jaguar. It was a Mondeo (top speed 121 mph). The first thing I noticed was that there was a zebra in the front passenger seat — one of those big fluffy toy ones. The back passenger-side door opened and Dad stepped out and paid the man, and the taxi drove off.

I won't go on about it. He didn't say much. He nodded at the zebra and said, 'That's for Max.'

'He's still asleep.'

'We won't wake them then.'

So we had a bit of a kick-around till the others woke up.

While we all had breakfast together, Max played with the zebra. He pushed it around the floor, making brum-brum noises.

Dad said, 'How's it all been?'

I said, 'We had a few problems with the insurance, but I've sorted them out.' Mam looked at me. I said I'd tell her later. 'Oh, and me and Marie can do oil changes now.'

Mam said, 'What brought you home?'

'I was in Harlech for a while, then I decided to move on. I went to look at the New Barrier. I was in London. I heard about this picture at the National Gallery that was something to do with Manod. I went to see it and it sort of persuaded me.'

Maybe you've never seen Marie's picture. I hadn't seen it myself at the time. I've seen it since on our wall. Everyone says it looked even better in the National Gallery – where it was the only picture. As

Dad says, 'They didn't need any other pictures. If you've got that on your wall, what else would you want to look at?'

The picture is thirty-five Polaroids of Max. They're all laid out next to each other, like words on a page, and they've got the date in the bottom left-hand corner. There's one for each day for thirty-five days. They all look pretty much the same. Except in the first ones he's got this long, curly baby hair, which we'd forgotten all about. At the beginning, he's a baby. By the end, he's a little boy. If you step back, they look like thirty-five pictures all the same. If you get close and look carefully, you can see the differences. You think you can see Time changing his face.

I suppose if you were Dad, you'd think it was a picture that showed you what you were missing.

Anyway, it was very popular. Especially with us.

Straight after breakfast we started unpacking the boxes. Because we weren't going to leave Manod now. I was with Dad when the Jaguar turned up and Barry and Tone got out. 'Can I help you?' said Dad. I was thinking, My dad was a bandit. He was on the run – but now he's home, what are they going to do to him?

They explained that there'd been some trouble and that they had this incriminating photograph of his children with a valuable painting. They showed him the Polaroid. Dad laughed, went indoors and came out with the painting by numbers of *Sunflowers*. He held it up for them.

'Painting by numbers,' he said. 'Three quid at Bala Sea Scouts car-boot sale. I think, gents, you have been taken for a ride.'

Barry and Tone looked uncomfortable.

Tone looked at me and said, 'They took twenty quid off us.'

Dad looked surprised. He said, 'That doesn't sound like them.'

Barry said, 'That's beside the point. We're here to talk about the Mini Cooper.'

'Oh, yes?' said Dad.

This was it. Now they really were going to arrest him for trying to defraud the insurance.

'It went missing and then it was recovered.'

'There's a stroke of luck, then,' said Dad.

'Any damage?'

'None whatsoever,' said Dad. 'Thinking of selling it on eBay.'

'Don't do that,' said Tone.

Dad looked at him. 'Why shouldn't I?' he said.

'Barry wants to buy it,' said Tone.

'I've always wanted one of them,' said Barry. 'Ever since I saw *The Italian Job*.'

'Right,' said Dad. 'That's good. That's very good.'

And it was very good. It was the best thing ever. Dad said he could get five grand for it on eBay. Barry said he didn't want to pay that much but he could pay cash there and then if the price was right, so they talked about prices for ages while Barry kept walking round and round and looking at the tyres.

'Bit worn on the inside front passenger side,' he said. 'Makes me worry about the tracking.'

Dad opened the driver's door and that's when Barry saw that the indicator arm had a little light on the end that flashed on and off. 'Oh,' he said, 'it's got the original thingy. Let's just take it.'

So they did. Barry handed Dad what looked like a triple-decker BLT but made of cash. Then he said, 'Hold on.'

And he took a twenty-pound note off the top of the pile and said, 'That's what your kids took off us. I'm having that back.'

Then Barry jumped in and started it up. The first thing he did was put the indicators on and giggle at them. Then off they went. I stood on the little wall and watched the two cars go all the way down the Blaenau Road (B5565). Every now and then the indicator on the Mini would randomly signal right or left, but the car just kept going until it was gone.

'I hope they're insured,' said Dad with a smile. Then he held up the wodge of money and said, 'We have now generated a small capital sum that we can invest in our business.'

Which is what we did. And soon everything was fixed. Which is exactly what my dad is good at. Fixing things.

22 August

MENU
THE BIG PICTURE – two sausages, bacon, egg, black pudding, tomatoes, toast
THE STILL LIFE (vegetarian option) – tomatoes, beans, egg, mushrooms, toast
THE SKETCH – sausage or bacon toastie with coffee
THE COLLAGE – selection of any five items with coffee
Welsh lamb casserole with barley
Welsh rarebit
Selection of cakes and coffees
Takeaway sales: Ms Stannard (2 Twixes and an 'FT')

Note: NO ONE LIKES BARLEY

We are no longer just the Snowdonia Oasis Auto Marvel and Copier Centre. We are now also a cafe, Manod's premier indoor attraction. Minnie wanted us to be called the Bandits' Hideaway, but she was out-voted. We're called the Masterpiece Cafe. We still keep a petrol log, but Mam's in charge of that now. I'm more involved with the menus. The lunch menu changes daily. I write it up in the petrol log and put some notes about it. For instance, no one likes barley. So everyone had Welsh rarebit. Which was a problem as we had to make each one separately, whereas the stew was in a big stockpot.

I remember we had to do twenty Welsh rarebits, because this is the day the paintings went back to the National Gallery. All the vans parked up behind the gate and all the drivers came in for lunch. Even Lester came in and had poached eggs on toast. He said he didn't eat eggs!

We'd solved the mystery of why Michelangelo never laid any eggs, by the way. She was a bloke hen. A cock. And we solved the mystery of why Donatello stopped laying. She'd had half a dozen little white chicks. We showed them to Lester and asked him to name them. He said, 'What about Splinter and April and Shredder and . . . I'm afraid I can't think of any more.'

I said, 'OK. Splinter, Shredder, April, Renoir, Monet and Massys.'

Later that day we walked up to the top, to get some sunshine. The barbed-wire fence had gone. One of the Technodromes was still there, but it was empty now. You could go right into the quarry. We walked all the way down into the big gallery and turned the lights on. It was, well, it was empty, a big empty space where all the paintings had been.

On the way home I stopped and showed Mam the drawings scratched on the boulder. She looked at the picture of the two women hidden under the moss and said, 'Blimey, you know who they are, don't you?' and she scrabbled around under the moss and, sure enough, right at the top of the boulder, someone had written two names.

Then Dad went and got Miss Elsa and Miss Edna and brought them over to the boulder and showed them the drawing and the writing. 'Elsa and Edna', it said. 'Turning Heads.'

Because the drawing was scratched into the rock, Elsa could feel the shape of it, which she could never do with a painting. Edna put Elsa's fingers in the grooves for her and helped her move them round the scratches. A big smile spread across Elsa's face. Because it was a picture of her all that time ago when she was pretty, and her dad must have drawn it, thinking of his girls on a cold day when he was supposed to be cutting slate. And here it was still, after all that time, a moment that was never going to go away.

If you ever feel like trying the Crispy Choc Constables in the Masterpiece Cafe, it's easy enough to find now. Just follow the sign for Manod on the A496 and keep going till the road ends. Lots of people do. We're so busy Dad's built a conservatory extension. It's called the Gallery. It's got Marie's picture on the wall. And one of the panels from the Elvis murals – the one of him in *Jailhouse Rock*. And our painting-by-numbers *Sunflowers*. And an exceptional view of the mountain.

Acknowledgements

The paintings of the National Gallery really were evacuated to the quarry at Manod during the Second World War. Jessica Collins of the National Gallery and Dafydd Jones of the Siop Llyfrau'r Hen Bost in Blaenau Ffestiniog were both extremely generous with their knowledge of this story. The lively and beautiful town of Blaenau Ffestiniog is nothing like my invented town of Manod. The story of Maria Pasqua is also true and can be found in a moving biography by her daughter, Magdalen Goffin. Luther Blissett is a real footballer, but it's a myth that he was bought by mistake. It's not true about liver; Denny made that up. But it is true that there is a great school in Gumbi. It's called St Martin's (www.guardian.co.uk/getinvolved). I know nothing about cars or the Welsh language. I asked Ian Millar about cars and Marc Evans about Welsh. Benedict, Gabriella and Chiara went with me down the mine and round the gallery. Inspiration came from the children of St Raymond's Catholic Primary, Netherton.

The editor was the immensely legend and hectic Sarah Dudman.

Above all I'd like to thank my parents. I first came across the wonder of art while holding their hands in the Walker Art Gallery, Liverpool, and later sitting next to my father while he studied the Renaissance for his OU degree in front of the television, very early in the morning.

F.C.B.

BONUS MATERIAL

CONTENTS

Dear Reader

I was always interested in art thefts. I thought they were generally more romantic and sophisticated than bank robberies, say. And in the summer of 2001 I got caught up in one. A big one. I'd taken my children to see the remote and lovely Drumlanrig Castle in Scotland. We were amazed by the art collection. They had everything: a portrait by Rembrandt, a Breughel, even a Da Vinci. And hardly any visitors. You could walk right up to the pictures and spend as long as you liked enjoying them. I thought it was great. That night in the pub, and next morning in a cafe, I told anyone who would listen what fabulous paintings they had stashed away up there and how you were allowed to walk right up to them. Someone must have been listening because the very next day someone went to Drumlanrig and did indeed walk right up to the Da Vinci (the *Madonna of the Yarnwinder*), lifted it off the wall and walked out with it. He put it in the back of his Vauxhall Nova and drove off with it.

I always felt that this was all my fault. I felt terrible about it. I was also disappointed that the thief had driven off in a Vauxhall Nova. I thought a proper art thief would have a helicopter at the very least. Possibly a personal jet pack.

After that I was always on the lookout for art-robbery stories. And I discovered that most of them didn't involve helicopters or jet packs. I've told the story in the book of how Vincenzo Perugia stole the *Mona Lisa* without anyone even noticing. The man who stole Munch's famous painting *The Scream* was a semi-professional footballer who took to buying increasingly flashy trainers after the robbery. And throwing them away at the end of each game. This would have been a

Daft Tom-like giveaway to the other players in his team. It so happened that five members of his team were policemen.

Given the daftness of art robberies in general, it didn't seem too far-fetched to have some children try to steal a masterpiece with the aid of some sheep and a packet of Quavers.

So I knew I wanted to write an art-robbery story, but I didn't have any idea where to set it or why the children would want to do it. In other words, it wasn't an idea. It was just a wish.

It was while I was thinking about this that I had an amazing piece of luck. I found an old notebook with a newspaper cutting inside about the evacuation of the National Gallery's paintings to a slate mine in North Wales. And suddenly the whole thing came to life for me – the rain, the grey town, the little boy who loved it, the paintings like treasure in a cave and the man from the gallery, guarding them like a dragon. The wish became an idea. I don't know why I cut that item out of the paper. I definitely don't remember doing it. But all the time I was writing the book, I kept thanking my younger self for putting that clipping away for my older self to find. People often ask writers where they get their ideas from. Well, one answer is that they come like this one did, in instalments.

Dwy'n hoffi partio!

Frank Cottrell Boyce

THE PAINTINGS

The (Im)perfect Crime
Mona Lisa, 1503–06, Leonardo da Vinci (1452–1519)

That Madonna Not the Other One
The Manchester Madonna, about 1497, Michelangelo (1475–1564)

The One with the Nuts
Still Life with Oranges and Nuts, 1772, Luis Meléndez (1716–80)

The One That Makes You Feel Good
A Grotesque Old Woman, about 1525–30, Quentin Massys (1465–1530)

The Party on Sticks
The Umbrellas, about 1881–6, Pierre-Auguste Renoir (1841–1919)

Not the Holy Grail
The Wilton Diptych, about 1395–9, artist unknown

The Prettiest Little Girl We'd Ever Seen
A Greek Captive, 1863, Henriette Browne (1829–1901)

Time Is Mutagen
The Arnolfini Portrait, 1434, Jan van Eyck (worked 1422, died 1441)

The One That Made Mr Davis Chainsaw Elvis
Bathers at La Grenouillère, 1869, Claude Monet (1840–1926)

A Different Angle
The Ambassadors, 1533, by Hans Holbein the Younger (1497/8–1543)

The One That (Nearly) Got Away
Sunflowers, 1888, by Vincent Van Gogh (1853–90)

You can visit some of these paintings at the National Gallery, Trafalgar Square, London WC2N 5DN or *www.nationalgallery.org.uk*

SOME PAINTINGS THAT DIDN'T MAKE IT INTO THE BOOK

The best bit about writing this book was having an excuse to hang around the National Gallery looking at the paintings. In fact, *choosing* paintings. I would walk around with some of my children and we'd pick which pictures could go into the book, as though we were on a fantasy shopping trip.

Some paintings we absolutely loved but never found a story for. One of these is *Whistlejacket* – a painting by George Stubbs (who came from my home town, Liverpool), showing a prancing racehorse on a plain background. Whistlejacket was a real racehorse, but in the picture he looks like a mythological creature – as fierce and light as a unicorn. We had seen postcards of the picture before we went looking for it in the gallery. When we found it, my daughter almost burst into tears. She'd had no idea the picture would be so big (you can't tell from a postcard). It's more or less life-size. Apparently, when the real Whistlejacket saw it, he tried to fight it!

Some paintings had great stories but we didn't like the pictures. There's a painting by Van Dyck of King Charles II on horseback. It's the biggest painting in the gallery. They called the crate it was in 'the Elephant'. When they were trying to move it to Manod on a lorry, it wouldn't fit under the railway bridge because it was so tall. They even let the tyres down on the lorry, but it still wouldn't fit. In the end they had to lower the road, and you can still see the dip in the road if you go to Manod today. I love this story, but the painting is rubbish! Van Dyck's a brilliant painter, but he couldn't do horses. The king's horse has a tiny head and it looks like it's made of mashed potato. We couldn't bear to put it in the book.

THOUGHTS ON BOOKS V SCREENPLAYS

I write films as well as books. In a film you're telling a story in pictures instead of words. I think that one of the things that drew me to the paintings in the National Gallery is that they're telling stories in pictures, just like in a movie. The difference of course is that in a movie you tell your story not in one picture but in twenty-five pictures *per second*. I became fascinated by the way the artists were able to freeze-frame a big moment so that you could see a whole story.

I'm currently working on the screenplay of *Framed*. Nearly everyone I meet says, 'The book is always better than the film.' But if you're writing the film, you have to want the film to be better, or at least different. Or else why bother.

One of the big differences between writing books and writing films is that although it takes a lot longer to write a book than it does to write a screenplay, it takes a LOT longer to *make* a film than it does to make a book. In film-making, if you think there's something not quite right about your story, you get years to fix it. You'll probably rewrite a film a dozen or more times while you're getting the money to make it, then there are rehearsals (weeks), shooting (months), editing (months and months). In a book, once you're done it's done. And a few months later it's out in the shops. I found myself driving around thinking of lots of ideas for *Framed* and then realizing it was too late now; the book was out. Making the film gives me a chance to use some of those ideas.

Of course, films are much simpler, more straightforward, than books. So I know I'm going to have to leave things out. I've already cut a couple of the paintings. I know they're sure to be someone's favourites. But one thing I hope the film will do is give me a way of showing the paintings themselves, of bringing them to life . . . and maybe showing the way that looking at paintings can change the way you see your own town.

QUESTIONS FOR DISCUSSION

Chatter Books

The following questions have been taken from the Macmillan Children's Books' reading guide prepared by children's librarian Jacob Hope, in association with Chatterbooks. To download the full guide, visit www.macmillanreadingguides.com.

1. Each member of the Hughes family is very different. Which of them do you think you would be most likely to make friends with and why?

Something to think about:

- Look on pages 23 and 24 where the family have different ideas for saving the garage. What do you think their ideas say about each family member?

2. Ms Stannard says *'Dylan Hughes, I believe you've been hiding your light under a bushel. I believe you're a lot cleverer than you let on.'* (p. 160)

Dylan is the main character in FRAMED and it is he who tells the story. Do you agree with Ms Stannard that he is a lot cleverer than he lets on?

Some things to think about:

- What do you like/dislike about Dylan and why?
- There are a lot of cases in the book where first impressions are wrong. Can you think of any?

3. *'I'm sad to leave the people, but really there's nothing here for us now.'* (p. 18)

In the book, lots of people leave Manod for other places, including Dylan's father. How does this make Dylan feel? Why do you think he loves Manod so much?

Some things to think about:

- Other people's reactions to Manod, for example, Lester.
- Do you think you would like living there?

4. '*As Splinter says in* Teenage Mutant Ninja Turtles, the Movie *(they're mean, green and on the screen): "Together,there is nothing your four minds cannot accomplish. Help each other, draw upon one another, and always remember the true force that bonds you."'* (p. 182)
Are people stronger in the novel when they work together?
What examples of this can you think of ?
Some things to think about:
• Look at how the Hughes family tries to develop the Snowdonia Oasis Auto Marvel.
• The change in Mr Davis when everyone helps out with the re-opening of the boating lake.

5. '*Everything's always changing, isn't it? Even the mountain is changing. Every second of every day, we get a minute older.*' (p. 127)
How important do you think change is in the novel?
Some things to think about:
• Dylan's entries in the petrol logbook – particularly regarding the weather.
• The way Marie reacts to the Misses Sellwood's painting, and the picture of Max that she makes.

6. '*How can something be a work of art if no one can see it? It's only a work of art when someone's looking at it. At least we're looking at this ceiling.*' (p. 154).
Do you think 'art' can be things other than paintings, for example a building, a book, a TV programme, etc.?
Some things to think about:
• Has FRAMED made you think about art in a different way?

7. How do the paintings influence the people in Manod? Think of all the things that change during the time the paintings are there. What do you think will happen to Manod after the paintings have gone back to London?

All Pan Macmillan titles can be ordered from our website, www.panmacmillan.com.

Also by **FRANK COTTRELL BOYCE**

Money can't buy
you happiness.

But it can buy:

1,434 Shogun Nude BMX bikes
15,291 travel-size Monopoly sets
18,816 stuffed-crust pizzas.

*We had millions.
Pity we had only days to spend it.*

Winner of the Carnegie Medal and shortlisted
for the Guardian Children's Fiction Award and
the Blue Peter Book Award

AN EXTRACT FROM *MILLIONS*:

It needed the two of us to carry the money back across the field towards the house. Think of that. More money than we could carry. I wanted to spread it all out on the dining table so Dad would see it when he got home and be of good cheer, but Anthony said we mustn't tell Dad about it.

'Why not?'

'Tax.'

I had to ask him what tax was.

'If Dad knew about it, he'd have to tell the government, and if they knew about it, they'd want to tax it. At 40 per cent – that's nearly half of it. We should just hide it and go to school.'

But we couldn't. We had to know how much was there. We tipped the money on to the table.

'Anyway,' Anthony said, 'if God had wanted Dad to have this, he would've sent him a cheque in the post.'

It was hard to argue with that.

I started to help him count. At first we just tried to count all the tenners using our ten times table, but we lost track of which ones we'd counted. The room seemed to be filling up with notes. Then Anthony had the idea of counting them into piles of a hundred, and then counting the hundreds. But even that was no good. After ten minutes the whole floor was tiled with wads of money. We couldn't find anywhere to sit, let alone count. So then we tried making them into piles of a thousand. There were 229 piles of a thousand. Plus 370 pounds change. That's 229,370 pounds. Or twenty-two million, 937 thousand pence.

For a while we just looked at it. Then Anthony picked up a thousand pounds and put it crossways on top of another thousand. Then he picked up another and put it crossways on top of that. Then I picked up a pile and put that on top of the other three. Then Anthony. Then me, and on and on, building a tower of cash. We got it almost as tall as me before it fell over. Then we both started laughing.

That was the first time we played Cash Jenga. We played it every night for the next week. The highest we ever got was Anthony's eyebrows. But that first time was the best, when it just sort of invented itself out of our excitement.

Cash Jenga is a great game if you can afford it.

Also by **FRANK COTTRELL BOYCE**

He wanted to see the world – but not quite like this . . .

Liam Digby is normal – but tall. Very tall.

Everyone thinks Liam's too big to be a kid any more,
but he's not old enough to be a grown-up either.
Or is he?

That's when things get confusing and Liam
ends up lost – in Space.

COSMIC *is a story about life's ups and downs –
for readers big and small.*

AN EXTRACT FROM *COSMIC*:

I discovered that if I pushed my feet against the wall, I could flit clear across the cabin, spin round and kick off again from the opposite wall, like Spiderman flying around New York. Then Florida popped up in front of me, making a buzzing sound with her mouth and miming a few passes with an imaginary lightsaber.

Looking back at it, I should have focused more on being dadly at this point. Because that's when DraxControl came on, asking us to move on to our task. 'You have a two-minute window to complete the task. Please commence now.'

All we had to do was press the right buttons in the right order, then we'd be all set for the trip home. Hasan and Max were still arguing about it. Samson Two put his hand up and said, 'Please, sir, I'd also like to press the button,' which was enough to get both Hasan and Max shouting at him. Maybe I should have just done it myself, but I was loving being a floaty Super Mario Matrix Jedi Power Ranger. Which is why I said, 'Let's settle it with lightsabers!' and took a buzzing swipe at them. They ducked and then bobbed up again, looking a bit confused. I realize now that they'd probably never seen *Star Wars*. They'd definitely never seen a dad trying to make a crucial life-or-death decision with an imaginary lightsaber.

I shouted, 'LUKE, I AM YOUR FATHER.'

Florida thought this was hilarious and shouted, 'You are NOT my father.'

'And you are not Luke.'

We were buzzing and laughing and laughing and buzzing. Then Max noticed Hasan was closing in on the buttons. He yelled, 'Hey! He's cheating!' and went after him. Samson Two dived in underneath them. Next thing, they were pulling and shoving each other in front of the multifunctional displays.

And the next thing after that: a long screeching noise. Then a jolt, as though we'd been caught on a bungee. Then we spun round. And round. And round. And over and round. Fast. And random. Like the cage of the Cosmic.

And a light strobed off and on and off like blue lightning.

And somewhere in the middle of it the voice of Drax Control was shouting.

Then it stopped.

Then it shouted.

Then it stopped again.

The Earth vanished.

And then came back.

Then vanished.

And then came back.

And then we stopped rolling.

And Earth was gone.

No one said a word.

We drifted over to the window and pressed our faces against the glass, looking for some sign of it.

It was very quiet. And very dark. And very, very scary.